PRIMAL
NEMESIS

JACK SILKSTONE

BOOKS

By Jack Silkstone

The PRIMAL Series

PRIMAL Origin

PRIMAL Unleashed

PRIMAL Vengeance

PRIMAL Fury

PRIMAL Reckoning

PRIMAL Nemesis

PRIMAL Redemption

PRIMAL Renegade

PRIMAL Deception

PRIMAL Exodus

PRIMAL Nemesis is dedicated to Deb.

Vinci Books

vinci-books.com

Published by Vinci Books Ltd in 2025

1

Copyright © Jack Silkstone 2015

The author has asserted their moral right to be identified as the author of this work in accordance with the Copyright, Designs and Patents Act 1988. This work is a work of fiction. Names, characters, places and incidents are the product of the author's imagination or are used fictitiously. Any resemblance to actual persons, living or dead, places and incidents is entirely coincidental.

All rights reserved. No part of this publication may be copied, reproduced, distributed, stored in any retrieval system, or transmitted in any form or by any means, including photocopying, recording, or other electronic or mechanical methods, nor used as a source for any form of machine learning including AI datasets, without the prior written permission of the publisher.

The publisher and the author have made every effort to obtain permissions for any third party material used in this book and to comply with copyright law. Any queries in this respect should be brought to the attention of the publisher and any omissions will be corrected in future editions.

A CIP catalogue record for this book is available from the British Library.

Paperback ISBN: 9781036701949

Printed and bound in Great Britain by Clays Ltd, Elcograf S.p.A.

Prologue

CARACAS, VENEZUELA

ANTONIO GRIPPED the flagpole with both hands and waved it furiously. The bandana obscuring his face hid a broad grin. In the last few minutes the ranks of the university demonstrators had swelled from hundreds to thousands. There was now a sea of brightly colored flags swaying as the army of students surged toward Altamira Square. Calls for free elections, less corruption, and more security filled the air as they surged forward as one. There was energy around them that gave Antonio hope. Hope that they could force change on a government bloated with corruption and nepotism. Hope that they could make a real difference.

He passed the flag to a supporter and fished his smartphone from a pocket in his jeans. The Twitter message he'd sent from an anonymous account had been retweeted over four thousand times. Word had spread and more and more demonstrators were joining the revolution.

The twenty-year-old student was one of a handful organizing the demonstrations. A leader in the secretive *Movimiento Estudiantil*, or Student Movement, his job was to use social media to rally thousands of students to key points around the city. They were always one step ahead of the police, the military, and the *colectivo* gangs. Of the three the *colectivo* politically motivated militias were by far the most dangerous. Lacking the discipline of the government agencies, they had already badly beaten dozens of young demonstrators. But even they couldn't stop what had been started. The revolution had gained too much momentum. The government would be forced to listen.

"Antonio, Antonio." One of the other protest organizers, Camilla his girlfriend, tugged his sleeve. The petite brunette held up her phone. "The police are rallying at the square."

"OK." He checked his own device. Numerous tweets warning of an imminent police response were filling his news feed. The *colectivos* were also starting to gather their forces. It was time for the leadership of the *Movimiento* to disappear. The demonstration would continue without them. He sent a message to the other leaders. They would meet tonight to plan the next round of demonstrations and evaluate their tactics.

He took his girlfriend by the hand and led her out of the crowd and down a side street.

"I feel terrible leaving them," she said once they were clear of the turmoil.

He pulled the bandana from his face. "We can't risk being arrested. Who'll organize the demonstrations if we're captured?"

"True." She remained quiet as they walked down the street heading back to where they had left their bicycles.

Antonio unchained them. "We'll meet tonight at your

place. The others will be there as well." He leaned across and kissed her. "We're doing the right thing, you'll see. Go home and study. Venezuela needs doctors." He mounted his bike and rode in the direction of his house.

The noise of the demonstration grew softer as he cycled away, replaced by the wail of sirens as a column of police cars raced past him. He suppressed a grin. By the time the police arrived most of the demonstrators would have already left. Only the hardliners would remain, those looking for a fight.

He pulled his bicycle up in front of his house and checked his messages as he climbed the stairs to the small residence. He had confirmation that all five of the *Movimiento* leaders would be at tonight's meeting. That was good news because they would have a guest attending, a member of the Voluntad Popular Party. The big players were starting to take notice of their growing influence.

"BOSS, you might want to check this out." Pete, the team's intel specialist was sitting in front of an array of screens in the corner of an old sugar warehouse.

James 'Jimmy' Scott, the leader of 'Team 1', hauled himself off a tattered couch and ambled over to the makeshift intel center. It was 2000 hours on a Friday night and his five Ground Effects Services contractors hadn't seen any action for over a week. "You got something useful this time fucktard?" he said as he stuck his Tom Selleck-inspired mustache over Pete's shoulder.

The geek had half a dozen windows open across the three screens. He knew it all went over Jimmy's head. The former DEVGRU operator was a door-kicker through and through. "I've been monitoring about fifty different accounts across Twitter and Facebook. These kids are smart; they keep closing them down and opening new ones just before each riot. But they haven't been smart enough to switch devices. They're using the same IP and IMSI addresses."

Jimmy shrugged. "That sounds great, dweeb. What the fuck does it mean?"

"It means I can find them once we get the bird in the air."

"OK, so let's get it up." He turned and yelled across the warehouse. "Hank, job's on!"

An oil-stained operator turned from under the hood of one of the team's vehicles. The self-trained mechanic was constantly working on the battered van they used to move discreetly around Caracas. Their black SUVs rarely left the warehouse. Hank was also responsible for maintaining and preparing their helicopter drone for flight.

Pete uploaded the individual device identifiers into the drone as Jimmy and Hank disappeared through the doors at the back of the warehouse. Located on the outskirts of Caracas, the facility served as the team's forward operating base as well as a hangar for the drone. They had made it as comfortable as they could, partitioning off an area to sleep, and arranging three moth-eaten couches around a television. One corner of the dusty floor space had been converted into a makeshift gym with kettle bells, an Olympic bar, rowing machine, and rings hanging from an exposed rafter.

The communications data for the targets had finished uploading by the time the roar of a helicopter engine emanated throughout the high-ceilinged building. A minute later the noise faded into the distance. Jimmy strode into the room and switched on the television. Hank went back to working on the van.

"Do we get anything other than goddamn soccer on this thing?" Jimmy tossed the remote on the equipment case that served as a coffee table.

"I can hook something up after I finish here," said Pete as he double-checked the waypoints he'd programmed. One of his screens displayed the navigation software for the drone.

"Focus on the intel shit dick-wad." Jimmy jumped off the couch and made his way across to the gym.

Pete glanced across as the team leader stripped off his shirt revealing heavily-muscled shoulders with intricate tattoos running down to thick forearms. He dragged an empty crate across to the rings so he could reach them. At five-foot-five, he was the shortest of the six contractors. Something none of them dared to heckle him about.

Jimmy grunted as he grasped the rings and hauled his compact frame toward the ceiling. Pete as focused back on his screens. He was the only non-shooter and as a result was treated as a second-class citizen. He didn't mind though, as he knew that he was getting paid significantly more than Jimmy and any of the operators. GES valued his skills.

Two of his screens now displayed the feed from the million-dollar Schiebel Camcopter 100 that flew above the city in the darkness. He kept the aircraft under a thousand feet and monitored its flight path. A pulsing icon indicated its progress along the route. A small box in the bottom of the screen showed the view from the helicopter's forward-looking infrared camera. Except for a handful of passenger jets in the vicinity of the airport, the night sky over the Venezuelan capital was empty. Since he'd already entered the details of the phones he was targeting, all he needed to do was fly the aircraft in search patterns until the onboard systems located one of them. Depending on how large the search pattern was it could take hours or it could take minutes.

He glanced back at the gym. Jimmy was doing some kind of hardcore circuit that involved pull-ups, burpees, and swinging a kettle bell around his head. Fucking operators, he thought. A tone sounded and one of the screens flashed a warning. A cluster of red dots had appeared on the map. "Boss, I've got a hit! Three of the handsets just pinged in the same location."

Jimmy dropped from the rings and swaggered over. He leaned forward, dripping sweat on the keyboard. "How far is that?"

Pete grimaced, wiped the sweat with his sleeve, and plotted a route on the map. "Five minutes or so."

"Hell yeah, let's hit it." He turned away from the screen, cupped his hand to his mouth, and yelled, "Gear up, boys, we're rolling!"

THE *MOVIMIENTO* LEADERS had agreed to meet in Antonio's girlfriend's ground floor apartment. Located in an affluent suburb, it was nicer than the other options that included a dormitory and his tiny flat. When they arrived he greeted the other four leaders and directed them to the living room where Camilla had laid out drinks and snacks.

One of the students filled a glass with water. "When are we expecting the Voluntad representative?"

Antonio checked the time on his phone. "Any minute now."

"We should think about making these meetings earlier."

The young man yawned. "I've been studying all day and need some sleep."

They made small talk, discussing the day's successful demonstration and the pending exam period. All five were students from the Central University of Venezuela, in their early twenties, altruistic, and focused on forcing change on the government.

There was a knock on the door and the room fell silent. Antonio opened it a crack.

"Is this the *Movimiento*?" a woman's voice asked.

"Yes it is, please come in." He opened the door.

The visitor was middle-aged, curvaceous, and dressed in a gray pencil skirt, heels, white blouse, and a jacket. Her features were soft and she had full lips that broke into a bright smile as she entered the room.

The rest of the group rose as Antonio introduced the guest. "Ladies and gentlemen, I would like to introduce Caitlin Bracho from the Voluntad Party."

After the formalities were complete he invited her to speak.

"First of all, I want to thank Antonio for inviting me here today. Secondly, I want to thank you all for your ongoing work. Without your support, our own cause would be so much more difficult, if not impossible."

The group exchanged smiles as she continued. "Every time the students of Caracas, your friends, your supporters, head to the streets and protest, we send a clear message to the government. A message of intolerance when it comes to crime, corruption, and inequality." Her voice rose in intensity. She spoke with a rhythm, like a beating drum calling the tribes to war. "My party needs people like you to continue your work. To be the resistance, to fight the fight, and let Maduro and his cronies know we will not let them continue to rape this country and grow fat while others starve."

"We will fight," declared Antonio, his hand clenched in a fist.

"We will fight!" echoed the other members of the group.

The sound of a heavy thud against the front door startled Antonio and he jumped to his feet. Wood splintered as the lock gave way and the door burst open.

His girlfriend screamed as a hulking brute wearing a balaclava burst into the house. He brandished an extendable baton in a raised hand and wore a pistol on his hip. More men charged in behind him.

"Run, it's the *colectivo!*" he screamed as he tried to slam the living room door. The baton flashed down on his shoulder, smashing his collarbone. He screamed in agony and hunched over on the ground trying to protect his face.

Through a haze of tears he watched as the intruders savagely beat everyone, including the political representative. The searing pain in his shoulder pulsed and he vomited as his girlfriend was dragged from the living room by her hair. She screamed hysterically until a gloved hand clamped over her mouth. Her assailant was short but powerful. She didn't stand a chance. Antonio staggered to his feet and managed to snag a handful of the thug's shirt, tearing the fabric. The last thing he saw before someone smashed the back of his head was the intricate tattoo emblazoned on the man's forearm; a dragon clutching a trident.

RESTON, VIRGINIA

Charles King lifted a glass of champagne from the waiter's tray and raised it to his lips. He sipped as his wife chatted to someone whose name he should probably have remembered. They were attending a gala hosted by his boss, Jordan Pollard. The former US Army Brigade commander turned investment banker was the majority shareholder in the security company King ran, Ground Effects Services.

He sighed and ran a hand over his shaved head. He hated these events and thought they were a veritable smorgasbord of self-absorbed assholes who only attended because Pollard's wife Caroline spared no expense on food, alcohol, or entertainment.

The phone in his pocket vibrated and he subtly tried to check it. His wife shot him a frown. He shrugged and answered the call. It was Jimmy, the GES Team Leader in Venezuela. Listening, he walked to a quiet corner of the ballroom. After a few seconds, he replied, "I'll get back to you." He left his glass on a table and moved across to where Pollard was talking to an elderly couple.

Well into his sixties, his boss still cut a lean figure in his tuxedo. With his wavy gray hair and chiseled jaw, many women still found him attractive. Charming and engaging, he was ever the perfect host. Not many knew how utterly ruthless the man was.

He waited for a break in conversation before speaking. "Sir, do you have a moment?"

Pollard fixed him with cold gray eyes before turning back to the couple. "If you will excuse me." He tipped his head for King to follow and strode between his guests, through a door, into an empty corridor.

"Having a good time, Charles?"

"Yes, sir."

"Liar. You hate these things as much as I do. But, we do what we must to keep our women-folk happy." The joviality in his voice dissolved. "Now, is this about the debacle in Mexico? Tell me you've tracked the bastards down."

"No sir, we're still working on that. We've got a very strong lead on Objective Red Sox."

"The German, Wilhelm or something?"

"Yes, the intel team is now set up in our facility. We'll find him in no time." He glanced down the corridor, confirming they were alone. "I just had a call from Team 1. They dealt with a resistance group tonight and inadvertently captured a member of an opposition party."

"Do they have a name?"

"Yes, it's Caitlin Bracho."

Pollard walked away and made a phone call. The conversation lasted thirty seconds before he pocketed the device and turned back. "Have her disposed of."

"Sir, don't you think that's a little extreme? I mean, she's a politician. They can intimidate her, release her, and create the required effect."

Pollard fixed him with a stare. "Are you getting cold feet, Charles?"

"No, sir, I just think it's unnecessary and risky."

"Don't get all self-righteous on me. What do you think your boy down in Mexico was doing? Handing out candy?"

"These aren't dirt farmers, she's a political leader. There could be blowback."

"Just make it happen."

He clenched his jaw. "Yes, sir."

"Good. Your boys are doing solid work down there." The corner of his mouth curled back in a snarl. "But they would want to be after your utter failure in Mexico."

"Pershing will find the men responsible for destroying the mine."

"He'd better, or he's done." The man's hard features softened. "Well, I guess we should get back to the gala."

"I need to call my man back."

"Text him."

He punched the message into his phone and sent it to Jimmy.

"Did you get a chance to try the lobster rolls?" Pollard asked when he was done.

"I did, they're amazing. Caroline always puts on the best spreads."

"That she does. I'll talk to you tomorrow, Charles."

"Yes, sir." King walked across to where his own wife was finishing her conversation.

"What was that about?" she asked.

He grabbed another glass of champagne. "Oh, nothing. Just something we've been tracking."

She put her arm around his waist. "Nothing too important, I hope."

"Just administrative issues. Have you tried the lobster rolls? Jordan recommends them."

RIO DE JANEIRO, BRAZIL

Kurtz drummed his fingers against the steering wheel of the rented minibus. Behind him the three other members of the rescue team were arguing whether now was the right time to move. He couldn't make out exactly what they were saying, just snippets. His hearing was yet to recover from a recent blast injury.

They had been watching the under-age brothel for the better part of a week. The seedy establishment was tucked away in one of Rio's wealthiest suburbs. Frequented by policemen, sex-tourists, government officials, and businessmen, it serviced the depraved needs of the rich and powerful. Everyone knew it was there. No one cared. Except, that is, for the small team of men in the bus.

The lanky German had been working with the Break Away organization for a little over two weeks. The not-for-profit's mission was to help rescue children from sexual slavery. Children who'd been kidnapped and forced into a life of pain and misery. Children like the three pre-teen girls being held in the brothel they were staking out.

Kurtz rubbed his unshaven jaw and slapped the steering wheel. "So are we doing this or not?" he asked loudly.

The leader, Brian, was a retired policeman from Kentucky. His voice wavered as he replied, "Yes, yes, we're ready. But, let's go over the plan again."

"*Nein*, we've been over it enough," said Kurtz. "The plan is good, it's simple, *ja*. We get in, we get the girls, and we get out. Then we take them away. Now is the time, we know there's no one there, just the caretaker."

"Yes, you're right," said another American. The other two volunteers in the back of the minibus were also former policemen. Like Brian, they were dressed in slacks and polo shirts. Kurtz, the most recent addition to the team was the youngest by at least ten years, and as such he had been relegated to the position of driver.

"OK, so we're going now, *ja*."

"Yes, let's go." Brian's reluctance was understandable. Previously these raids had been left to the local authorities. The expatriate team usually only conducted the initial recon, identifying under-age brothels by posing as potential clients. However, the police had refused to act this time and it was only at Kurtz's urging they had decided to conduct the raid themselves.

Kurtz checked the mirrors as he pulled out from the curb. It was early morning and the quiet leafy streets were empty. In half an hour it would become busy as people drove their children to school and headed off to work. By then the team would be long gone.

He turned the minibus into a laneway between two rows of townhouses. The brothel used a nondescript back door that allowed patrons a discreet means of slipping back to their cars. He braked gently when they were opposite.

One of the retirees in the back slid the door open and stepped down to the street. He grabbed the door handle to the building and tried to yank it open. It wouldn't budge. "I can't get it open," he yelled.

"Let me try." Brian jumped out the front of the vehicle and joined the other two men on the street. He pushed them aside and grabbed the handle. It still wouldn't budge. "Damn, it's locked." He shook his head. When he'd visited the brothel during the recon phase he'd simply walked in. Posing as an American sex-tourist, he'd been welcomed and shown the girls.

"*Dummkopfs*," mumbled Kurtz as he climbed out of the driver's seat. In the back of his mind he wondered if the brothel had been tipped off and knew they were coming. He made a quick assessment of the door and identified that it swung inward. "Get out of the way." He kicked hard directly below the handle. There was a crunching sound as the lock tore from the jamb and it swung open with a crash. "One of you stay with the van," he said as he stepped into the corridor.

He felt naked without his armor and a weapon. It was

an alien feeling for the former PRIMAL operative. Break Away, a not-for-profit organization, had a policy of never carrying weapons. In fact this was their most aggressive mission in their two year history.

Brian pushed past him and lumbered up a set of stairs. "This way." He reached the top and grunted as a baseball bat thudded into his chest.

So much for one caretaker, thought Kurtz as he spotted the youth who'd hit Brian. The kid with the bat wore a crazed expression and his eyes bulged from his head like an insect. He raised the bat and was about to deliver a killing blow when Kurtz leaped into action.

He jumped over his colleague and raised an arm to deflect the bat. It stung as it glanced off his forearm away from Brian's skull. With a grunt he thrust his knee forward. Ribs snapped and the kid collapsed to the ground gasping for air. Kurtz grabbed the bat and left him spluttering and whimpering on the tattered carpet. With the bat in hand he strode down the corridor. A door secured with a padlock barred the way. The lock sheared off with a single blow.

What he saw when he entered broke his heart. Huddled together on a single stained mattress were three young girls. They were dressed in ill-fitting lingerie, their faces smeared with makeup and tears. Kurtz collapsed against the wall and lowered the bat, his eyes misting with tears of his own.

The Americans entered the room. One of them shrugged off a backpack and handed the girls tracksuits. "We're here to take you home," the man repeated over and over, in Portuguese.

Kurtz stepped back into the corridor and found himself face to face with another gangster. The muscular assailant lunged with a knife. He managed to deflect the blow but the attacker reacted even faster, lashing out with a kick that knocked his bat to the ground.

The knife-fighter saw he was outnumbered and backpedaled down the corridor, the knife extended in front of him.

"*Schweine,*" Kurtz hissed between his teeth as he strode forward and lunged. He grabbed the wrist of the knife-wielding hand and fired a savage punch at the man's face. It connected with a crunch. Driving forward with murderous rage, Kurtz struck again and again splitting the man's eyebrow open and pulverizing his cheekbone. The knife dropped to the ground and he delivered a devastating front kick. The force of the blow knocked the man backward and sent him sprawling on the carpet.

Kurtz picked up the bat and was about to finish him when Brian called out. "Come on, we need to go."

He turned and saw the others had the girls and were ushering them down the stairs. He gave the two injured gangsters a cursory kick and followed. When he got to the minibus one of the others was already in the driver's seat. He jumped into the passenger seat and slumped in the chair.

Glancing in the rear-view mirror he stared directly into the eyes of one of the rescued girls. Emotion choked him and tears welled up again. The little face smiled and Kurtz looked away. Catching one of the other volunteers staring at him he took a deep breath and struggled to contain himself.

An hour later Kurtz was back in his room at a cheap hostel. He'd managed to slip away from the rest of the men who were celebrating in a local bar. The girls were safe, handed over to a local agency who would work with the authorities to return them to their families.

Kurtz should have felt good; he'd saved the day and the

girls were safe. Job well done, as Bishop would have said. He clenched a fist as his thoughts turned to his former teammates. It had been over a month since he'd abandoned them in Tokyo. A month filled with self-loathing, self-doubt, and heavy drinking. He grabbed the bottle of rum on the nightstand and took a swig. "Fuck Bishop and fuck PRIMAL," he mumbled as he wiped his mouth on his sleeve. He fell back onto the hard mattress and wept. "I'm sorry, Karla, I'm so sorry."

Chapter One

KINGSTON, JAMAICA

NORMAN MANLEY INTERNATIONAL AIRPORT was small by modern standards. A single runway jutted out into the emerald green waters of Kingston Harbor and the terminal was capable of handling only half a dozen airliners.

The airport sat on one of two islands linked by a land bridge that supported a dual lane highway. The furthest island housed a Jamaican Coast Guard base and a marina. The closer island accommodated the airport, including a freight handling area with an array of hangars. It was inside one of these hangars that PRIMAL had established a Forward Operating Base.

The makeshift facility had been rented to enable PRIMAL operatives to rapidly adjust to targets in Venezuela and North America. Chen Chua, the vigilante organization's intelligence chief and second-in-command, had forward deployed with a small team that now included his lead analyst Flash, the operatives Bishop, Saneh, and Mirza, and Mitch, PRIMAL's technical guru.

Aden Bishop sat on a stack of black equipment cases inside the hangar, dripping perspiration. His dark hair was drenched in sweat that ran in rivulets between his eyes, over the bridge of his nose where it clung for a second before dropping to the floor.

For someone in his mid-thirties he was in good shape; his body lean, his arms and shoulders muscular. But tropical humidity had always played hell with his body's cooling system. He turned to his partner, a former Indian Special Forces soldier. "Mirza, how in hell are you not sweating your ass off?"

The dark-skinned operative grinned. "Compared to New Delhi this is lovely. If we could open the hangar doors we might even get a sea breeze."

Mirza Mansoor, like Bishop, was a covert operative for PRIMAL. He was shorter than the Australian, about five-foot-nine, with a wiry runner's build. Half Nepalese, his features were angular and complexion dark. An experienced sniper, he was renowned for a cool temperament that offset Bishop's audaciousness.

Bishop wiped sweat from his brow and downed half a bottle of sports drink. "Yeah, but then we wouldn't be covert would we?"

The pair were wearing low visibility chest rigs, concealed pistol holsters, and carrying integrally-suppressed Tavor assault rifles. They'd been training in close quarters combat for most of the morning, running dry fire drills, and practicing entry and clearance procedures. It was exhausting in the stifling humidity of the iron-sided hangar. Despite the industrial air conditioner that had been rigged to one of the windows the temperature almost reached a hundred degrees.

"Hey if you can't stand the heat, lads, get out of the kitchen!" The British accent came from the fuselage of the Gulfstream business jet that was parked in the middle of the hangar. A pair of coverall-encased legs dangled from a hatch to the rear.

"Like you'd know, ball bag," said Bishop. "We're the ones kicking doors while you tinker with gadgets and toys."

"Whatever, Rambo, just remember who saved your bacon in Mexico." Mitch Freeman jumped down and slid the hatch on the underside of the jet shut. The upper half of his coveralls were rolled down to his hips with the arms tied around his waist. His brown T-shirt was drenched in sweat and clung to his muscular frame.

Bishop gave him a smile. "You did alright for a geek."

"Better than alright," added Mirza.

"There you go giving him a big head again." Bishop grabbed an ice-cold bottle of sports drink from a cooler and tossed it to the PRIMAL technician. "Even though that melon of yours couldn't get any bigger."

"If you've finished stroking each other's egos, you're all wanted in the office for a briefing."

All three men turned to the voice of Afsaneh Ebadi, PRIMAL's only female operative. Bishop was a little taken aback to see that the former Iranian assassin was dressed in skin tight leggings and a Lycra sports bra that did little to hide her ample bust and athletic figure. Her full lips pursed together and she frowned as the men continued to stare at her. "You never seen a girl in her gym gear before? Now, get a move on, Chua is waiting."

"Yes, ma'am." Mitch and Mirza strode across to the transportable office building at the far end of the hangar.

Saneh placed a hand on Bishop's shoulder. "You alright?" She wore a concerned expression.

He ignored the pain in his joints as he stretched. The mission in Mexico had taken its toll and he still hadn't had a proper opportunity to rest. At least the nightmares had stopped. "I'll be OK."

"You need to start taking care of yourself. You're not getting any younger, Aden."

"Tell me about it." For a moment he was lost in his former-lover's brown eyes.

"You could always take a few months off. Work in the bunker with Vance and the team."

"Why the sudden concern?" asked Bishop as they walked across to the office.

"For a former intelligence officer you're an idiot sometimes," she whispered before stepping through the door.

Bishop shook his head and followed her inside. Chen Chua, PRIMAL's Chief of Intelligence, had established a makeshift version of their command and control facility on Lascar Island. A row of laptops sat on a pair of rickety wooden tables. Two flat screens secured to the rear wall displayed a digital map and the latest intelligence feeds. Working at one of the computers was 'Flash' Gordon, PRIMAL's electronic intelligence specialist. The portly former-NSA officer wore a black snapback cap and a Led Zeppelin T-shirt. He glanced up from his computer and gave Bishop a nod as he dumped his armor and rifle inside the door. Chua, a slightly built Chinese American, was standing in front of one of the screens wearing an expression that reminded Bishop of his ninth grade math teacher.

"Last man," Bishop said as he took a seat.

Chua took a swig from a can of energy drink and placed it next to his laptop. "Now that we're all here I'll get started.

First things first, Vance wanted me to pass on a well done for the operation in Mexico. Our initial post op assessment indicates that the Chaquetas Negras Cartel has been completely destroyed and the mine is out of action. Our contact on the ground has also confirmed that the gold from the mine has been shifted to the town hall. Through an intermediary we've found a legitimate broker in Mexico City who's willing to pay market rate for the raw product. The wealth is going to be redistributed to those impacted by the mine."

"And the Sinaloa Cartel?" asked Bishop. "Are they still supporting the farmers?"

"It seems that way."

"What about that bloody murdering bell end, Pershing?" asked Mitch. Pershing had been identified as a former CIA officer and was the security contractor responsible for targeting Mexican ranchers in order to secure their land. He'd employed the services of a particularly vicious Mexican cartel to achieve this.

"Well, if you'd let me get to that."

"Sorry, mate."

"Getting a big head, champ," whispered Bishop.

"Look, I know you're all keen to get hunting Pershing but the reality is he's only small fry. Even Ground Effects Services, the company he works for, are small timers. We need to take down the private equity fund behind the entire operation," continued Chua.

"Manhattan Venture Investments," said Bishop.

"That's the one." Chua nodded at the analyst sitting to his side. "Flash has been working on a detailed intel pack for MVI. These guys take their OPSEC very seriously so it's taking a little time. However, we're confident in the next few days we'll have dug up enough information to get you guys out on the ground. It's the main reason we've forward deployed, so we can react quickly as information becomes available."

Bishop raised his hand. "Do we have any more information regarding the links between GES and the CIA?"

"Not yet, but we do know they have a number of CIA contracts. We're ninety percent sure they're not a CIA front company even though we know for certain Pershing is ex-CIA."

"Not great news," mumbled Mitch.

"Bottom line, we're up against a formidable enemy with deep pockets and highly trained operatives. We know their next move will be in Venezuela. That's why we're here. The problem is we have zero fidelity on what they're planning. In saying that we do have two potential sources to acquire that information; the MVI staff in New York City and the GES staff in Virginia. Flash and I are working on identifying weaknesses in both areas. Once we've finished that planning we'll brief you."

"So is Venezuela off the cards in the short term?" asked Bishop.

"Yes, until we know what they're up to and exactly how GES ties into it. We've revealed the tip of the iceberg. As yet we don't know how deep this thing goes. We need to be ready to roll at a moment's notice. Stay sharp, Flash and I will let you know as soon as we have something actionable. OK, that's it for now."

The group dispersed with Mitch and Mirza heading out into the hangar, chatting. Flash quickly became absorbed with his laptop. Bishop approached Chua as the intelligence officer was about to do the same. "Hey Chua, have we heard anything from Aleks about Kurtz?"

"No bud, I'll let you know if we get anything."

Bishop sighed and left the office. Outside Saneh was waiting.

"Do you want to join me for some green tea?" she asked.

"Maybe a coffee."

"Tea will do you good. Come on."

They strolled to the far corner, beyond the business jet, to a little kitchenette. Beside a water boiler Mitch had set up a plastic travel case containing a range of beverages. He called it his Combat Café.

Bishop watched as Saneh spooned green tea into a French press.

"You know you really should think about taking some time off. It would do you wonders. My trip to Bali really helped clear my mind and refresh my body." She filled the press with boiling water.

He had to admit she looked amazing. Her olive skin was tanned and her long brown hair shone. He, on the other hand, felt like a wrecking ball had hit him. He caught his reflection in the stainless steel water boiler that hung over the sink. His eyes had dark bags under them and his skin was pale.

"Maybe when this is over."

She poured the green tea into two mugs and handed him one. "Aden, I'm serious. You need to start caring for yourself. You can't keep rolling from one mission to another. The stress alone will kill you." Her voice softened. "Look at Japan, some of your decisions were definitely impacted by stress."

"It's not a bad idea. Let's just get through this next mission and then I can do something about it, OK?" He sipped the beverage. It tasted bland, exactly as he expected.

Saneh smiled as she drank. "It's not that bad and it's very good for you."

"It would want to be. Tastes like dirt."

"Look, we've got some down time now. Maybe I could show you a few yoga breathing exercises?"

Bishop raised an eyebrow as he glanced down at her outfit. "Do I have to dress like you?"

She laughed. "Only if you want to."

GES FACILITY, VIRGINIA

Terrance Howard sipped from a can of sugar-free energy drink as he drove his hire car through the Virginian countryside. A chain fence lined the road, at least fourteen feet tall and topped with razor wire. Signs every few hundred yards warned the site was restricted and trespassers would be arrested.

He slowed the car at the security checkpoint to the Ground Effects Services facility. A uniformed guard inspected his CIA identification before raising the boom gate and letting him through. It was a short drive to the main administration building. He parked in the lot with the other employees' vehicles and approached the low-slung concrete and glass building. He used the reflection in the glass window to adjust his clothes. His poorly-knotted green tie clashed with his loosely-fitting cream chinos and blue sports jacket.

The woman who stood waiting behind the automatic sliding doors was tall and could have been a fashion model. "Good morning, Mr. Howard. Welcome to Ground Effects

Services. We've been expecting you." She handed him a security pass.

"Thanks, sweetheart." He smiled, so far so good. "Where am I working? Close to you I hope."

She managed half a smile. "This way." She led the plump CIA analyst down a long corridor and through another door to a waiting All-Terrain Vehicle. "We have a SCIF out near the ranges. That's where you'll meet the rest of the team." She was referring to the Sensitive Compartmented Information Facility, a high-security space where classified information and operations are managed.

"Wow, impressive," he said as they drove along a narrow asphalt track through a leafy forest. He was staring directly at her breasts.

"Yes, we have four weapons ranges, two kill houses, an advanced driving track, twenty five hundred hectares of close terrain, accommodation, classrooms, and the SCIF."

They drove out of the trees and she parked the buggy alongside two others outside a tall fence. They swiped their access cards, passed through a gate, down some stairs, and into the foyer of an underground facility.

"What's with the bunker?" asked Howard.

"It used to be an ammunition storage facility. This is as far as I go, Mr. Howard. This gentleman will take it from here." She gestured to a burly guard manning a reception desk.

"OK, well maybe we could catch up for a drink later?"

She ignored his offer and walked away.

"What a cold bitch," he murmured as he watched her rear end disappear up the stairs.

The guard registered Howard's iris in a biometric system that gave him access to the secure area. Then he made a call informing someone inside he had arrived.

A moment later a solid steel door swung open and a tall gentleman dressed in a suit greeted him.

"Terrance, glad you could make it." George Henry Pershing was a former CIA officer turned GES consultant. Forty-five years old, he was tall and lean with hawkish features, a receding hairline, and ears that stuck out from the side of his head like radar dishes.

"Mr. Pershing." Howard tentatively shook the Texan's hand. It was their first meeting in an official capacity. Previously, Howard had known him as 'Source 88'.

"I was just about to brief the rest of the team. Come on in."

They passed through a retina scan activated gate before stepping into the workspace. The layout of the SCIF was no surprise to Howard. It was configured like any other. An open floor plan for most of the team, facing a wall of screens, with a series of offices across the back wall for the managers. He was surprised to see the number of analysts gathered in the room, at least eight that he could see at first glance. Three were women and out of those one was mildly attractive.

"Team, I would like to introduce Mr. Terrance Howard. He's our CIA liaison officer and lead analyst." He gestured for Howard to take a seat. "For those of you who are unaware, four days ago this organization was the victim of a significant terrorist attack. A mining venture we were paid to protect in northern Mexico was attacked by environmental terrorists and completely destroyed." Pershing scanned the room letting the severity of the comments sink in. "This has directly affected American citizens and substantial investment. We've been contracted on behalf of the CIA to find the people responsible and help bring them to justice." He turned to the analyst. "Mr. Howard, can you give us an update on what the CIA was able to uncover?"

"Now?" He hadn't expected to be briefing right away.

Pershing nodded.

"Umm, OK. Have you all read the background report that was released to GES?"

A few people nodded.

"OK, good. Well our number one suspect at the moment is this dude Aden, Objective Yankee. We know for a fact he was at the mine and was working with criminal elements to sabotage it. We think that he's part of an environmental terrorist group that also includes a former German Police officer called Wilhelm Jager. Jager is Objective Red Sox and is the next link in the chain, and the key to getting to the entire... Major League Network." Howard smiled, he'd made that up on the fly.

"The latest intel I've got on Jager dates back to 2008 when he was removed from GSG 9 and the police force for beating a rapist to death. From there we have nothing. I want to know where he went after that. Did he immediately join the Major League Network? How did he avoid jail? These are the questions we need answered."

Pershing clapped his hands. "OK team, so that's where we are at. Let's get to work. Mr. Howard, if you don't mind." He gestured to one of the rooms at the back of the SCIF.

Apart from a cowboy hat hanging on a hook on the wall the office was bare.

"Looks like we're back in business," drawled Pershing as he sat in his chair.

"What the hell happened at the mine? I saw the satellite imagery, dude, the place was trashed."

"Objective Yankee managed to sabotage a number of

the facilities then turned the Black Jacket Cartel against us. Without security in place there was little we could do when his militia attacked."

"Holy crap."

"But that's not what I wanted to talk about." Pershing tipped back in his chair. "The German. Wilhelm or whatever, have you got an address?"

Howard shook his head. "Not for him, just his parents. They live in Bavaria."

"Good, we're going to need that."

"Do you want me to go over and interview them?"

Pershing smiled. "No, I've got someone a little more persuasive in mind."

Chapter Two

KINGSTON, JAMAICA

BISHOP INHALED the fresh air as he sat cross-legged on a yoga mat. Saneh had snuck him under the fence to the beach behind Norman Manley Airport. The sun was low in the sky and there was a cool breeze coming off the sea. He peeked through one eyelid to see if Saneh was still holding her pose; she was.

"You opened your eyes didn't you," she said.

"Nooo." He closed them tightly and tried to focus on the waves crashing against the gray sand. No matter how hard he tried he couldn't stop thinking. A maelstrom of thoughts raced through his head. He sighed; he just wasn't cut out for meditation.

"Don't get frustrated, Aden. It takes a lot of practice to be able to let go. It will come, with time. You need to focus on your breathing. Long and deep inhale, long and deep exhale."

He tried the breathing exercise and for a moment it calmed him. Then he opened his eyes and scanned the beach. There wasn't another person in sight. Just him, Saneh, and a few seagulls. "So, this is what you did everyday for two weeks?"

"Not just meditation. I also practiced yoga and ate organic food in a pristine environment. It was about spiritual as well as physical healing. Oh and massages; Ulaf had the most amazing hands."

"What!" Bishop turned to face her. "Ulaf?"

She laughed. "It's so easy to wind you up."

He lay back on the mat and pulled his baseball cap over his face.

"Oh now you're sulking?" She laughed.

"No, I'm meditating."

"I did a lot of thinking. About you and me, about what we do, about how sometimes we hurt people."

He sat up and lifted the cap so he could see her face. She wore a pained expression that worried him.

She continued, "What happened in Japan is going to bother me for a long time. Not just what happened with Karla but everything. When I was in MOIS, I never questioned my mission. I never worried if I had to take a life. I had no choice. But this, this is different. We're the judge, jury, and executioner, and I'm not sure that's right."

"We're not soldiers, Saneh. We shoulder the burden of decision as well as execution. It's not a light load to carry."

"Sometimes I think it's too much."

"You're probably right but if we don't do our job then who will?"

"Is it worth it?"

"I think so. We're only one pin prick of light in a world of darkness, but we make a real difference."

"I just worry that darkness will consume us, or maybe it already has."

Bishop gazed out at the ocean. "In Japan I was forced to make a decision. I chose your life over someone else's. It's a decision I've replayed in my mind hundreds of times. Do I wish I was never put in that position? Yes. Can I change what happened? No. If I had to do it again I would make the same decision."

She looked at him intently. "Would you have done the same for anyone else on the team?"

"In an instant. Because this team is my family."

"So, your decision had nothing to do with... us?"

Bishop nodded. "At that moment it didn't. It was a tactical decision made in the heat of the moment. My feelings for you are strong, but they didn't cost Karla her life. Her actions did."

She was silent.

"I'm the first to admit I was too harsh on Kurtz."

"Harsh? He already had post-traumatic stress and then you shot a teenage girl right in front of him. You've got to have a little more empathy sometimes. He was on your team. You had a responsibility to make sure he was OK."

He stared out to sea and swallowed hard. "I know."

She touched his arm. "I'm sorry."

He blinked off tears and glanced at her. "It's OK."

"We all make mistakes. It's what we learn from them that defines us."

They watched the waves crash on the sands for a minute. Then he broke the silence. "We should head back." He rolled up his yoga mat and waited for Saneh to do the same. "Thanks," he said as they walked back to the airport fence.

"For what?"

"For listening." He lifted the bottom of the perimeter fence and she shimmied under. "I wonder if Aleks is getting close to finding Kurtz."

"If anyone can find him it's Aleks. He knew him the best."

He crawled through after her and they walked toward the hangar. "I feel a bit sorry for the rest of the CAT." Bishop referred to the Critical Assault Team, PRIMAL's high-risk combat squad.

"Why is that?"

"Because with Aleks gone, Kruger is in charge and that guy lives by the ethos 'train hard, fight easy'."

She smiled. "I'm sure the boys are having a great time."

NEW YORK CITY

The boardroom of Manhattan Ventures Investments was an elaborately furnished space on the 34th floor of a skyscraper in Lower Manhattan. Floor to roof glass windows ran down one side giving the occupants a sweeping view of the Brooklyn and Manhattan bridges.

Jordan Pollard, the Chairman, sat at the head of a polished mahogany table with a scowl on his hawkish features. "I want the Mexican government to bleed for this. I want to sue them for every single dollar we can get. We were assured a safe and cooperative mining environment not a goddamn revolution." He eyeballed each person at the table.

The three directors of MVI were present: Charles King, also the CEO of Ground Effects Services, Ian Macmillan, the company's Chief Financial Officer, and Wesley Chambers, a former investment banker responsible for raising capital. A fourth person, a female lawyer, had also been invited to the meeting.

"Ian, what has this cost us?"

The CFO adjusted his spectacles and coughed. "About five hundred million."

"Five hundred million," Pollard snapped. "They cost us five hundred million."

"Yes sir, and a five year forecast of an additional six hundred million, possibly more."

"Over a billion dollars, gone up in smoke." He jabbed a finger at his attorney. "Where do we stand with our legal recourse?"

The lawyer was plain looking, with her hair in a bun and a suit that could have belonged to a man. She hadn't been hired for her looks. One of the best in the business, she was a Columbia Law graduate with a decade of experience in international business law. "Sir, I've assembled my team and we've initiated legal action against the Mexican Government. We anticipate serving the defendant by the end of the month."

"And you're confident you will be successful?"

"Yes, sir. Like you said, under the North American Free Trade Agreement, the Mexican Government was obliged to provide you with a secure environment to conduct your business. They failed. There is no doubt in my mind they're accountable for the loss of your investment and your future earnings. It's covered under Chapter 11 of NAFTA."

For the first time in days Pollard smiled. "This may turn out to be lucrative after all." He gestured to the door. "Now if you would excuse us, my dear, I would like to talk privately with my colleagues. I will see you later in my office."

"Yes, sir." She left the table and Pollard waited till she was out of sight. He pointed at Charles King, the director responsible for security and the CEO of Ground Effects Services. "Charles, I want an update on our progress with finding the people responsible."

"Yes, sir, the intel team has assembled in our GES facility and have commenced working with the CIA to find Objective Yankee. We've discovered that he has an associate who is German, Objective Red Sox. I have an asset traveling to interview this associate's family in Bavaria. We're confident he will unlock the identity of Yankee and the rest of what we are calling the Major League Network."

"And these are the people you let destroy the mine?" asked Wesley Chambers.

King glared at the thirty year old. The investment banker was by far the youngest in the room and, as far as King was concerned, the biggest security risk. "Yes, that is correct."

"Oh OK, so what are you doing to make sure they're not planning to take down any of our other ventures, like Venezuela, or the DRC? I mean, dude, you did such a good job of protecting the Chihuahua mine."

"Shut the hell up!" Pollard, the Chairman, snapped.

King continued, "You'll be happy to know, Wesley, that as a direct result of your inability to maintain your own security, I'll be assigning you and the others with a personal security detail." He referred to a previous incident where the PRIMAL operative Mirza had accessed Wesley's phone and installed hacking software.

Wesley looked shocked. "What? You mean a bunch of your goons are going to follow me around all day? No way, dude. It's bad enough you make me carry one of those shitty company phones."

Pollard stabbed a finger. "You'll comply with the security requirements or you can find another job. It's that simple."

Wesley chewed his lip and remained silent.

"That concludes our meeting, gentlemen. We won't convene as group again until the security situation has improved. That will be all."

Wesley and the CFO gathered their things and departed. The investment banker was still complaining about the security changes as he walked out.

"That idiot is getting on my nerves," said King when they were gone.

"He'll be dealt with in good time," replied Pollard. "My main concern is neutralizing the Major League group. If we don't, I have no doubt that our other CIA contracts will quickly evaporate. Need I remind you exactly how lucrative arming rebels and running rendition ops is?"

"No, sir. Shrek is heading to Bavaria as we speak. He'll interrogate the parents of the German. The rest of his team is postured to exploit."

"And the situation in Venezuela?"

"Good. Jimmy's boys have been very effective. Since their last mission there has been a significant drop in demonstrations."

"As I predicted, targeting the facilitators would be the key to success."

"Indeed sir, and how are the contract negotiations progressing?"

"We're in the final stages. Once they've been signed Team 1 will transition from covert operations to the site security force. Try not to repeat your screw up in Mexico."

The veins on the side of King's shaved head bulged as

he packed up his notes. "We'll have the Major League criminals neutralized by then."

Pollard rose and made his way to the boardroom door. "You'd better. We literally can't afford any more mistakes."

CARACAS, VENEZUELA

Antonio's eyes opened and he panicked. All he could see was a blur of bright white. His brain throbbed and his arms failed to respond as he tried to sit upright so he could see what was going on.

"Steady, steady." The voice was warm and feminine. Gentle hands pushed him back into the bed. "It's OK, you're in hospital. You're safe."

"Where's Camilla, is she OK?"

"I'm sure she's fine. You need to rest."

The room spun and Antonio closed his eyes. Images from the attack flashed through his mind. The forearm with its intricate tattoo was etched in his memory. For what felt like an hour he focused on the image. Then he forced open his eyes. The fog had started to lift and he could almost see clearly. A young nurse was watching him intently, a clipboard held in her hands. "Did anyone else come in with me?"

"Yes, there were a number of you."

"Are they all OK?"

"I would have to check."

"Can you help me sit up?"

The nurse wound the bed to a sitting position and left the room. A minute later she returned with a tray of food. "Eat slowly or you'll be sick."

He was so groggy that he hadn't realized his left arm was strapped across his chest. His shoulder and upper arm were bandaged heavily. Then he remembered the savage blow that must have shattered his shoulder.

"Antonio, how are you?"

He turned his head toward the new voice. One of his fellow demonstrators, Chabi, was standing in the doorway. The student was sporting a black eye and stitches in the brow above it.

"You can go in," said the nurse as she walked out.

His friend approached slowly and stood next to the bed.

"How is Camilla?" Antonio asked.

"She's alive." Chabi's face was grave.

"Where is she?"

"They've got her in the room down the hall."

Antonio threw the blankets off and swung his legs out. Fighting the urge to vomit he grabbed the IV stand next to the bed for support.

"You need to stay in bed."

"No, I need to see her." He staggered to the door. "Show me the way."

His friend shook his head but led him to the room down the corridor. "She hasn't spoken since they brought her in."

Antonio made it to his girlfriend's bedside and took her hand. "Camilla, it's me. I'm here."

She stared at the ceiling with lifeless eyes. Her hand was cold and limp.

"Camilla, speak to me."

A single tear ran down the pretty brunette's cheek and hit her pillow.

"They did horrible things to her," his friend whispered.

"Do her parents know?"

"Yes. They are coming today."

"Who else was hurt?"

"The others are fine but..." Chabi fell silent.

"But what?"

"They found the body of the woman from the Voluntad party."

The news hit him like a punch to the chest. "The *colectivo* killed Caitlin Bracho?"

His friend nodded solemnly.

"They can't get away with that! We'll hold them to account."

Chabi shook his head. "The fight's over. Look what they did to Camilla. Look what they did to you. We can't fight them. The *Movimiento* is finished, it's over. Stay here with your girl and take care of her."

He turned and watched another tear stream down Camilla's face. He knew he wasn't going to be able to walk away from this. There was no way he would run scared from criminals who didn't deserve the freedom he and his friends fought for. They would pay. He would find a way.

KINGSTON, JAMAICA

Paul 'Flash' Gordon leaned back from his laptop screen and rubbed his eyes. He'd been hunched over the keyboard for two hours sifting through all the intel he had on the private equity firm, MVI, and GES, the security company. There was a lot to process, not just what he'd managed to pull from open sources but also the information they had hacked from MVI's servers. The connection had been severed but he still had plenty of material to work through.

"Hey, Flash, how you tracking?" Chua entered the office

with a can of energy drink in each hand. He tossed one to the analyst.

"Thanks, bro. I won't lie, I'm hurting tonight."

"You've been working for nearly 48 hours straight."

"Made some good headway."

Chua dropped onto a chair. "What have you got?"

"Couple of things that are interesting. MVI have definitely got a big deal going down range in Venezuela. It's mentioned in a few different emails. They've been building capital for something big."

"Another mine?"

"Possibly, they've got a history of it. Their last major project before Mexico was a rare earth minerals mine in the Congo."

"There seems to be a *modus operandi* developing here. Unstable environments and ruthless resource exploitation. They provide the capital, their in-house mining company does the work, and GES deals with any local security issues."

"Or GES could be working to destabilize the government. That would tie into CIA objectives and possibly pave the way for MVI to strike a deal with a new regime."

Chua nodded. "So how do we get some fidelity?"

Flash popped his can of drink with a hiss. "Well, it just so happens I may have found a way in."

"Go on."

"One of the main guys in MVI goes by the name Wesley Chambers. From his emails I think he's some kind of investment banker. Brings in the big cash from high net worth individuals and other brokers."

"Mirza met him in New York, right? You got him to hack his phone."

"Yep and from what these emails are saying, this clown

likes to party hard. The CEO of GES thinks he's a liability. He was real pissed when they discovered his phone was hacked."

"That aligns with what Mirza told us. Do you know what Jordan Pollard thinks about it?"

"Not sure, he rarely sends emails. I've got a feeling he does most of his business face to face or over a secure phone link. However, King, the GES boss, does remind the CFO to limit Wesley's exposure to operational details."

"So neither of them trust him?"

"Nope, and Wesley likes bitching about King to some of his other banker buddies. Even after the phone hack. This guy's OPSEC is looser than a—"

Chua cut him off. "OK, I get it. That's our in. We go after Wesley in New York and monitor King at the GES facility in Virginia. He's got a residence on the estate when he's not at his apartment in New York. Spends most of his time there."

"What about Venezuela?"

"Ivan's already in country." Ivan was one of PRIMAL's deep cover agents. A 'blade' as Chua called them; someone who, when they had enough warning, could infiltrate a target country and establish HUMINT networks and safe houses. "He's going to set up a base of operations and start putting feelers out. Do you have anything for him to investigate?"

"Not yet. MVI's next project might be linked to one of their CIA contracts; they've got a few. Problem is all the payment invoices are generic. I've got no idea what they're actually doing or where they are doing it. They might even be running independent operations for a private client."

"Keep digging. I'll brief Vance on what we've got. Once

we get the teams out on the ground we should be able to uncover more."

Flash finished the can of caffeine-laced sugar, crushed it, and flung it into the trashcan. "I'll ride this wave for a few more hours then I'm gonna get my head down."

"Copy that."

Chapter Three

GES FACILITY, VIRGINIA

PERSHING DROVE his buggy in through the sliding doors of the GES holding area. The massive shed contained everything a special operations team needed to discreetly train, plan, and prepare for a mission. There was an indoor range, accommodation, kitchen, planning room, and a vast hangar where mockups could be built for rehearsals. It was an impressive facility, out of sight from prying eyes, that was occasionally used by the CIA, FBI, and JSOC.

He brought the ATV to a stop and strode across the concrete floor to where Shane 'Shrek' Cameron and his five-man team were running through a vehicle drill. A black SUV was parked in the middle of the hangar.

"Ambush right, vehicle disabled." The bald-headed goatee-wearing team leader was standing in front of the vehicle in his assault rig.

Pershing watched as the doors on one side of the vehicle burst open and the Team 2 operators exited smoothly. Dressed in cargo pants, T-shirts, and assault vests, they moved into fire positions behind the SUV and started engaging targets on the far side with paint rounds from their AR carbines. They fired over the hood, under the chassis, and from the back of the trunk. Then, after an initial volley of rounds Chris, Shrek's blonde-haired second-in-command, issued an order. "Go, go go!"

The team peeled around the back of the SUV and assaulted directly toward the targets, riddling them with the paint rounds as they advanced.

"OK, that's a wrap!" bellowed Shrek.

Pershing smiled. He'd seen the team in action in Mexico and knew their slick drills transitioned seamlessly into the field. Shrek's team was a finely tuned killing machine that was itching to be released against the Major League Network.

Shrek strode across and thrust out a gloved hand. "Henry, you found those assholes from Mexico yet?"

Pershing grasped his hand. "The bloodhounds are baying, Shrek. It's time to go hunting."

"Hell yeah! What have you got for us?"

They walked across to a bench where the men were refilling their magazines.

"Any of your boys speak German?"

"Yeah, Matt does. Spent five years with 10th Group in Stuttgart."

A tall operative wearing tactical wrap-around glasses glanced up and gave Pershing a nod.

"Excellent, the two of you need to get packed."

"What about the rest of the boys?"

"Keep training. I've got a feeling you're gonna be out hunting before the week's out. Your colleagues in Team 1 have been killing it in Venezuela. Soon it's going to be your turn."

"Fuck yeah," said Chris, the 2IC.

"You might get a chance to hit that dude who chest shot you," joshed Mikey, a handsome square-jawed former SEAL.

The team laughed and Chris shook his head. "You motherfuckers, that shit hurt."

Pershing joined the laughter then slapped the bench. "Shrek, once you're ready, drop by the SCIF and I'll brief you on the job." He spun on his heel and strode back to the buggy.

"This going to be wet work?" Shrek yelled after him.

"Not yet," Pershing said as he walked. "Not just yet," he added under his breath.

PATONG BEACH, THAILAND

Aleks slumped at the bar and waved over the Thai bartender. "Vodka."

The man slid a shot glass over and he downed it in a single gulp.

He had spent the better part of three nights searching the beachside town of Patong for Kurtz. This seedy dive was exactly like others he'd visited. Pop music blared from tinny speakers and neon signs barely lit the dark corners. To say he was disappointed was an understatement. For nearly a week he'd been searching Thailand for any trace of Kurtz. At least three expats had remembered the tall blonde-haired German but no one knew where he'd gone.

Aleks pushed the empty glass away. "One more."

The Thai flashed him a toothless grin and sloshed in more vodka. Aleks sighed and let his broad shoulders drop before he tipped back the glass.

"More?" the man asked.

He shook his head. The alcohol took the edge off his stress but last thing he wanted was to get drunk. He already felt guilty about leaving the Critical Assault Team. Kruger was a capable leader but the CAT was his responsibility. Being intoxicated would just make that guilt worse. He needed to focus on finding Kurtz and getting him back to the team.

The pair had often discussed where life would have taken them had it not been for PRIMAL. Kurtz had always said if he hadn't fallen in with the vigilante group he would have ended up in South East Asia rescuing young girls from sex slavery.

He felt an arm snake around his waist and turned to face a moon-faced girl with long black hair. She winked at him. "Hey mister, you seem sad. I bet I could make you smile."

He reached into his pocket and took out a photo of Kurtz. "Have you seen this man?"

She studied the photo and shook her head. "No, but if you want I can do a special deal for two."

"No, thank you." He paid the bartender and walked out into the throng of tourists exploring the nightlife of Bangla road. He wasn't sure where to go now. He had visited most of the go-go bars and spoken to everyone involved in rescuing children.

"Come on, big boy. I could make you so happy." The girl from the bar had followed him out to the street.

He stopped at a vendor selling coconuts and bought one. "You want?" he asked the girl.

"No, I've got my own right here." She pushed her breasts together to form a deep cleavage.

He laughed and paid for two coconuts. The vendor hacked a triangle out of each green husk with a machete, popped in straws, and passed them over. Aleks gave one to the girl.

"See, you like me." She fluttered her eyelids.

"No, you have it wrong. I think if you're drinking coconut you'll be quiet."

"You aren't like the other Russians around here. Are you just searching for your friend?"

"Yes."

"Have you tried where you last saw him?" She slurped coconut juice through the straw.

Aleks sighed. "No, he won't go back there."

"What about his family. Has he gone home?"

He'd already thought about that. It was his next port of call, a final lead that he had not wanted to use. Kurtz had left his parents' address on file, as his next of kin and sole beneficiaries, but Aleks knew the German had not visited them during his time in PRIMAL. It would probably be a dead end and rub salt into wounds not yet healed.

He pulled out his wallet and took out a hundred baht note. Pressing it into the girl's hand, he turned and stepped onto the street to hail a cab. It was time to book tickets to Germany.

LASCAR ISLAND

Kruger scanned the jungle through his dual-sensor fused night vision goggles. He had chosen to ditch his full-face helmet in favor of a lighter, and cooler, head harness. Despite being the early hours of the morning, the air was stifling and humid. The trees were alive with the screech of insects and god knows what else.

The jungle was the South African's least favorite operating environment. The six-foot-five former Recce sergeant was much happier in the African bush. At least there you had a chance to see the animal trying to kill you. "You boys got anything?" he whispered into his throat mike.

"Negative," replied Miklos. The Czech was patrolling to his left. Through the state-of-the-art night vision goggles he appeared in shades of red and orange against the monochrome backdrop of the jungle.

"Nothing, comrade," confirmed Pavel from the right where he trained a suppressed MK48 machine gun down a slope that ran into a creek.

The three-man team was missing one vital component, Aleks, their leader. He was still searching for Kurtz, leaving the Critical Assault Team with an uneven number.

All three CAT operators were dressed in mottled green battle fatigues, faces painted with camouflage cream. They wore matching lightweight body armor festooned with pouches.

"Advance." Kruger stalked slowly, his Tavor assault rifle held at the ready. He placed his feet gently, avoiding any sound that could give away his presence over the buzz of the jungle wildlife. As he scanned ahead he caught a glimpse of movement and a heat signature. He instinctively fired a series of rapid shots, the subsonic 300BLK rounds barely audible through the integral suppressor. "Contact front!"

Pavel opened up with the machine gun. Tracer flashed

through the darkness and the reek of gunpowder replaced the musky stench of rotting undergrowth.

More of the glowing man-sized targets appeared behind the first and the team bounded forward, blasting the jungle with lead.

"Check fire," Kruger commanded. The aiming laser on his weapon switched off.

The jungle fell silent.

"All clear left flank," transmitted Miklos.

"All clear right," added Pavel.

He cocked his head to one side and tried to identify what sounded like a faint whistle in the air. "Incoming!" He dove to the ground as an explosion flashed through the trees and the ground shook.

Another blast followed the first, closer. Mortar fire was being adjusted toward them.

"Peel right, peel right!" he yelled as he leaped to his feet and ran. He almost collided with Pavel as the smaller man struggled to maneuver his machine gun in the dense jungle. They slid through leaf litter down a slope into a creek.

Behind more bombs rocked the ground. He glanced back and angry explosions of energy flashed in his goggles.

Miklos was the last in. He skidded off the bank and disappeared underwater. A second later he reappeared, spluttering, "I found a hole."

The creek offered protection from the blasts on the ridgeline above. Kruger checked his iPRIMAL strapped to his forearm. It had automatically updated the location and navigation path displayed inside his goggles. It led them straight up the creek. "Let's keep moving, *ja*!"

The three operators waded through the waist deep water, scanning the banks for any heat signatures. After a minute the explosions above them ceased and the jungle went silent. A few more minutes and the insects restarted their orchestra with vigor. Fuck I hate the jungle, Kruger thought as he swatted at a mosquito buzzing in his ear. He swore he'd find leeches inside his pants once this was over.

A few hundred yards further along the creek he led them up the bank through a patch of thick undergrowth to the edge of a clearing. He clenched his teeth as his goggles started fogging. Fifty-thousand dollar night vision technology and they still used a stick of anti-fog wax to ward off the humidity. He adjusted the goggles pushing them further from his face and focused on a cluster of buildings ahead. The hostage they were searching for had to be inside one of them.

"No sign of security," whispered Miklos.

"We'll clear the three buildings starting with the closest. I've got point. Miklos with me, Pavel covering."

He moved through the knee-high grass to the first building. It was small, about the size of a motor home. He slid in next to the door and placed his hand on the knob. Once Miklos was in position opposite he tried the door. It was unlocked. He pushed it open.

Miklos swung into the room and engaged a target with a double tap. Kruger was a split second behind and did the same, dropping the other hostile in the room. "No sign of hostage, coming out."

They moved to the second structure, repeating the process. They finally found their hostage in the third building. Kruger heaved the body over his shoulder. "Objective secure, boys. Let's get out of here."

They met Pavel on the other side of the clearing. There was a path that ran down a ridgeline toward the coast of the tropical island. Taking turns with the 180-pound 'hostage', it took them forty-five minutes to reach the beach where a high-powered ATV was parked with headlights on.

"Nice one, team." Vance, PRIMAL's Director of Operations was waiting for them. The barrel-chested bald-headed African American was dressed in a Hawaiian shirt and Panama shorts. "Drinks are in the cooler."

Kruger dumped the dummy hostage into the back of the ATV and grabbed a sports drink. "Those mortar sims were a nice touch. Wasn't expecting that."

"You handled it well. Let's load up and get you guys back to the Bunker."

He jumped in the passenger seat as Miklos and Pavel piled into the cargo bed. "Any news from Aleks?" he asked as they sped off.

"Yeah, he's heading across to Germany to talk with Kurtz's parents. Once he's done there he'll be coming home."

"Then we'll be deploying to Jamaica with the others?"

"Possibly. We need to be ready to respond to a range of contingencies, not just in South America." Vance drove the buggy off the beach onto a tarmac runway. The headlights lit up an old rusted hangar that butted against a towering cliff.

"I think we should probably do some HAHO and HALO practice then," Kruger said referring to the high-altitude parachuting techniques.

"Good idea." Vance drove inside the rusted out hangar and stopped in front of the solid rock wall. "I'll schedule some jumps for tomorrow afternoon."

The cliff face at the back of the hangar rumbled as it split. A gigantic hidden door slid apart. Once the gap was wide enough Vance raced into PRIMAL's hidden headquarters.

No matter how many times you saw it, the PRIMAL hangar was still impressive, thought Kruger. The floodlit cavern was home to the organization's aircraft. There were two parked in the hangar: a hulking Ilyushin-76, its engines currently in pieces, and an AW609 tilt rotor. The third jet in the fleet, a Gulfstream G650 nicknamed Sleek, was deployed in Jamaica.

Vance drove the ATV around the Il-76 transporter and cut across the nose of the tilt rotor. He parked next to the cargo elevator and jumped out. "Sort your gear out, boys, and get some rest. I've got a feeling you're going to be in the thick of it in no time."

KINGSTON, JAMAICA

Chua had let the team enjoy their breakfast before herding them inside the office for a pre-mission briefing. His own meal, a burrito, was sitting cold and limp on his desk among a pile of empty energy drink cans. He'd been up all night planning via video link to the Bunker. His right eye was already starting to twitch from fatigue.

"Looking pretty tired there, brother," said Bishop as he took a seat in front of the main screen. He looked refreshed from his morning yoga session with Saneh.

Chua nodded as he watched the others file in. Only Flash wasn't present; he was getting some much-needed sleep.

"OK team, I'm going to start with a quick update on the work Flash has done since last night. As you're all aware we've been working our way through the intel that Mitch and Mirza enabled us to pull off MVI's secure servers."

"Well done, lads," said Bishop.

Mitch punched his fist in the air and gave it a victory pump.

"MVI has since tightened their security procedures limiting collection to what we already have. We've exploited almost all of that information now and one of the conclusions that has dropped out is a rift in the relationship between two of the directors. Wesley Chambers, their capital raising guy, and Charles King, the head of security and boss of GES, hate each other. King has identified Chambers as a significant risk due to his hedonistic social life and unwillingness to comply with security protocols. Mirza had the opportunity to meet him last week when he was undercover." He glanced at the PRIMAL operative. "Did you have anything you wanted to add?"

Mirza rose. "Yes thank you, Chen. Chambers is very much a Generation-Y child. I spent some time on his yacht, the *Nemesis*, and can confirm he's entitled, has an overinflated opinion of himself, and is fixated on wealth, power, women, and cocaine."

"Sounds like a hell of boat ride," said Bishop.

Everyone laughed except Mirza who frowned. "It was most enlightening."

"Bet it was," added Mitch, nudging him as he sat down.

"So there it is people, our first target. Saneh, Vance and I think this guy is a prime candidate for a honey trap. You'll have the lead on this and Mirza will back you up. Your mission is to get close to Chambers and identify any opportunities to exploit him. Mirza's already intimate with Chambers and his cover was blown, so his support will need to be discreet."

Saneh nodded solemnly then turned and gave Mirza a wink.

"Bishop," he continued. "You and Mitch will be targeting the GES facility in Virginia. We still have very little on the organization but we do know King spends most of his time at his residence on the estate. The calendars we pulled off the email server indicate King is due to be staying at the residence for the next week. I need you to infiltrate and exploit any opportunities. We're particularly interested in the locations and type of work they're doing. And any links to the CIA."

"What about Venezuela?" Bishop asked.

"Ivan's on the ground already," Chua said referring to his deep-cover operative. "Once we get any additional information I'll let you know."

Bishop nodded.

"OK, guys, I'm going to get my head down for thirty minutes. Once you've got your initial plans ready start prepping your gear." He checked his watch. "Be ready to back-brief your plans at eleven hundred hours. Wheels up at midday. Any questions?" He paused. "No? I'm out."

Chua left the room leaving the pairs to discuss their individual missions. Bishop sat behind one of the laptops and accessed the iPRIMAL imagery database. He found the facility in Virginia and zoomed in. "Looks like a pretty standard training setup." He turned the screen so Mitch could see.

"Yeah, got kill houses, admin facilities, ranges. Even if security is tight we're probably going to be able to get in through the forest," said Mitch.

"It'll provide us with cover all the way to the residence. That's got to be where King lives." He pointed out a mansion in the middle of a dense forest. It was located a half mile from the sprawling training facilities but was still within the perimeter security fence.

"We can bounce a laser off the windows and eavesdrop. Maybe plant a bug."

"Good plan, mate, simple." Bishop turned to see Mirza and Saneh already talking through their own problem. "How come you always get the good jobs?"

They both turned to face him.

"What do you mean?" asked Mirza. "Your job is much simpler."

"You get New York and a beautiful woman. I get Virginia and Mr. Tight T-shirts."

Chapter Four

VIRGINIA

AFTER DROPPING Saneh and Mirza in New York, Bishop and Mitch flew south to Chesterfield County Airport where they parked the Gulfstream and hired a station wagon. From there it was a three hour drive south through lush green forests, rolling farmland, and quaint townships.

Mitch was driving with Bishop riding shotgun. As they turned off the interstate Bishop's eyes were glued to the iPRIMAL tablet on his lap. "This is the very edge of the GES facility."

"Not very welcoming are they," said Mitch.

The road followed a tall fence bordering a thick wall of trees. There was a gap of fifteen yards between the wire fence and the woods.

"Probably got ground sensors, CCTV, dogs, tripwires, patrols, drones..." the Brit said.

"OK I get it. It's not going to be easy to get in."

They continued along the fence for another four miles

before seeing the sign for the entrance to the training and operations facility. As they drove past Bishop gave the entrance a quick glance. "So far you're right on two accounts. They've got CCTV and dogs at the front gate."

"So we slip in somewhere else, yeah."

Bishop turned his attention back to the tablet. "The property's huge, over five thousand hectares. That's a lot of fence line to manage. There'll be a few spots where we can slip in."

"That's all good. What about the live fire ranges?"

Bishop flashed him a grin. "What's wrong, champ, getting cold feet? I thought you loved being in the field."

"I'm not real keen to get shot by accident wandering onto a bloody rifle range."

"Good point; there could be some kind of patrolling training going on. We're going to need some decent camouflage anyway."

The pair had come prepared for a surveillance operation but they had packed light. Having traveled in the US before Bishop knew there wasn't much they couldn't buy from a local outdoor store.

"I don't know about you, buddy, but I could do with a bite to eat and a cup of joe," said Mitch in his best American accent.

Bishop glanced up from the tablet with a frown.

Mitch shrugged. "Just trying to blend in."

"You've got a beard and a flannel shirt. You fit in here just fine."

They finally reached the end of the fence and the road continued for a few miles before reaching a town. It was small, only a few thousand people. Mitch pulled the wagon into a truck stop. "We better fill up while we're here."

"I'll take care of that. Can you grab me a coffee and a chili dog?"

"Will do."

Bishop jammed the gas pump in the fuel tank and leaned against the car as it filled. He stared absentmindedly at the buildings on the other side of the street as a rented sedan pulled alongside. He glanced sideways as a badly dressed and overweight thirty-something man got out of the car. From behind his shades he rolled his eyes; didn't these people exercise?

As Bishop was pumping gas Mitch was trying to work out how to extract coffee from a grubby urn located at the back of the shop. He pushed a button on top and managed to squirt brown lukewarm liquid onto the bench. In the end he gave up, grabbed his room temperature burrito and Bishop's chili dog and walked across to the fridge. He waited for an overweight guy dressed in chinos and an ill-fitting suit jacket to select six cans of sugar-free energy drink from the fridge before grabbing two of his own. He dumped them on the counter next to 'chino guy' and waited for his turn to pay.

Mitch watched as the man reached in his pocket and pulled out his wallet. At the same time his ID card with a lanyard fell to the floor. Mitch bent down and picked it up.

"Thanks, dude," said the man stuffing it back into his pocket.

Mitch gave him a nod, paid for his supplies and gas, and followed the man out through the sliding doors. Bishop was waiting in the station wagon and Mitch handed him the food and drink through the window before jumping back in the driver's seat. As the hire car in front of them turned back toward the GES facility he followed.

"Thought we were heading into town to buy gear?" said Bishop.

"I want to see where this guy goes."

"Why? You want to ask where he bought those awful pants? Or are you looking for some dietary advice?"

Mitch tried not to laugh. "No, he dropped his ID card and I picked it up."

"So he's a GES guy?"

"No," replied Mitch. "He's CIA and his name's Howard."

"No shit." They followed the car as it drove down the road, slowed at the sign to GES, and turned into the security checkpoint. "Well that confirms the CIA and GES are definitely in bed together," said Bishop.

"That a problem?" asked Mitch.

"Nope, let's go buy some kit."

NEW YORK CITY

While Bishop and Mitch searched for an outdoor store Saneh and Mirza were preparing for their own mission. They caught a cab from Newark International Airport to the apartment Saneh had chosen on a short-term rental website. The two-bedroom apartment was only a block from the building that housed the MVI offices.

"Wow, you did well, Saneh. This is a nice place." Mirza dragged two black bags into the living room.

The accommodation was ultra modern, painted off-white, with original pieces of art on each wall.

"It'll do." She placed her own bags on the floor and nodded at a long glass table. "We can set up here." She unzipped her laptop case and started setting up the secure network link back to the Bunker.

Mirza brought his own computer over and plugged it in.

"So what exactly happened down in Mexico?" she asked as she connected an encryption module to the Wi-Fi receiver.

"What do you mean? Chua briefed you on what happened. We shut down the mine."

"Yes, I know that part. I was just wondering about how it all started. I mean, one minute you and Bishop are heading to New York and the next minute you're on a mission in Mexico. You were supposed to be on a holiday."

"We were, but Chua sent Bishop on a mission."

"To Mexico?"

"No, here in New York. Aden met with a journalist who Chua was concerned might be investigating PRIMAL. He didn't know she was investigating the dodgy mining operation in Mexico. Bish walked into the middle of an attempted kidnapping and saved her."

She looked up from her laptop. "So, let me get this straight. Aden chased a girl down to Mexico and you and Mitch had to bail him out?"

"No, not exactly. He agreed to go to Mexico to help expose what was happening with the mine and then things... kind of escalated."

"This girl, is she pretty?"

"Yes, but not like you."

She arched an eyebrow. "Oh, is that right?"

He laughed nervously. "It wasn't like that. He went down to Mexico to make sure she stayed safe, that's all. She needed to get photos of the mine and he wanted to find out if what she was telling him was true. It turned out to be worse. The mine had hired cartel gunmen to force farmers from their land. They murdered old men, tortured young boys. She was wounded when the cartel went after them."

"Is she OK?"

He nodded. "Aden got her out, then refused to abandon the farmers. You know the rest. He has a big heart. You should know a lot of it belongs to you."

The former Iranian intelligence operative tried not to blush. She redirected the conversation back to their current mission. "So we know where Mr. Wesley Chambers works and we know he owns a boat. But what we really want to know is where he likes to party."

"There's a club on 10th called Avenue. He seems to be there a fair bit."

"How do you know that?"

"I Googled him." Mirza spun his laptop so she could see the pictures on the screen. There were half a dozen showing the banker with pretty girls and men in suits.

"Might be a good place to start then."

"I've already checked out the metadata on the photos. If his routine is the same as the last three weeks, he should be there tonight."

She smiled. "You've become quite the agent, Mirza Mansoor."

"Well, I've learned from the best."

She pretended to grimace. "Aden Bishop, super spy."

He laughed. "You guys are so perfect for each other it's disgusting."

Her eyes narrowed. "Really? Grab your jacket, Mirza. I'm going to punish you for that comment."

"What? Where are we going?"

"Shopping. I need something to wear tonight and you're going to carry the bags."

CARACAS, VENEZUELA

The bus door opened with a clunk and Antonio stepped onto the street. He winced as the step down jarred his shoulder. His arm was in a sling and it was the reason he was using the bus instead of his bike.

He walked stiffly beside the busy main road passing throngs of pedestrians. Tall office blocks overlooked the tree-lined street and he checked their numbers as he passed. Finding the one he wanted he entered through the front door and paused in the lobby. Massive posters of freedom fighters were plastered on the walls. Nelson Mandela, Mahatma Gandhi, Mother Teresa, and Martin Luther King all seemed to watch him from the powerful black and white images. He took a moment then walked slowly up the stairs to level one, the national office of the Voluntad party. If anyone was interested in seeking justice for the dead politician, and his traumatized girlfriend, they would be here.

He buzzed the intercom and smiled at the middle-aged receptionist he could see through the glass.

"Can I help you?" she asked through the intercom.

"My name's Antonio. I called earlier."

He watched her check a list then reach for a phone. A moment later she buzzed him in. She gave him a sad look and directed him to the plastic chairs in the waiting room. Minutes passed before a door opened and a man dressed in a tweed jacket appeared. He was thin and wore thick black glasses that magnified his eyes.

"Hello Antonio, my name is Dante."

It was the man he had spoken to on the phone.

"You mentioned you had information regarding the

disappearance of Caitlin Bracho." He led him inside a modest office and offered him a chair. "Do you need anything?" he asked once Antonio was seated.

"No, I'm fine. Miss Bracho came to visit us on the night of her disappearance."

"Yes, you are with the *Movimiento*?"

He nodded. "That's correct. She came to speak with my group. Not long after she arrived the *colectivo* burst in and took her." He pointed to his shoulder. "They did this to me, beat my friends, and raped my girlfriend."

"And you think they killed Caitlin?"

"I know they did. Who else could it be? They took her from my girlfriend's apartment. Then she is found dead in a gutter."

"We have many enemies, Antonio. It could be any number of government organizations or criminal groups. Yes the *colectivo* are violent, but they rarely kill."

"Well, this time they did." He clenched his jaw.

"OK, let's say they did. What are we supposed to do now? Go to the police and complain? Expect them to do anything other than laugh? They hate us just as much as the *colectivo*."

"They killed your colleague, an innocent woman, and you're going to do nothing?"

"No, we will mourn her loss and we'll continue to fight for a change in government. We honor her loss by lobbying for change so in the future women like her can live without fear, can have good jobs, and can provide for their families. That is what we will do. You're a leader of students, Antonio; you know how important it is to force the government to have fair elections. Then and only then can we give justice to you, your friends, and to Caitlin."

He rose and stormed out of the office in disgust, slamming the door behind him. Of all people he thought the Voluntad would want to find Caitlin's killers and avenge her death. Now who could he turn to? The police? Dante was right, they wouldn't give a shit what happened to a member of the Voluntad party, or the *Movimiento* for that matter. They would probably arrest him, frame him for the murder, and throw him in jail to rot.

He strode past the posters of his heroes and out to the street. There was no one else to turn to now and no way of finding the men who had killed Caitlin and raped Camilla. All he had was the image of a dragon clutching a trident. It was an image he would never forget.

Chapter Five

VIRGINIA

BISHOP AND MITCH found an Outdoor World store twenty miles from the GES facility. The sprawling complex was an outdoorsman's wet dream. The storefront was modeled to resemble a lumberjack's cabin complete with a pool teeming with trout, an American flag dancing in the wind, and fake log walls. It even had deer antlers on either side of the automatic sliding doors.

"Welcome to Virginia," said Bishop as they entered. "The home of moonshine, hunting, fishing, and shooting stuff."

"Blimey!" added Mitch as his jaw dropped.

Bishop gave a low whistle as he scanned the shelves. The place looked like someone had opened an outdoors store in a museum. The walls were covered in hunting and fishing paraphernalia including rifles, rods, mounted deer, fish, and fake trees. He was blown away by the level of effort the store's designers had made to immerse their customers in the make-believe outdoors.

"Let's get what we need and get out," said Bishop.

"Good idea. We spend much time in here, mate, and I'm going to buy a boat load of junk I don't need." Mitch grabbed a shopping cart and they started exploring the indoor, outdoor wonderland.

"Hunting is over there." Bishop pointed as he passed the aquarium in the fishing section and walked to the sign-posted area. Surrounded by mannequins dressed in camouflage outfits he scanned for the items he needed.

"Can I help you, sir?" The shop assistant startled him. He was dressed in the same garb as the mannequins and wore a similar cheesy grin.

"Yeah, I'm trying to find gillie suits." He referred to the shaggy camouflage suits commonly worn by snipers.

"Yes, sir, they're right over here. What type are you looking for? Laser cut leaf pattern, plastic strand, or a more traditional hessian design?"

"Something traditional, for use in the forests around here."

The assistant showed him three mannequins dressed in the camouflage coveralls. One of them wore exactly what Bishop wanted. "We'll take two of those."

The assistant pulled them off a shelf and placed them in Mitch's cart. "Is that all you need in clothing? We've also got some excellent wet weather gear. The rain this time of the year can put a dampener on things."

Bishop glanced at Mitch and shrugged. "I'm good. You want a jacket?"

"Do you think we'll need it?"

"Ooh, I love your accent," said the assistant, clapping his hands.

"I think we're fine." Bishop pushed the cart out of the clothing section. They stopped in front of a long rifle rack and cabinets filled with pistols.

"Almost as good as Warmart," said Mitch, referring to PRIMAL's extensive armory.

"No way, do you see any rocket launchers?"

"True, can we even buy guns here?"

"Sure can, no waiting period, and no license required." Bishop grinned.

"Awesome! You can't buy an air gun in the UK without a bloody permit."

"Mitch, this is the home of the brave and the land of the free. You can buy anything you like to protect your own liberty." He sauntered up to the counter and asked for two Beretta Px4 Storm Compact pistols, holsters, spare magazines, and a couple boxes of ammo.

"Good choice," said the weapons attendant as he piled the boxes on the cabinet. "Great little concealed carry weapon." He lifted his shirt to show them his own pistol. "I carry mine everywhere I go."

Mitch caught Bishop's eye and his eyebrows rose.

He managed to hide his smile and signed for the weapons with a Virginia ID. While he filled out the form the attendant verified the ID on his computer.

"All good! None of that waiting period nonsense here, brothers," continued the man. "Just get out in them there hills and start shooting."

Bishop nodded as he put the boxed weapons in the cart and they wound their way through the store stocking up with some basic camping equipment. He put two sets of rudimentary night vision goggles and a spotting scope in the cart along with spare batteries, a couple of boxes of protein bars, beef jerky, and camouflage cream.

When they got to the counter he paid with the credit card linked to the fake ID. Then they piled the gear into the back of the station wagon.

"Where to now?" asked Mitch as Bishop handed him his pistol.

He put on his best Virginian drawl. "Now, we get out in them there hills and start shoot'n."

―――

NEW YORK CITY

Wesley Chambers was in his element. Surrounded by leggy models, splashing out on champagne, he was enjoying impressing some of Wall Street's up and comers in the best club in town. The only thing putting a dampener on his night, he lamented, was the muscle-bound buffoon who was now permanently attached to his hip thanks to that asshole King.

"Who's the meathead?" asked a fellow banker dressed in a smart pinstripe suit.

"Security." Wesley rolled his eyes.

The man laughed. "What sort of dodgy shit are you up to Wes?"

He shrugged and smirked. "You know me, always up to no good."

"No good is right, just like the Mexican deal you got me in on. Tanked big-time, bro."

Wesley waved their hostess over and ordered a bottle of Patron and shot glasses. "Hey, you win some, you lose some. You make a good return on the Congo gig I got you?"

The banker shuffled across on the leather settee he was

occupying and waved a blonde model over to sit next to him. "You're right, that one was good."

"Don't worry about Mexico, it'll come good in the long run. Our legal team is going to rape the Mexicans for every buck they owe us."

The banker had his hand on the thigh of the blonde. "Nice. You got anything else for me? Something new?"

A waitress approached and was forced to wait for the bodyguard to move before reaching the table.

"Get the hell out the way, moron," snapped Wesley over the background music. "Can't you see we're trying to have a good time? You're being a dick."

The guard shuffled out of the way and maintained a passive face.

Wesley turned back to his buddy. "The anal retentive dipshits I work with are paranoid. Some environmental lunatic blows up a mine and they think we're under attack." He sloshed premium tequila into the shot glasses.

"Could be something in it, Wes. People are talking, saying MVI is pretty much done."

Wesley downed a shot and grabbed another. "Look around, dude. Do I seem done? Trust me, we've only just got started. You need to double down now." He touched the side of his nose. "You know what I mean."

"What have you got going, buddy?"

"Something big, real big, down in Venezuela. Got the support of the government, going to make a goddamn killing." Wesley handed him a shot glass.

"No one gets into Venezuela. Their commie politicians hate US investors."

"Not MVI, man, they love us." Wesley signaled for one of the girls to move closer to him. He lodged a shot glass in her cleavage. "Titty shots!"

Both men had forgotten about the security guard standing mere feet behind them. He was close enough to hear the conversation over the club's music. As Wesley and his friend sucked shots from the model's bosom, he pulled a phone from his pocket and thumbed a text message.

From the other side of the club another set of eyes were watching Wesley. Saneh had positioned herself at the bar where she had a clear view of the VIP area.

Entry to the exclusive venue had been relatively easy. The door security had taken one look at her long brown legs, plunging cleavage, and exotic features, and fallen over themselves to pull back the velvet rope. The dress that Mirza had helped her choose had performed its job perfectly.

Once inside she'd given the place a once over. It was classy, two stories of leather furnishings and French polished woodwork were designed to give the club an opulent plantation mansion feel. The throbbing music was smooth and low enough that you could hold a conversation.

She continued to watch Wesley and his ensemble as she sipped on sparkling mineral-water. The dynamic was interesting. The young banker was drunk and trying to impress one of his friends. They had gathered a posse of buxom blondes who all wore too much makeup and exposed far too much skin. The bodyguard was alert; he could potentially a problem. If she could break into the group she was going to have to maneuver Wesley away from him.

"Hey, gorgeous."

She turned to the voice. Its owner was another limp-wristed suit emboldened by a generous dose of overpriced alcohol. She glanced back at the VIP area where Wesley was drinking. She eyeballed the bouncer guarding the roped-off lounge and strode across to him leaving the would-be suitor in her wake.

"Hello." She smiled.

"This is a private function." The bouncer's eyes dropped straight to her cleavage.

"I know, I was wondering if I could join?" she asked seductively.

A female hostess appeared at his elbow. "Sorry, doll. Invited guests only."

"Could you ask the gentleman if it would be OK for me to join them?"

The hostess shrugged, strutted over to Wesley's table, bent down, and said a few words. He glanced at Saneh. She smiled at him and waited for the hostess to return.

"He said it's a lovely offer but he only likes blondes. Sorry, babe."

Saneh quickly retreated to the bar where the suit was still watching her. "So, do you want to buy me a drink?"

The man smiled. "OK."

She couldn't leave straight away so she may as well enjoy the attention. Then she would call Mirza and get him to pick her up outside. They would have to develop a new plan to target 'Mr. I only like blonde porn stars'.

Chapter Six

CARACAS, VENEZUELA

THE HOTEL IVAN had chosen was low key and reasonable value. It suited the identity he had selected for this operation. According to his travel documents he was Igor Kozar, a project manager for a Russian company scoping investments in Venezuelan oil projects. It was a cover he had used once before and one that was layered deep enough that even the most comprehensive security check would be unlikely to find holes in it.

He ran his fingers through his salt and pepper hair and checked his suit in the mirrored walls of the hotel elevator. Studying his face, he noticed a number of new wrinkles at the corners of his eyes. This business was all about details and he saw everything. It was why he was so good at what he did. Nothing was ever left to chance. This mission would be no different.

He had read the PRIMAL mission pack on the Alitalia flight from Rome. The intelligence was patchy at best. All they knew was MVI likely had an interest in resource exploitation, and there were indications that GES could be involved with anti-government groups. Chua had given him two tasks; one, establish anti-government contacts and two, locate a local safe house. The second was easy. He'd already arranged a number of inspections with a realtor. The first task of finding local contacts would be more difficult. However, like everything it was covered by a plan.

A chime announced that the elevator had reached the ground floor and Ivan strode out through the lobby. The hotel had arranged a car and a driver, and he had a number of meetings organized with mid-level officials in PDVSA, the state-owned oil and gas company. He doubted any of them would offer insight into MVI's undertakings. However, they would add legitimacy and depth to his cover.

His driver was an elderly gentleman who smelled of cigarettes. Ivan lowered the window as he entered the car. He preferred the humidity to the stench of tobacco.

"Where do you want to go?" the driver asked in Spanish.

Ivan gave him the address. He was fluent in five languages: Russian, English, French, Spanish, and German, and able to deliver them all with a convincing accent.

It took ten minutes to navigate the inner-city traffic a half-mile to the destination. It was not the offices of an oil and gas company. That would come later. His priority today was to establish contact with those opposed to the government.

The driver waited at the curb as Ivan walked into a building and took the elevator to the second floor. He crossed the street using a sky bridge to another building. Then he walked down an escalator and strolled another hundred yards along the street. Entering a shopping mall, he chose a magazine from a stand and examined the cover before doubling back out to the street. Confident he wasn't being followed he continued along the street and arrived at his destination, the Voluntad head office.

He scanned the black and white posters on the walls of the foyer as he climbed a set of stairs. The faces of famous freedom fighters and peace activists looked down at him. Pausing to announce himself through an intercom, he waited for the receptionist to open the door. A minute later he was sitting in the office of a scholarly gentleman wearing thick black-framed glasses.

He offered the Voluntad politician his hand. "A pleasure to meet you, Dante. Thank you again for agreeing to see me at such short notice."

"No problem."

He placed a gray device the size of a TV remote on the table. "I hope you don't mind. It's a security precaution." A green light flashed on top of the box.

The man stared at it.

"It scrambles any listening devices. Standard procedure for my company." He smiled. "So, I guess you're probably wondering why a representative from one of Russia's largest energy corporations is talking to you?"

Dante nodded. "That did cross my mind."

"*Da*, I can see you are very interested."

The man nodded again. "Intrigued."

"Well, my company thinks change is on the horizon. Soon Venezuela will move to democracy. This is inevitable. And when that happens once again deregulation will occur and my company will be able to establish operations here."

"That's certainly an optimistic view."

"Take Russia. For years we slaved under the yoke of

communism and now we're free. This will happen here too."

The man sighed like he had heard it all before. "And you're here to do what exactly?"

"I'm here to offer funding and support, discreetly of course."

"And in exchange we will give you access to the oil when and if the time comes?"

"Yes, you will give us the opportunity to make a deal and establish operations. But in the short term we would also like information. We would like to know what other oil companies are talking with you."

"You're the only one so far."

"Good." Ivan took an envelope from his jacket and placed it on the desk. "I would like to be informed if that changes."

The man picked up the envelope and glanced inside. "Your generosity is appreciated. I'll make sure this is put to good use. Funding has been difficult since the government crackdown."

"We can offer you other types of support if you need it."

Dante adjusted his glasses. "What do you mean?"

He shrugged. "Anything you need, anything that would help." He touched the side of his nose. "We have people who specialize in helping influence change."

"That is not something this office would want to discuss." Dante glanced down at the scrambler device. "But, I could put you in contact with others who may appreciate that sort of thing. The students running the demonstrations have come under increasing pressure from the *colectivos*."

"The *colectivos*?"

"Government sponsored criminal gangs. They've escalated their standover tactics to include murder. The police do nothing. They turn a blind eye or worse. The only thing the students can do is hide. Your people may be able to help."

"I would be happy to talk with them."

Dante took a piece of paper and scribbled a number on it. "The student's name is Antonio. His group is one that has recently been attacked. Now, I'm sorry but I have other meetings."

"It has been a pleasure." Ivan shook his hand and pocketed the paper and the scrambler. Minutes later he had reversed his counter-surveillance route and was back in his vehicle. The meeting had gone better than expected. He now had a contact.

VIRGINIA

Bishop and Mitch parked their station wagon in a secluded location. Posing as hikers, they humped their backpacks through the woods that adjoined the GES facility. Moving under the cover of darkness they followed the tall chain fence, searching for a way in. They had correctly assessed that the security was unlikely to be as tight away from the main road. Through their night vision goggles they could see the fence was alarmed but the CCTV towers were much further apart. It was possible to find a piece of fence that was unwatched.

"That's our spot." Bishop pointed to a place where heavy rain had eroded a channel under the fence. Animals had taken advantage of the breach digging it out till it could accommodate a small deer and, with a little work, a man.

Mitch kept watch as Bishop crawled forward and dug out the scrape. When it was large enough he pushed his pack under the fence and slid through. Crouched in the woods on the other side he waited for the Brit to follow.

He chuckled as Mitch struggled to fit his broad shoulders through the gap. "Time to lay off the 'roids."

"This is one hundred percent natural, mate. You'd get the same if you laid off the yoga."

"Yoga?" Bishop scoffed as they moved deeper into the forest.

"Yeah, yoga with your sweetheart. Getting all sensitive new age on me."

He shook his head and shielded the glow from his iPRIMAL as he checked the navigation app. "We're about three miles from the house. Got to cross two tracks and avoid the rifle ranges. If we move steadily we should be in position before dawn."

"You want to gear up here?"

Bishop flipped a flap back over the device. "No, there's a good spot to the west of the house. We'll change there." He heaved his pack onto his shoulders. "You sure we need all this crap?"

"Nope, but better safe than sorry." Mitch shouldered his own pack with ease.

"You gave me all the heavy stuff, didn't you?"

"Too much yoga, not enough lifting." Mitch snickered.

Bishop bumped him as he passed.

It took them four hours to make their way through the woods. They avoided two vehicle patrols and slipped behind the stop butt of a range being used for a night shoot. Then, when they reached their lay-up point they rested for a few minutes and ate a protein bar before Bishop pulled a gillie suit from his pack. "I'll go forward and recce a good spot, case the security." He rubbed the suit in the underbrush getting leaves and moss to tangle in the shaggy coat. He pulled the suit on over his clothes and camouflaged his face with cream. Using a knife he cut a flap in the forearm so he could use his iPRIMAL. Finally he checked his Bluetooth earpiece was activated.

Mitch pulled out the spotting scope. "You let me know what the security's like and I'll prep the gear."

"Roger."

Bishop stalked slowly through the trees, stopping every dozen yards to listen and scan with his night vision goggles. It took him twenty minutes to reach a point where he had eyes on the house. He dropped down onto his stomach and watched. The house was dark and showed no sign of life; not surprising considering it was four in the morning.

He slithered forward to get a clear view across the back lawn to the rear patio. The house was two stories with a gabled roof and large windows. That was good, plenty of glass for them to eavesdrop through. The backyard showed no sign of children, or worse still, dogs. However, the house did have CCTV cameras and motion-sensitive floodlights hanging under the eaves. Much more than Bishop would have thought necessary. He spotted a raccoon sniffing around the base of the barbecue at the end of the patio. The critter's presence hadn't tripped any of the infrared sensors that controlled the floodlights.

The heavy security quashed any thoughts of a break-in. If they tripped any of the sensors a heavily armed response team could be only minutes away and he wasn't keen to fend them off with just a pistol.

Chapter Seven

NEW YORK CITY

JORDAN POLLARD WAS SITTING at his desk examining a box of fishing flies. The chairman of MVI was dressed in khaki cargo pants, matching shirt, and a baseball cap. On the floor in front of his desk lay a rod, waders, fishing vest, and a picnic hamper. At least once a month he would abandon his tailored suits for this fly-fishing attire.

A helicopter would take him from the roof of the office building to the Catskills, a hundred miles to the north, where he would spend the better part of the day fishing. It was something he'd been doing for the last five years, a cherished part of his routine. His staff knew it wasn't to be interfered with. Even King had conceded on the need for a security detail. That was why the knock at his door surprised him. He glanced up from his collection of flies and saw it was Ian Macmillan, his Chief Financial Officer. "Come in." Pollard glanced at his Rolex. "This better be quick, Ian. I leave in ten minutes."

"Yes, sir." The CFO stood awkwardly at the door.

"For god's sake man, come in and start talking."

Macmillan walked in. "Sir, it's... well, we've been fielding a lot of inquires from other funds."

He pulled a fly from the box and examined it. The mayfly was a favorite and had been very successful on his last trip. "Isn't that normal?"

"Yes sir, but two of them have asked specifically about Venezuela."

He put the fly back in the box and locked eyes with Macmillan. "Do you know where they're getting their information from?"

"I have my suspicions."

"Do we need any more investment?"

"No, we've reached our targets."

"Very good, thank you for this information, Ian."

The accountant nodded and backpedaled out of the office.

Pollard rested his elbows on the desk and folded his hands. It was time he had some of the risk mitigated from the organization. He stabbed a finger at the secure phone on his desk. It rang twice before connecting.

"Sir," answered Charles King over the speaker.

He grabbed the phone and pressed it to his ear. "I've just had Ian Macmillan in my office with some disturbing information."

"Yes sir, I'm aware of the situation."

"I want you to find out if–"

"It's true, sir. His security detail confirmed it this morning."

Pollard exhaled slowly. "Take care of it. Make it look like an accident." He dropped the phone on the cradle. He checked his watch as the thud of helicopter blades penetrated his office. Right on time. He collected his equipment and made for the stairs.

KINGSTON, JAMAICA

Chen Chua wiped the sweat from his forehead for the fifth time in half an hour. It was only mid-morning and the temperature inside the rusty hangar was almost unbearable. The air conditioning had broken down within hours of the Gulfstream taking off. Neither Chua nor Flash had the skills required to get the industrial unit back online.

"At least the fridge is working." Flash tossed Chua a cold can of energy drink. "Have the teams dialed in yet?"

"Not yet, I'm expecting them any minute now." Chen had a headset on and was using the secure iPRIMAL system to monitor the deployed personnel. On his screen an icon resembling a chess piece flashed. He clicked on it. "Aden, how are you?"

"Good, mate," Bishop's voice came through at a whisper.

Chua could see on his map that the chess piece was adjacent to King's residence at the GES facility. "We're just waiting for Saneh to come online."

"Roger."

On cue Saneh's icon, a flower, also flashed. Chua added her to the conference. "Morning Saneh, I've got Bishop here so we can get straight into it. Aden, I'll get you to report first."

"Right on, morning Saneh. We infiltrated last night and were in position by 0400 hours. The household awoke at around 0600 and we've been eavesdropping with a laser ever since. We can confirm it's Charles King's residence and he's in loc, but as yet we've got nothing worth reporting. Opportunities for infiltration are limited due to an extensive security system and regular patrols by GES security."

"Copy, how long can you maintain your position?" asked Chua.

"We have enough supplies for twenty-four hours. However, Mitch is confident he can rig a remote system to eavesdrop on King's office for about six more after we pull out."

"Good to know. I'll leave it up to you when you want to extract."

"Roger."

"Saneh, what's your status," Chua asked.

"Mirza and I are reevaluating our plan after last night."

"Why, what happened?"

"It would seem Wesley Chambers has a taste in women more aligned with blonde porn stars."

"Right."

Bishop chuckled.

"Anyway," continued Saneh. "We're going to check out his yacht to see if there are any opportunities to get onboard and bug the vessel. Then we'll work out how and when to grab him, if it is in fact viable."

"OK, a minor setback," said Chua.

"Worst case, you can get some bleach and a shorter skirt," said Bishop.

"I thought you were supposed to be in a clandestine OP?" snapped Saneh.

"OK, moving along. My only update is Ivan is now active in Venezuela and has established a safe house in Caracas. He's out on the ground getting a feel for the situation. Now if neither of you have any questions I'm going to let you get back to work."

"I'm good," said Bishop.

"Me too," confirmed Saneh.

"Very well, stay safe. Jamaica out." Chua terminated the conference call and removed his headset. "The teams are in position. Hopefully they'll have some new intel in the next twenty-four hours."

"And if they don't?" replied Flash. The tubby hacker's T-shirt was drenched in sweat. "How long are we going to stay in this shit hole? I thought Jamaica was going to be girls like Rihanna and Rum Collins on a beach."

Chua grinned. "I had you pegged as a punk rocker not a Rihanna type of guy."

"I don't like her music, bro, I just think she's hot. But not as hot as this shitty hangar. You think we could open the doors now the jet is gone?"

He sighed. "Do I have to explain to you again what covert means?"

CATSKILL MOUNTAINS, NEW YORK STATE

Pollard flicked his line in under the bank and teased the fly across the surface. He knew there was a brown trout lurking in the still water, lying in wait for an unsuspecting insect. He'd spotted the fish soon after arriving and for the last hour they had been playing a game of cat and mouse. Pollard jiggled the fly with finesse, hoping to make the trout believe it was alive.

The fly was soon out of range and Pollard relaxed as he wound it in. He was standing knee deep in the crystal waters of a mountain stream, deep within the Catskills. A long way from the hustle of Manhattan and the stresses associated with MVI's projects. His phone was off and the helicopter pilot knew not to pick him up until late afternoon. It gave him at least another five hours of uninterrupted, peace.

As he prepared for another cast he cocked his head to one side. He swore he could hear the dull thud of a helicopter. He ignored it and cast under the bank. It was probably another fishing charter or a fire spotter.

The beat of rotor blades grew louder and Pollard's eyes narrowed. He glanced over his shoulder and spotted the helicopter approaching down the valley. It was a black Hughes 500; a small, short-range helicopter highly suitable for maneuvering in close terrain. He wound in his line as the chopper landed behind a copse of trees. There was no way the fish was going to bite with all this racket.

He heard the turbine spool down as he as unfolded the stool attached to his lunch hamper and sat to enjoy a sandwich. The intruders were here to stay; probably another fisherman. After lunch he would move further downstream and try his luck again. He was not going to let this ruin his day.

He was chewing a salami, pickle, and cheese sandwich when he heard rustling. He turned expecting to see another fisherman. Instead he spotted a man in a well-cut dark blue business suit, white shirt, and a gray herringbone tie.

"Jordan Pollard, I trust you're having a relaxing morning." Thomas Larkin's title was Director of Contracts for the National Clandestine Service, the covert operations arm of the CIA. He was middle aged with jet-black hair and a pronounced jaw that reminded Pollard of a barracuda. The likeness to the voracious fish was fitting considering how ruthless the man was when it came to contract negotiation.

"Thomas, I didn't know you were a fisherman. Although you appear to be a little overdressed." Pollard rose and offered to shake his hand.

Larkin laughed, keeping his arms folded. "No, I'm more of a hunter myself."

"Each to their own. All that walking is bad for my knees. I leave the hunting to my men."

"And how's that going? Have you tracked down the terrorists who shut down your operation in Mexico?"

His brow furrowed. "We're working on it."

"I know, I'm paying the bills."

"We'll find them."

Larkin's lip curled. "You had better get it sorted fast. That's if you value the work you do for the Company."

He swallowed hard. The contracts GES had with the CIA were now its greatest source of income. With the loss in Mexico they could ill afford to lose them.

"I thought as much. Now, I'm assuming all your resources are focused on neutralizing this threat. You wouldn't have anything else on the side distracting you, would you?"

Pollard glared as he finished the last of his sandwich.

"You know what the problem is with you straight-leg infantry guys?" Larkin continued, referring to Pollard's time as a brigade commander in the Army. "You don't cover off on all the contingencies. Oh you can plan, but you're constrained by your training and indoctrination, your fears, your morals and ethics. This is why ultimately you will fail. You're lucky you've got men like Pershing and King to pick up the slack."

"GES has never failed the Company," growled Pollard.

"True, but when you can't keep your own house in order it hardly fills me with confidence."

He clenched his jaw.

"Sort it out, Jordan." The senior CIA officer spun on his heel.

Pollard watched him disappear back into the woods. A moment later the whine of a turbine filled the air. He waited till the chopper was airborne before he reached inside his hamper and turned his phone on. He dialed King. "Where are we at with the German?"

"Shrek will be on the ground in a matter of hours. What's wrong? You're supposed to be—"

"I just got a visit from Larkin."

"Oh, shit. What did he want?"

"He's obsessed with the Major League Network. He's threatening to burn our contracts if we don't wrap them up fast."

"Have no doubt that he's willing to follow through on that threat. I worked with him on a few operations back in the Unit. He's driven by success. He literally only cares about outcomes, that's it."

"Well you understand the imperative. I want you to take care of this personally. I'll be down there in a few days and we'd better have made some progress."

"Yes, sir."

He terminated the call and placed the phone on his stool. Grabbing his rod, he waded back into the steam, determined to not let Larkin spoil his day. He cast and the fly caught on an overhanging branch. He whipped it hard, snapping the line. His favorite fly was now stuck on a branch over the deepest part of the stream. "Son of a bitch!"

Chapter Eight

DENKENDORF, GERMANY

THE BAVARIAN TOWNSHIP of Denkendorf was small, housing a population a little less than five thousand. It was an unremarkable town set against a landscape of rolling green fields. It was also where Wilhelm Jager, AKA Kurtz, was born and raised. The Jager family home was on the outskirts; a stately mansion backing on to an estate of a few hundred hectares.

"Nice place you've got here," Shrek said as he stomped into the living room and smiled at the elderly couple sitting on the couch. "Must be worth a buck or two."

Matt, his offsider, was standing in the corner of the room watching them intently.

"That 7-series Beemer out front is pretty nice too. So what did you do for a living, Mr. Jager, you a banker or something?"

"No, I'm a surgeon. Now, what do you want?" Dieter Jager held his wife protectively.

"I want to know where your son is."

There was a long pause before Dieter responded quietly. "We don't know. You're scaring my wife. Please leave."

He stepped forward and leaned in close. "Scaring her? If you don't tell us where your son is I'm going to do a hell of a lot more than scare her."

"We haven't seen him for over six years. Ever since the incident."

"The incident?"

Dieter shook his head. "Look, who are you people? Do you work for the American government? Has Kurtz done something wrong?"

Shrek glanced across at Matt then back to the couple. "Your son has been linked to an act of terrorism."

Anger flashed in the old lady's eyes. "That's not possible! Wilhelm used to be a policeman. He would never do anything like that. He is a good boy."

Shrek shrugged. "A person can change a lot in six years. Now, tell me about this incident."

"He did something silly and was forced to leave the police force."

"Silly? What, like joining a terrorist organization?"

"No, his girlfriend was raped by a gang. He hunted them down and beat them. One of the criminals died in hospital."

Shrek nodded. "Sounds like your boy's a bit of a bad ass. So what happened to him after that?"

"He disappeared. We haven't seen or heard from him since," snapped the mother.

"That's because your dear little boy ran off and joined a group of terrorists and criminals."

She looked away and shook her head. "Not my Wilhelm. He wouldn't do that."

"Then tell me where he is."

"Are you deaf? We don't know!"

His eyes narrowed. "Shut the fuck up you old bag. I'm done talking to you." He directed his attention to Dieter. "Now, I'm pretty damn sure you don't want anything to happen to frauleine bossy britches here." He flicked his knife open.

The old man's face went white. "He sent us a number. For emergencies."

"Dieter, no!"

"I thought I told you to shut your mouth! Matt, you got a pen and paper?"

"Yeah, bro." He tossed Shrek a khaki notebook holder.

He undid the velcro and pulled out a pencil. "OK, let's have the number, gramps."

Dieter pulled up the number on his phone. "Here it is."

Shrek grabbed the phone and scribbled the number down. He pocketed the device as he walked across to the kitchen and called Pershing.

"So, have you found him?"

"We've got the next best thing."

"And that is?"

"A phone number." Shrek read it off the notepad.

"Good work."

"What do you want me to do with his parents?"

"Get me proof of life then make them disappear."

"Yes, sir." He terminated the call, walked back to the living area, and wedged himself on the couch between the elderly couple.

"Now, before we go for a drive I thought we might grab a photo. Matt, if you don't mind." Shrek had a grin on his face, his massive arms around Mr. and Mrs. Jager, as Matt snapped a few shots.

"Right, now let's go for that drive. Matt, can you grab the car?"

Outside, an equally intimidating operative was also searching for Kurtz. Aleks had parked his hire car a couple houses down from the Jager estate. The PRIMAL operative felt a little uneasy about meeting the parents of his best friend under these circumstances. He'd never met them and still wasn't sure what he was going to say. He had flown direct from Thailand and it had been all he thought about on the long flight.

As he approached the entrance to the estate a man walked out the gates and across to a sedan. He wore tactical wrap-around sunglasses, short hair, and the biceps under his T-shirt bulged. Aleks gave him a nod, pretended to check the mailbox next door then ducked into the neighbor's yard. He reached for his pistol then remembered he wasn't carrying one.

The car engine started up and Aleks glanced around the end of the fence, watching as it drove into the Jager address. He ran past the thick hedge that grew along the road and glanced through the gates into the gardens. The sedan drove up a short gravel path and stopped alongside a black BMW in front of the manor.

The driver disappeared inside and Aleks ran quickly up the drive. The mansion was three stories and made of stone with a red tiled roof. He waited around the corner from the entrance, pressed himself against the wall, and listened.

A woman's voice cried out, "Let go of me, it hurts!"

"Get the fuck in the car." The accent was American.

When Aleks stepped out from around the corner the short-haired man was holding the door of the sedan open. Another man, a bald-headed brute with a goatee, was pushing an elderly couple toward it. Aleks strode forward. "What do you think you are doing?"

The man at the car turned to face him. "This is none of your business."

"I just made it my business."

Short hair pulled a knife from his pocket and flicked it open. He lunged at Aleks but the barrel-chested Russian moved surprisingly quickly. He sidestepped and threw a straight right to the jaw. The man collapsed and slumped against the car tire.

Aleks turned to the bald-headed kidnapper. "Your friend was a little tired. Do you need a nap as well?"

"You should have walked on by, pal," he said taking a fighter's stance.

Kurtz's parents took the opportunity to escape back to the house as Aleks sized up his opponent. The American looked younger and fit. He was slightly shorter but had massive shoulders leading up to a thick neck. With a roar the man launched his attack aiming a front kick to Aleks' midriff.

He jumped back as the attacker followed up with a volley of punches. Taking the blows on his forearms, he counter-punched but the blow glanced off the American's skull to no effect.

Street fights are usually over in a matter of seconds but this one was becoming a toe-to-toe boxing match as they hammered each other. Aleks managed to deliver a solid uppercut to the stomach. As the American doubled over, he shoulder charged, knocking him to the gravel. He pounced, attempting a chokehold with a thick forearm.

His opponent clenched his jaw, forcing it to his chin to stop the hold encircling his neck. He wedged his hand under Aleks' arm and drove his elbow back into the Russian's ribs.

Aleks grabbed his own hand and used it to add additional force to the hold.

The American screamed as the straining bicep compressed his face. He smashed his elbow back again and a rib cracked. Reaching up he managed to slip his fingers under the arm, break the hold, and roll away.

By this time the first man Aleks had knocked down was standing and nursing his jaw.

The goateed bald-headed assailant was also on his feet and eyed the PRIMAL operative warily. "You're fucking dead."

Aleks ignored the pain in his ribs and cracked his neck. *"Ebat' tvoju mat'"*

The sound of police sirens filled the air.

"Next time, you commie fuck," snarled the hulking American. He helped his partner into the car. The sedan spun its wheels on the gravel, took off down the drive, and disappeared around the corner.

A moment later the flashing lights of a police car appeared. It pulled in to the estate and skidded to a halt in front of Aleks.

"Show me your hands!" an officer yelled in German as he jumped out the car aiming his pistol.

Aleks winced as he held them up. Behind him a woman's voice called out. "Leave him alone, Ulrich. He's the one who helped us."

The police officer holstered his sidearm and helped him to his feet. "You're a very brave man stepping into stop a kidnapping."

"I was walking past and something was wrong." Aleks' German was flawless. "Do you know who they were?"

"Just hooligans," said the old lady. Aleks could see the family resemblance to Kurtz. He knew it had to be his mother.

"Do you want to make a statement?" the police officer asked.

"Yes dear, Dieter will come down to the station later. Let me take care of this young man first. Say hello to your mother for me."

"OK. Just let me know if you need anything else." The policeman got into his car and drove off.

"He used to play with my son. Such a nice boy. Now come inside, Dieter has brewed some coffee."

Aleks glanced down the drive as she guided him into the house; there was no sign of the Americans. She sat him at the kitchen table in front of a steaming pot of coffee and a plate of cake.

"Are you sure you're alright? We can drive you to the hospital if need be."

"No, I'm good thank you."

"OK then, my name is Barbara and this is Dieter." She introduced her husband as he sat at the table.

"A pleasure to meet you. My name is Aleks." He paused. "I'm a friend of your son, Kurtz."

Barbara shot her husband a glance. "Wilhelm?"

"Yes, Wilhelm Jager. I know him as Kurtz."

"Did he send you?"

"Not exactly. I'm trying to find him."

"So were those men."

"Did you tell them where he is?"

The gray-haired lady shook her head. Aleks spotted a tear forming in the corner of her eye.

"We don't know where he is, Aleks. We haven't seen Wilhelm in six years." She used her sleeve to wipe the tear away. "But my silly husband did give them the contact number he left."

"He left a number?"

"Yes, only for emergencies."

Aleks pulled his **iPRIMAL** from his leather jacket. "Well, this seems like an emergency to me."

Chapter Nine

GES FACILITY, VIRGINIA

PERSHING WAS in his office at the back of the underground SCIF when his phone rang. It was Shrek. He called Howard in, shut the door, and put the call on speaker.

"Shrek, I've got Howard in here with me, the CIA analyst."

"Roger, boss, just wanted to let you know we got jumped by some big bastard at the Jager place."

"What, someone was waiting for you?"

"Nah, the dumb shit was walking along the street when we were trying to get the old fuckers in the car."

"And he jumped you?"

"Yeah, might be a friend of this Wilhelm guy."

Pershing ran a hand through his receding hairline and leaned back in his chair. "Or those sneaky sons of bitches could know we're on to them."

Howard shook his head. "No, there's no way they could know. It would have to be a random—"

Shrek's voice interrupted through the speaker. "Listen, the fucker knew how to handle himself. One-punched Matt, knocked him the hell out."

"Alright, so there's a good chance he's part of the Major League Network," said Howard. "So do you have a description or a photo?"

"No photo. He's a big bald-headed commie fucker with a beard. Sounded Russian."

Howard rolled his eyes. "Wow, that's real useful, dude. I'll be sure to put out a BOLO on that."

"Who the fuck is this prick, boss?"

Pershing glared at Howard and held his fingers to his lips. "Just a CIA guy, Shrek."

"Well tell him to shut his fucking trap. Any time he wants to get in the field and go head to head with a goddamn Spetsnaz wrecking ball then he can mouth off." There was a pause. "So what do you want us to do, boss? We could get our hands on some steel, go back, and finish the job."

Pershing rocked forward on his chair. "No, you guys have done well getting the phone number. Get your ass back stateside."

"Copy."

Pershing terminated the call. "I've got to go down and report to King in fifteen minutes. Where are we at with the number?"

"I literally just received the initial analysis from my NSA dude," said Howard.

"And?"

"It's a Skype number."

"What does that mean?"

"It means it's a number that forwards to a Skype account where you can leave a message. Then the user logs on to their account and checks them. It makes it very difficult to track."

"Difficult, but not impossible."

Howard shook his head and his chins wobbled. "No, not impossible. My guy has located the account. He's just waiting for someone to log in and that will give him a location."

"Can't he tell us where it was last accessed from?"

"Yeah, he already did that. It was down in Brazil, Rio to be precise. About a week ago."

"Excellent!" Pershing jumped out of his chair, grabbed his ten-gallon hat, and strode through the SCIF. Outside the building he commandeered a buggy and raced through the woods to King's residence. The short drive was pleasant and he found himself whistling as he followed the paved path.

The guards at the front gate waved him through and he parked in front of the manor. He waited at the front door for one of the house servants to let him in and direct him to the study.

King was sitting behind his desk working on his desktop computer when he arrived. He glanced at Pershing and gave a curt nod. "George, come on in." He pointed a remote at a box on the wall turning on the room's active security measures. "What news have you got for me?"

Pershing hung his hat on the stand and sat down in a plush leather chair. "We've got our first solid lead, sir."

"Good, Jordan Pollard is arriving in a few hours. He's expecting progress."

"Oh, we've got progress."

LESS THAN FIFTY yards away Bishop was lying on his stomach with the spotting scope pressed to his eye. The arrival of Pershing had interrupted his breakfast of beef jerky. It was their second day watching the house and the first time they had seen anything worth noting.

"Check out this guy," Bishop said passing Mitch the spotting scope. They were laying at the edge of the woods that bordered King's backyard.

"That's the wanker from the mine," said Mitch as he peered through the scope into the office.

"Sure is. Can we listen in?"

Mitch handed the spotting scope back and turned his attention to an eavesdropping laser mounted on a compact tripod. The device was designed to capture vibrations striking a surface, turn them back into audio, then transmit them to a headset. Mitch adjusted the laser, double-checking it was aimed at the window of King's study. After a minute of fiddling he shook his head. "Sneaky bastards."

"What?"

"They're running some kind of scrambler that's messing with the vibrations. I'm getting three-fifths of bugger all."

"You're kidding me. We've been lying here for over a day and now they turn on their countermeasures?"

Mitch tried the laser on another window. "The whole house is covered."

He continued to watch the two men through the window of the study. Pershing was telling his boss something important, that much was clear.

"Mate, we might want to pull back," said Mitch.

Bishop lifted his eye from the scope and saw two gardeners as they rounded the building with a wheelbarrow filled with tools. "Wow, could this get any worse?"

The two workers started raking leaves from the back

lawn. A moment later the back door to the patio opened and two of the house servants appeared. One carried out a cooler, placing it next to a large stone barbecue. The other proceeded to fire up the barbecue. A raccoon appeared, searching for food. One of the gardeners chased it away with a rake and the animal scurried back into the woods.

"Looks like King might be expecting company," said Bishop as he started snaking back through the bushes. Within a few yards he and Mitch turned, stood up, and made their way to where they had hidden their packs.

Mitch pulled a case the size of a paperback from his pack and unclasped it. "I've got an idea." Inside, packed in foam, was what looked like a dead wasp.

"What the hell is that?" Bishop asked.

"Nano-drone with a built-in audio recorder. Little fella can fly out, stick to anything, and will record up to four hours of conversation."

"So we just fly it inside the house?"

Mitch shook his head. Under the gillie suit hood the bearded tech resembled Chewbacca from Star Wars. "No, it can only fly in a straight line. I was thinking we put it near the barbecue and see what we get."

"Could be worth a try."

"The only thing is…"

Bishop's eyes narrowed. "What?"

"Well, it's not one hundred percent reliable."

"How do you mean?"

"It flies out good enough. I point a laser at the target and it lands right on the mark. It's just sometimes it stays stuck and doesn't want to come home. It's a temperamental little bitch and since it can't transmit…"

"You're saying one of us has to go and get it?"

Mitch grinned. "Potentially. Dibs not!"

KING MET Jordan Pollard's helicopter when it landed at the helipad next to the administration buildings. He watched as the crew opened the side door of the Eurocopter and the gray-haired Chairman strode across the grass toward him. "Goddamn, I'm starving."

"Sir, we've got a briefing at the SCIF and then lunch."

Pollard scowled. "Your house is secure isn't it?"

"Yes, sir."

"Then you can brief me over lunch."

King drove him the half-mile from the landing zone to the house. When they arrived he sent the housekeeper out to check on the barbecue and led Jordan to his study. He activated the security measures and made to pour a whiskey.

Pollard waved the glass away. He glanced out the window as a housemaid placed a tray of meat alongside the grill. "You got ribs out there?"

"Yes, sir, but not as good as the ones you make, of course."

"Of course, but we can make do."

They went outside and King excused the housemaid. He reached into a cooler next to the barbecue and passed Pollard a beer.

The chairman positioned himself in front of the cooker and checked to see the coals were cherry red before he tossed the rack of ribs on the grill. "I envy you, Charles. This sure beats the hell out of working in New York all the time."

He sipped from his beer. "Yes, it does."

Pollard watched the meat sizzle for a moment then

turned to face him. "When are you going to deal with that weasel Wesley?"

"Tonight."

"Good, he's a goddamn liability." Pollard took a long pull from his beer and smacked his lips. "Damn, that's good. So what did your boys uncover in Germany?"

"We've got a strong lead, sir. The parents of Objective Red Sox had a means of contacting him. A phone number we've traced to Brazil. Pershing's team is ready to go as soon as we have more fidelity."

"Fidelity?" Pollard checked the meat. "How long is that going to take?"

"A few days at most. Our CIA liaison has NSA working on it."

"And you don't think it would be a good idea to pre-position the team?"

"I'm waiting for two of them to return from Germany. They arrive tonight." He paused. "We also think they ran into a member of the Major League Network."

"In Germany?"

"Yes, someone was watching the house. He jumped our boys on the way out."

"How many?"

"Just one man. The police arrived before Shrek could finish him off."

Pollard clenched his jaw. "Who the hell are these people? We need to pick up this Red Sox guy as soon as possible."

"We're waiting to confirm support from the CIA station chief in Rio."

"Did you have to run it past that piece of shit Larkin?"

"Yes, sir, I did."

"So he's abreast of the situation?" Pollard turned the ribs.

"He is now."

"That bastard's up to something, I just know it."

"What do you mean?"

"He's just taking way more interest in this than he should. There was no reason for him to interrupt my day off in the Catskills. Our independent operations have no impact on the government contracts we already have."

"Do you think he knows about Venezuela?"

Pollard shook his head as he turned the ribs again. "No, if he did he would want in on it. You know as well as I that the CIA struggle to get any ops off the ground in that country. You've worked with him before, right?"

King nodded.

"Try to find out what he's after. Why the sudden interest? Now, these ribs are ready." He transferred them to a plate. "I'm guessing your wife has whipped up some of that amazing potato salad of hers?"

"Sure has."

"Good, let's eat. Then you can show me around your intel facility."

As King grabbed the tray of ribs Pollard glanced up at the wooden frame that supported the all-weather awning. "You might want to get your maintenance boys to search for a wasp nest, Charles. He pointed at the yellow and black insect perched high on the frame. "That's a big sucker."

RIO DE JANEIRO, BRAZIL

Kurtz sat on the edge of the bed in his cheap hostel room. In his hands was an extendable baton. He snapped it open with a flick of his wrist then collapsed it by driving the point against his palm. He had purchased it at the street markets. After the incident during the last rescue, he was taking no risks. Confident the Chinese-made baton was functional he stashed it in his backpack that also contained pepper spray and a dagger.

He lay back on the lumpy mattress and stared at the ceiling. His mind wandered to thinking about his old PRIMAL teammates. Aleks was probably enjoying Lascar Island's pristine beaches during his down time. He hated to admit it but he missed his old team. He missed the camaraderie, the challenge of a new mission, and the thrill of combat. But, then images of Karla's death flashed through his mind and his hands shook. He sat up and reached for the bottle of rum on his nightstand. It was empty. His anger boiled and he threw it at the door. It gouged a hole in the cheap particleboard and thudded onto the thin carpet.

"*Scheisse!*" He swung his feet off the bed, grabbed his backpack, and left the room. He descended a flight of stairs, past the elderly gentleman manning the reception desk, and stormed out to the street.

It was midday and the sun was harsh. The bottle shop was a block away. He changed his mind and ducked into the internet café next door. It was air conditioned and sold chilled water. The woman behind the counter knew him by sight and smiled. She was middle-aged and had told the tall German he was very handsome.

He bought a bottle, sat down at a computer, and logged

on to an anonymous email account. He was waiting for a reply from Escape, another not-for-profit organization operating in the region where the Brazilian, Paraguayan, and Argentinian borders met, an area where sex slavery and smuggling was rampant. He was tired of working with his current team of retired police officers. Escape had a reputation as a more professional outfit, run by young war veterans from the UK.

There was an email in his account but it wasn't from Escape. It was an alert from his Skype account. Someone had left a message. It could only be his parents as they were the only ones with the number. Opening the account he listened to the message.

"Wilhelm, it's me your mother. One of your friends is here. He has a message for you."

There was a pause.

"Kurtz, it's Aleks. Someone's searching for you. They came after your parents but they are safe now. Call the Bunker as soon as you can."

That was it. A short message that hit home harder than anything he had ever felt. He couldn't believe PRIMAL would stoop so low as to use his parents to try and track him down. It angered him even more coming from Aleks.

He logged off, deleted the browser history, and grabbed his backpack. He considered heading back to the hostel but he had all he needed on him. New clothes could be easily purchased and it would take PRIMAL next to no time to track him to the internet café. They probably already had people in Rio. As he left the building he ran into Brian, the retired police officer he had been working with.

"Hey Kurtz, where are you going, buddy? We've got a briefing in half an hour."

He scowled. "Count me out. I'm leaving." He grabbed the retiree by the front of his shirt. "If anyone comes looking for me, we never met."

He strode away from the confused man and headed for the bus terminal.

Chapter Ten

NEW YORK

IF FIRE ever broke out among vessels berthed at the Newport Marina it was going to bankrupt at least a dozen insurance companies, thought Saneh. The floating pontoons on the western banks of the Hudson were home to some of the most expensive yachts she had ever seen.

"Wow!" she exclaimed as she used the telephoto lens on her camera to inspect Wesley Chambers' pride and joy, the *Nemesis*. The sleek motor cruiser resembled a cross between an offshore racing powerboat and a stealth fighter. Nearly 120 feet long, the Wally 118 sported a chiseled dark-green hull crowned with an angular glass superstructure. With its high bow and lines sweeping back to a low stern it looked fast, even bobbing at its moorings. "You're not wrong, Mirza, she's beautiful."

"You should see it go." Mirza was inspecting a tourist map as he leaned on the park rail next to her. The pair had caught the subway across town and walked to the marina where, from his previous experience, he knew Wesley kept the boat moored. The park opposite the rows of motor cruisers and yachts offered an excellent vantage point for their reconnaissance. With Wesley's social life proving to be a challenging target they had decided to look for another way to exploit him. His boat provided an opportunity to plant a listening device or possibly stage a kidnapping.

"And Wesley arrives by chopper?"

"Correct. The helo pad is at the end of the second row of pontoons."

She angled the lens and spotted the floating deck. "So does he live onboard?"

"I'm not sure. It's big enough."

"Probably just brings models back for drug-fueled orgies. But you wouldn't know anything about that would you?" She lowered the camera and gave him a wink.

Mirza struggled to think of a retort. He had been exposed to Wesley's playboy lifestyle when he'd gone undercover as an investment banker.

She laughed and returned to scanning the marina. Saneh wasn't at all surprised to see access was tightly controlled. It bristled with CCTV cameras and she noticed that while one of the security guards was patrolling the other remained in the box monitoring the camera feeds. "How far is the local police station?"

He checked on his iPRIMAL. "Less than four minutes."

"They'll have them on speed dial."

She lowered the camera and frowned. "The best way onto the boat is to swim."

"Doesn't look very inviting." The two hundred yards between them and the sleek vessel was thick with trash. Plastic bags, Styrofoam cups, and empty soda cans bobbed in clusters.

"I'll go tonight." Saneh nodded at the park on the foreshore. "Plenty of trees and no lights. I'll slip under the handrail."

"You sure? I should go."

Saneh turned to him, her eyebrows arched. "Did Bishop tell you to stop me from doing anything dangerous?"

Mirza shrugged. "He doesn't have to say anything, Saneh."

She stared at him then turned away. "Mirza, five years ago, before PRIMAL, I was part of a team who kidnapped an Israeli scientist from a resort at Ashdod. The mission went bad and I swam over a mile towing my dead partner to get back to our boat. I think I can handle this."

Mirza nodded. "We need to find a sports store. You're going to need a wetsuit and fins."

GES FACILITY, VIRGINIA

Night had fallen and it was raining as Bishop and Mitch lay in the bushes watching King's house. The lights in the downstairs level were all out, except in the kitchen where one of the maids was working. The head of GES had retired upstairs with his wife. Since the barbecue the PRIMAL pair had been looking for an opportunity to recover the wasp bug. As Mitch had predicted, the experimental nano-drone would not detach from the awning and fly back.

Bishop was wet, uncomfortable, and bored. His gillie suit offered little protection from the torrent of rain that had blown in after sunset. The downpour had soaked through the camouflage strands adding extra pounds and drenching him. "This is shit," he mumbled under his breath.

"What was that, old man?" whispered Mitch. "Something about it being a beautiful night?"

"You would enjoy this, bloody sadist. You grew up with this shitty weather."

"I'll have you know Wales is beautiful this time of year."

He rolled his eyes and went back to looking through the spotting scope. "Hey, check it out, our little buddy's back." The raccoon who'd been lingering around the garden climbed onto the barbecue and scavenged for scraps. He watched the animal for a moment, noting none of the security lights had come on. "Mitch, you reckon the rain is affecting the infrared sensors?"

"For sure, the range would be impacted. The CCTV won't be great either."

"Right, well it's been over five hours and I don't think this weather is going to lift. Should I duck in and grab the bug so we can get the hell out of here? I mean, no one's coming outside any time soon."

"Sounds good to me, only an idiot would be out in this," whispered Mitch.

Bishop smirked as he set off. He methodically worked his way through the trees and bushes. At the edge of the woods he paused, checking the house for any sign of movement. The light was still on in the kitchen; the maid was hard at work.

"You're all clear," transmitted Mitch.

He crouched and paced steadily toward the barbecue. The raccoon eyed him suspiciously from its perch. The back door creaked open and light streamed out into the backyard. He froze. The raccoon turned to face the noise.

"The maid's at the door," Mitch's voice came through in his earpiece.

Bishop lowered himself to the ground as he watched her. She was standing on the porch holding a plastic bowl. He crawled forward until the stone barbecue blocked her from his sight.

"She's just standing there," Mitch reported.

The raccoon chirped and Bishop heard the woman call out to it. The little animal leaped from his perch and made for the back door.

Mitch sniggered. "No wonder he hangs around. She's feeding him scraps."

A minute passed before the door swung shut leaving the backyard in darkness. Bishop quickly climbed onto the barbecue, grabbed the bug from the under the weather awning, jumped down, and sprinted to the tree line. "Let's get the hell out of here."

NEW YORK

Saneh walked along the foreshore wearing a coat and carrying a sports bag. She stopped in the shadow of a cluster of trees and gazed out across the inky black waters of the Hudson. On the other side of the river Manhattan sparkled. Twin pillars of pale blue light shot skyward over the financial district, a stark reminder of the evil that lurked in the world.

She removed her coat, revealing a three-quarter length wet suit. The three-millimeter thick neoprene clung to her skin accenting every curve of her athletic figure. She pulled a set of fins from the sports bag as well as a small dry bag containing her equipment. A razor sharp dive knife was already strapped to her forearm. She stuffed the jacket inside the empty sports bag and hid it under a shrub. The dry bag was secured around her waist with a strap.

"Mirza, where are the guards?" A short-range waterproof earpiece was in her right ear and she wore a throat-mike.

"They're both inside. You've got a jogger heading your way. Once he passes you're all clear." Mirza was positioned closer to the marina where he could observe both the guard shack and the footpath.

Saneh waited for the runner to disappear from sight before she stepped out from the bushes, crossed the path, and slid under the railing. Dangling from the edge of the sea wall she lowered herself slowly into the frigid water. It was only a few feet deep and she balanced on one foot as she fitted the compact fins. Then she slid into the darkness, a lithe black predator in search of prey.

Swimming low in the water she was careful to keep her head clear as she delivered powerful kicks with the fins. She crossed the channel quickly and within minutes was alongside the sleek hull of Wesley's boat. Once at the stern she dragged herself out of the water onto the swim platform.

She peeled off her fins and wetsuit, and toweled herself with the microfiber chamois from the dry bag. She stashed the wetsuit in a locker and clad only in a black one-piece swimsuit she padded across the smooth teak deck to the glass sliding doors. Crouching she pulled her lock-pick kit from the dry bag. As an afterthought she tried the door. It slid open.

She crept through the doors and slid them shut behind her. The inside of the luxury cruiser was dark without the lights on. The cabin's tinted glass dulled the marina's lights.

She waited for her eyes to adjust. Slowly the detail of her surroundings emerged from the gloom.

The *Nemesis'* main cabin was spacious. She walked through a lounge area that could accommodate at least ten passengers in comfort. Avoiding the stairs in the middle of the floor that led below decks, she climbed to what served as the bridge.

The upper level was unlike any vessel she had ever seen. The console with its controls was familiar but the presence of what could only be described as a boardroom table was not. In fact, the entire top floor felt more corporate than nautical. She took a listening device the size of matchbox from the dry bag and stuck it under the lip of one of the cabinets that lined the walls. She returned down the stairs and placed another device behind the lounges. Then she walked down into the hull, pulled a small flashlight from the dry bag, and switched it on.

A narrow corridor with doors on each side split the lower deck of the *Nemesis*. She guessed the end room, in the bow, would be the master bedroom. Her assumption was correct. The bedroom was twice the size of an average New York apartment and in dire need of a woman's touch. Suit jackets, shirts, and underwear were strewn across the bed. She almost trod on a champagne glass as she made her way past the bed and checked the ensuite bathroom.

There was a crackle in her ear as she searched for somewhere to hide another bug.

"Saneh… copter… in…" The transmission was distorted and broken, probably due to the shielding effect of the carbon composite hull.

She slid the last bug under the bed and trotted back down the corridor and up the stairs. "Mirza, you there?" she asked as a helicopter roared over the boat.

"Chopper's inbound. You need to get off the boat."

She slid the rear doors apart as the helicopter touched down on the pad sixty yards from the *Nemesis*. Sliding them shut behind her she stayed low, running down the stairs to the swimming platform. She contemplated dashing across the gangplank but when she peeked over the side she could see someone in a suit staggering along the pontoon supported by another, larger man. The drunk was singing boisterously. It was too late to jump into the river unnoticed so she dove into a sunken lounge setting.

Lights snapped on bathing her hiding place in a soft glow. She climbed under a table. "Mirza, I'm going to have to wait a while," she whispered.

"I don't think that's going to take long. Wesley was struggling to walk."

"Let's hope the security guard doesn't give the boat a sweep."

Wesley stumbled through the cabin's sliding doors and collapsed sideways onto one of the couches on the lower level. He sprawled on his back and stared up at the ceiling that appeared to be rotating slowly. He had no idea how he'd managed to extract himself from the club and get to the helipad for pickup.

"Sir, you need to sober up."

He turned his head toward the voice and recognized his bodyguard. Now he remembered how he got to the helicopter. The big oaf had pretty much dragged him kicking and screaming from the nightclub. "Hey oaf, thanks." He laughed and looked back to the ceiling.

"Sir, you've got a meeting in six hours. You need to sober up."

"Screw them," Wesley mumbled. "I need another drink." He staggered off the lounge and managed to make it up the steps to the bridge. There was a selection of liquor in a cabinet. He yanked it open and pulled out bottle of tequila. He held it high so the guard could see it. "Shots?"

The burley GES operative took something from his suit pocket and threw it on the glass table. "We need to get you sober."

Wesley eyeballed the bag of white powder and smiled. "That's a brilliant idea, Jeeves." He shuffled over, emptied the bag on the table, and used his credit card to chop it into lines. Before he hoovered one up he glanced at the bodyguard. "Hey man, you're alright." He used a rolled-up bank note to snort the line off the table and waited for the rush to hit.

A split second later he knew something was wrong, very wrong. His heart raced and he fought the sudden urge to puke. He turned to the bodyguard as he clutched his chest. The man was watching him intently. As Wesley keeled over he wondered why the guard was wearing rubber gloves. Clarity hit him the same time as the deck.

Crouched under the outdoor setting Saneh was listening to everything happening inside. Mirza was retransmitting the audio feed from the listening devices over her earpiece. Prompted by the commotion she crept up to the glass and peered in. "Mirza, he's not trying to help him." Wesley was lying on the ground convulsing as his bodyguard watched calmly from a seat at the table. "I can't just let him die. I'm going in."

"Saneh, wait."

She drew her Riffe dive knife from its sheath and padded forward. The rear doors were still open. She slipped through and stalked across the floor, the knife hidden behind her forearm. The bodyguard was watching Wesley and didn't see her till she was climbing up the steps to the bridge.

"Where the hell did you come from?" His eyes locked on to her cleavage.

"I was waiting for Wesley." Saneh flashed him a doe-eyed look and thrust out her chest as she walked toward him. "Oh shit, is he alright?" She cupped her free hand to her mouth.

"He's fine. Had bit too much to drink."

That's a lie, thought Saneh. Wesley was still convulsing on the floor.

"You want a line?" The bodyguard flicked his chin in the direction of the table.

She shot him a sultry smile. "I don't need drugs to have fun."

The man reached inside his jacket. "You should have a line," he said as a pistol appeared from under the coat.

"I'm on my way," Mirza transmitted.

She glanced at the handgun then back down at Wesley. "What are you doing? Please don't hurt me." The banker was clutching his chest, hyperventilating, and his lips were blue.

"No one's going to get hurt if you do what you're told."

Another lie, thought Saneh as she took a hesitant step toward him. "He's dying, isn't he?" She exploded into action. A long brown leg flashed through the air kicking the gun free from his hand. Simultaneously she lashed out with the knife.

The bodyguard was fast and he avoided the knife strike.

Saneh knew she was overmatched. The GES operative was bigger, stronger, and just as quick. She reversed the knife strike and launched another kick. The slash cut through cloth and flesh but the guard caught the kick and with a grunt tossed her across the room.

She hit one of the uprights supporting the ceiling and landed dazed on her side. The bloody knife was still clutched in her hand.

The man pulled back his jacket to reveal a blood-soaked wound in his flank. "You fucking bitch," he snarled as he turned and dived for the pistol under the table.

As Saneh moved to throw the knife it was plucked from her hand.

Mirza spun the blade in his palm and leaped up the steps to the bridge level. The guard retrieved his handgun as the PRIMAL operative thrust the dive knife down between his shoulders, burying the blade in his spine and heart. Screaming, the guard tried to reach back and grab it. Slumping forward he hit the ground and twitched in a rapidly expanding pool of blood.

Saneh staggered to her feet. Mirza had dumped his backpack next to Wesley and was checking his vitals.

"How is he?"

Mirza shook his head. "We need a med kit. I haven't got adrenaline or a defib. He's going into cardiac arrest." He rolled the skinny banker onto his side. "A boat this size should have a proper med kit. Check the galley."

She rushed downstairs. The first door she opened was the empty crew quarters. The second was the galley. She flicked a light switch and pulled open cupboards. Above the sink she found the medical kit. Grabbing the bag she ran upstairs, ripped the defibrillator unit from the pack and handed it to Mirza.

He waved it away. "I need adrenalin."

Her hands trembled as she hunted through the pack's compartments and pouches. She found a clasp of injectors and handed Mirza a shot of adrenalin. He plunged it into Wesley's thigh.

The banker sat bolt upright and screamed. Mirza clamped his hand over his mouth and the two of them held him down as he thrashed. After a few seconds he went limp. "He's got a pulse but we need to keep him warm." The wiry Indian scooped Wesley off the deck like he was a child and carried him across to the lounge. "We need a blanket."

Fifteen minutes later Wesley was stable and passed out on the lounge. Mirza had rigged a giving set and placed a heart rate monitor on him. He sat beside Saneh on the couch opposite.

"How did you get past the security?" she asked.

"I used a trick Bishop taught me."

One of her eyebrows arched. "You blew something up?"

He laughed. "No I pulled my cap low and strolled on in."

She gave a chuckle. "He has his faults but a lack of courage isn't one of them. So, what are we going to do now?"

He shrugged. "I don't know, team leader, what are we going to do?"

She nodded to Wesley. "We've secured our primary objective. Now we just need to figure out how to get him the hell out of here."

"Can I make a suggestion?"

"Of course."

"Well, we're on a boat."

Saneh smiled. "Yes, we are."

Chapter Eleven

VIRGINIA

BISHOP WAS behind the wheel of the station wagon as they sped through the rain-swept countryside. A torrent lashed the windshield and the headlights cut through the darkness illuminating the road ahead. The extraction from the GES facility had gone off without a hitch. Their gillie suits, stinking and muddy, had been thrown in a dumpster at the last town where they stopped for coffee and donuts.

"How's it going?" Bishop glanced across to see how Mitch was progressing with the bug. He had plugged the tiny device into his iPRIMAL and was using a single earphone to listen to the six hours of recording.

"Good, none of the data has been corrupted."

"That happens often?"

"The micro memory in this thing is cutting edge, but not exactly bomb proof yet."

He frowned. "You mean there's a chance we went through this for nothing?"

Mitch shrugged. "There are always risks, mate."

He concentrated back on the road. It was three in the morning and the coffee they'd drunk was doing little to keep his eyelids from drooping. He needed to keep talking to stay awake. "Mitch, can I ask you a question?"

"Shoot."

"What do you think I should do about Saneh?"

Mitch stared sideways at him. "Not sure what you mean."

"Should I make a go of it?"

"Look, I'm not an expert on women or relationships. But, I reckon if you love her, you should. God knows she's nuts about you."

"What? She hates me."

Mitch snorted. "Champ, she hates self-destructive, high-speed, leap before you think, Bishop. She's angry because she can see what you could be if you dropped all your baggage."

He frowned. "So she wants to change me?"

"No numpty, she doesn't want you taking risks and getting yourself killed."

He grunted.

"Mate, your cowboy days are over. But, you already knew that."

"What's that supposed to mean?"

"The last job in Mexico. Your decisions were cool, calm, calculated. That's more Mirza than you."

His eyes narrowed. "Yeah OK, character assassination is over. How about you find me something interesting to listen to."

Mitch turned his attention back to the tablet. "OK, I've trimmed the track to when King and Pollard are talking. Audio's pretty shite though, can't quite make out the words.

I'll run it through an enhancer and see if we can clean it up."

"How long will it take?"

"A few seconds." As the software completed its rendering Mitch plugged the tablet into the car's audio system. "OK, we're live."

The speakers crackled and Bishop could make out faint voices. He turned the volume up.

"When are you going to deal with that weasel Wesley?"

"That's Pollard," said Mitch.

"Tonight."

"And that's King."

"Good, he's a goddamn liability... Damn that's good. So what did your boys uncover in Germany?"

Germany? Bishop's hands tightened on the steering wheel. "Mitch, Aleks was in Germany."

Mitch put his finger to his lips. "Listen."

"We've got a strong lead, sir. Objective Red Sox's parents gave up a means of contacting him. A phone number we've traced to Brazil. Pershing's team is ready to go as soon as we have more fidelity."

"Fidelity? How long is that going to take?"

By the time they'd finished listening Bishop's hands were crushing the steering wheel. His foot was pushed almost to the floor and the needle was touching ninety miles an hour. "Call Chua."

Mitch enabled the secure communications app on the tablet.

A dial tone sounded over the speakers. "Gentleman I trust you're—"

"Listen, Chua," Bishop snapped. "You need to warn Saneh. Pollard is going to have Wesley killed."

"OK."

"There's more. Somehow they know about Kurtz, they've been sniffing around in Germany. You've got to let Aleks know."

"Guys, great work getting this info. It corroborates what's happened in the last twelve hours."

"Is everyone OK? We can be back at the jet and airborne within the hour. Fly to New York by morning and backup Mirza and Saneh." He spoke at breakneck speed.

"That's not necessary, everyone is fine. They're not going to be in New York for long. Saneh and Mirza have commandeered Wesley Chambers' boat and they'll be underway in the next few minutes."

Bishop raised his eyebrows. "How the hell did they do that?"

"Saneh was onboard when Wesley's bodyguard tried to kill him using spiked cocaine. She and Mirza intervened, saved him, and killed the guard. They're about to sail the boat down the Hudson."

"Do either of them know how to sail a vessel that size?"

"Yes, it seems Saneh was trained as a helmsman for a mission when she was with Iranian intelligence. With Wesley's help they're confident they can get underway and escape. They might need some technical support so Mitch should standby for a call."

"Will do, mate," responded Mitch.

"OK, so we were a little late with that intel." Bishop backed off the accelerator and the torrent of rain hitting the windshield eased. "But, what about Aleks? Has he found Kurtz?"

"No, but he did thwart an attempted kidnapping. Two ex-military types tried to abduct Kurtz's parents. They're both safe."

"That's what King was talking about," said Mitch.

"Did you get a recording?" asked Chua.

"Yes, Mitch can send it to you now." Bishop paused. "Chua, those guys Aleks bumped were GES operatives. I think we've seriously underestimated the resources and audacity of these people. They're half-way to tracking down one of our own."

"And that's why we need to regain the initiative. Vance has activated the CAT and they'll be in my location in twelve hours. Aleks is meeting them here to head it up. If GES get Kurtz we'll have to be prepared to do a recovery op."

"But we still don't know where Kurtz is."

"That's why I need you to take over the search for him. We do know the last time he checked his Skype account he was in Brazil, downtown Rio."

"OK, Mitch and I can fly there directly."

"Negative. I need Mitch back here to assist in extracting Saneh and Mirza. Get him to drop you at Miami International. I'll arrange a ticket to Rio for you. Contact Aleks and get a verbal handover. We'll deploy a team to support you once we've reconsolidated here in Jamaica."

"Makes sense."

"I know I don't need to tell you to keep a low profile.

GES are probably already in Rio and we don't want to deal with them until the CAT is ready."

"Roger."

"I'll check back in when I've arranged your ticket. Drive safe."

"Will do."

NEW YORK

Saneh checked the time on her watch; it had just passed three in the morning. She glanced out the bridge windows of the *Nemesis* at the Hudson river. There were only a few boats cruising past. New York might not sleep but she was definitely at her drowsiest in the early hours.

She turned to where Mirza was checking on the now conscious investment banker. "We have to get this boat underway."

He nodded. "Wesley, we need you to start the engines. Are you feeling strong enough to stand?"

"Yeah." The banker was staring at Mirza with a confused expression. "I know you, don't I?"

Mirza shook his head. "No, I don't think so." He helped him off the lounge.

"Yes, I do." Wesley was shaky as he walked across to the helm. Halfway across the room he stopped and his face lit up. "You're the miner! The Indian guy. You're the one who bugged my phone. You sneaky shit!"

Saneh grabbed his shoulder, holding him steady. "Hey, Wesley, let's focus on the job at hand. Your dead bodyguard probably has other friends, yes? They could be on their way here now."

"Oh, yeah, OK." He leaned against the console. Mirza slipped out through the rear door of the cabin.

He dropped his head and mumbled, "Hey, I haven't had a chance to thank you yet. So... thanks."

Saneh shrugged. "At least now you know what your boss thinks of you."

The young man sniffed and rubbed his nose. "Those dirty pricks. They'd be nothing without me. I brought in hundreds of millions of dollars of investment."

She gave him a wink. "And now you get to help us take them down."

"You're working with the Yankee guy aren't you? The one who took down the Mexican operation."

"Let's just say we're here to right some wrongs. Now are you going to help me power this bad boy up?"

Wesley sighed. "She's a lady. Nemesis was a goddess..." He managed a wry smile and shot her breasts a glance. She was still wearing her black one-piece swimsuit. "Just like you."

"Eyes on the console, Romeo."

"Yeah, OK." He reached across and pressed a button. The touch screen came to life. He entered a four-digit code and the engines commenced their initiation procedure. "You can tell your buddy to cast off."

Saneh relayed the order through her radio. "Let's keep the running lights off," she added as Wesley checked the engines were green across the board. "I was expecting a more complicated start-up process."

He shook his head. "No, I had her upgraded last year. Single digital console, pushbutton start, and automated engineering settings. Extra two million on the thirty I paid for her."

"Wow, you really must have the world's smallest dick."

He frowned. "That's a bit harsh."

"You'll get over it."

Mirza reappeared in the cabin a moment later. "We're free of the pontoon. No sign of the guards."

"You're kidding me. With the berthing fees I pay I would have expected more. Look, if you're not going to let me use the running lights maybe we should kill the internals."

"Good idea." Mirza hit the wall-mounted switch.

The glow of the boat's console cast an eerie glow in the cabin as Wesley pushed the throttle forward and spun the wheel. The sleek vessel pulled away from the dock and slowly nosed its way out onto the river.

"You got it from here? I'm not feeling great."

"Sure." Saneh took the helm and aimed the bow down river. Once they were a few hundred yards from the dock she activated the running lights and eased on the throttles. The touch screen indicated the boat was making headway of eight knots. The digital map showed their position being slightly right of the river's centerline. Off the port side the lights of Manhattan were bright.

She eased the throttles and brought the high-performance motor-yacht to a cruising speed of fifteen knots. The diesels thrummed under her feet as they surged forward. She noticed there was another set of throttles for the 5,600 horsepower jet turbines. She searched the screen to see if they were online and identified a button for the start-up sequence. That might be handy later on, she thought.

Mirza joined her, having laid the Banker on the lounge behind them.

"How is he?" she asked.

"As good as can be expected. We're just lucky he's got a high tolerance for drug abuse."

"Kids these days."

"So what's the plan from here?"

She swiped the touch screen accessing the navigation system. "I've plotted a route from here to Jamaica. At twenty knots we'll be there in forty-eight hours."

"She'll go that far?"

"She'll go further if we're just cruising on the diesels. Once we're far enough offshore we can ditch the body." She nodded at the dead bodyguard that Mirza had wrapped in a blanket.

"And the authorities? What if the boat is declared missing?"

"We'll get Wesley to call in and tell them he decided to take her for a cruise."

"Good thinking."

"Mirza, I need you to setup the iPRIMAL satellite uplink so we've got comms. I also want you to secure Wesley in his bedroom. Then you should get some rest. We're going to be pulling four hour shifts once underway."

"Roger, Skipper. I'll get things sorted. Oh, one more thing. Mitch sent me a message to remind you to disengage the mode A and B AIS transponder, whatever that is."

"Well done, Mitch."

As they passed between Liberty and Governor Islands she found the menu for the Automatic Identification System, a transmitter that let other ships and the authorities know the *Nemesis*' location. She switched it off then glanced out the windows at the Statue of Liberty. Powerful spotlights bathed her in light, like an angel watching over them. She whispered a quiet prayer as they sailed past.

NEW YORK CITY

King had flown to New York first thing in the morning. The corporate helicopter transported him to the roof of the MVI office building and he took the elevator to his office on the tenth floor. He took a number of calls as soon as he was in the office. None of them were good. There was a saying King used when he was in the army; bad news didn't get any better with age. With that in mind he left his office and stabbed the button for the top floor of the building. When the doors opened he gave the receptionist a nod and walked past Wesley Chambers' empty office to Jordan Pollard's, where he knocked.

"Come in."

He pushed open the door and stood in front of the chairman's desk. The former Brigadier glanced at him with cold gray eyes. "I trust things have been taken care of?"

"There's been a problem, sir. Wesley and his bodyguard are missing."

"Missing?"

"Yes, that damn boat of his was last seen heading down the Hudson at 0500 hours. At 0730 Chambers rang the marina and told them he was sailing to the Hamptons."

"And you've tried to contact your man?"

"I'm unable to reach him."

Pollard shoved his chair back and stood. "Goddamn, what the fuck's wrong with you people. You just keep screwing shit up, don't you? I mean, I give you basic tasks and you keep letting me down. Time after fucking time!"

He'd never seen an outburst like this before. The chairman rarely lost his temper and when he did it usually manifested itself in a brooding silence followed by calmly delivered threats.

Pollard turned his back and gazed out his office window. He sighed. "How much does he know about the Venezuelan project?"

"Next to nothing. He doesn't know about Jimmy and his boys."

"But he does know enough to bring the Feds sniffing."

He shrugged. "But they're not going to find anything. Our OPSEC is watertight."

Pollard spun to face him. "Watertight? We've got some kind of covert special ops organization breathing down our neck and you're telling me your operational security is watertight? What if they've got their hands on Chambers? What happens when he starts talking? In 48 hours I'm going to be in Caracas closing this deal. If anything interferes with that..." He clenched his fists by his side.

"Nothing will, sir. We'll locate Wesley and neutralize him, and whoever is with him. I'm heading back home to Virginia tomorrow and I'll manage this personally."

Pollard dropped back in his chair. "Where is Pershing at with the German?"

"His team are inserting tomorrow. They're ready to take this guy down."

"We can't afford any more mistakes. If he screws this up, he's done."

"Yes, sir."

"Now, get the hell out of my office."

King retreated down the corridor to the elevator. When he was back in his GES office he used a secure line to call Pershing at the intelligence facility in Virginia. They needed every asset available searching for the damn boat.

Chapter Twelve

CARACAS, VENEZUELA

IVAN SHRUGGED out of his smart suit jacket, turned it inside out, and put it back on. He ruffled his hair and pulled a pair of thick-rimmed glasses from his satchel. An armful of papers completed his outfit and he left the public toilets, crossed the road, and strolled along the shaded footpaths of the Central University of Venezuela.

His driver had dropped him three blocks closer to town at an expensive restaurant popular for business meetings. Slipping away had been as simple as finding the delivery entrance and ducking out. It was a short walk to the public restrooms opposite the campus.

As he strolled purposefully through the university grounds. he was impressed by the sheer size of the campus. The buildings were old and a little tired but still functional. Throngs of students paid him no attention as they spilled out of classrooms and lecture halls. Others gathered in the shade of the leafy trees that grew in the spaces between the buildings. He stopped to inspect a poster taped to one of the broad trunks. It used bold communist era graphics to call the students to action against the government. He'd noticed them scattered across the campus.

He spotted the central library from a distance. The postmodernist structure had bright red walls and towered at least a half-dozen stories above the rest of the campus. Ivan angled toward it, following one of the paved footpaths that criss-crossed the green lawns. He reached the main entrance stairs, peeled off to one side, and sat in the sun. Pretending to examine his papers, he scanned the route he'd just taken. Anyone tailing him would have nowhere to go except into the library.

After five minutes he packed away his papers and strolled inside. He walked past the front counter, made his way up three flights of stairs and into a hall marked ARCHIVES.

The musty smell of old books hung in the air. Ivan found it comforting; it harkened back to a simpler era where information was written down and not stored in the cloud. It made him wonder how long it would be until people like him were completely replaced by technicians and computers.

He found the study area he was searching for past rows of bookshelves, tucked away in the back corner. Secluded and rarely used, it was a good spot for a meeting. What's more, Ivan had identified no less than three exit points including a fire escape and a window leading out onto the roof of the lower levels. He spotted a red baseball cap and sat in the cubicle next to the owner.

"Do you know when the library closes?" the baseball cap-wearing student asked.

He recognized the voice from their phone call. "Around

five. You should probably check with the front desk," replied Ivan.

The young man stood and stiffly attempted to pull his chair in next to Ivan. He was in his early twenties, slightly built, with collar-length wavy brown hair and a clean-shaven face. One arm was strapped across his chest in a sling.

Ivan reached out, grabbed the chair, and pulled it into his cubicle. He saw pain in the boy's eyes. It was something he'd seen many times before. "You must be Antonio. You can call me Igor."

"OK, Igor, what did you want to talk about?" Antonio said as he sat.

"I work for an organization with an interest in fostering democracy in Venezuela."

Antonio lowered his voice to barely a whisper, "Are you CIA?"

He smiled. "No, I'm from a private organization."

"OK, so what do you want from me?"

"I want to help you in your struggle."

Antonio snickered. "Didn't the Voluntad tell you? You're too late. The *colectivo* has shut the *Movimiento* down. They killed a politician that supported us and raped my girlfriend." He made to leave.

Ivan reached across and held his good arm. "And that makes you want to give up? Don't you want justice? Don't you want to fight back?"

The student slumped back in the chair. "What can you do to help?"

"I can help with security and intel. I can help you against your enemies." He reached into his jacket and pulled out an envelope. "Do you need cash? I can supply funding."

Antonio's eyes narrowed. "What do you really want?"

"You're a smart man. I need eyes and ears on the ground. I need to know if there are any other foreigners working with the anti-government movement."

"I have friends who may have met some Americans. You might have to pay them for information, but I will help you for free."

"Whatever works for you."

"But, I want you to find someone for me."

"Who?"

He reached inside his backpack and pulled out a sketchbook. He opened to a picture and placed it on the desk. "I want you to find me the man with this tattoo. He was one of the *colectivo* who attacked us." The hand drawn sketch was that of a dragon clutching a trident.

ATLANTIC OCEAN

The twin-engine Ocean Sentry Coast Guard surveillance aircraft was cruising at 20,000 feet as it flew south along the eastern seaboard. Based in Cape Cod, the aircraft had been on a routine patrol when it was vectored to search for a vessel of interest.

"We've got a contact twenty five nautical miles out, south, south east," Lieutenant Junior Grade Harley Neilson reported over the intercom. As the co-pilot of the aircraft he was watching the radar surveillance screen in front of him.

Lieutenant Frank Hadaway, the aircraft captain glanced across at the scope. "What about the AIS?" he said, referring to the transponder that all ocean-going vessels were required to carry. Each Ocean Sentry had direction finding equipment capable of locating the beacon.

"No reading."

"Could be our ship. Let's go in and check." He banked the aircraft bringing them on to a track that would take them within a few miles of the contact.

"Who the hell steals a 33 million dollar boat?" said Neilson as they leveled out.

"Someone with bigger balls than me." The captain laughed. "Was there any extra info in the report?"

Neilson glanced down at the notes he had made on the pad strapped to the thigh of his flight suit. "Nope, US flagged ship *Nemesis* departed New York, heading south. Wallypower 118 class vessel stolen 0500 hours this morning."

"Yeah, I saw a show on Discovery. That beast is capable of hitting 75 knots, it's powered by three turbines. Hell, it's got more horsepower than we do."

"Well she's not traveling that fast at the moment." He glanced at his watch. "It's 1245 now which means she's been underway for nearly seven hours." He checked the distance from New York. "By my calcs she's only doing about twenty."

They flew in silence for a few minutes. When they were five nautical miles out from the target Neilson switched on the Electro Optical and Infrared search camera located under the nose of the aircraft. Using a joystick next to the screen he panned the camera, searching for the contact. "Hello my pretty." He centered the screen on a black shape trailing wake and zoomed in. A low sleek vessel filled the screen. "Thar she blows."

"You sure that's her?"

"No doubt about it. Look at those lines, she's one seriously sexy boat."

"Take a photo you weirdo."

"Oh it's already in the spank bank. You want me to report it in?"

"Yeah, I'll hold off here so we don't spook them."

Neilson thumbed the radio transmit button. "Cape Cod, this is Charlie Golf 4583, over."

"Charlie Golf 4583 send, over."

"We've located the *Nemesis*." Neilson read out the lat-long from the camera feed. "She's heading south at a speed of twenty knots."

There was a moment's silence before Cape Cod responded. "Acknowledged, Charlie Golf 4583. You are to remain on station, shadow, and report *Nemesis's* position every thirty minutes. Charlie Golf 7040 will replace you in three hours."

"Roger, Charlie Golf 4583, out."

The captain tapped his finger on the screen. "We're in for some rough weather. Wouldn't want to be onboard that sexy cruise of yours."

Neilson shook his head. "You kidding? She loves it rough."

GES FACILITY, VIRGINIA

Howard clapped his hands and threw both arms in the air. "Boom, we've got a hit." He was sitting at his desk in the front row of the GES SCIF in Virginia. "A Coastguard bird has located her thirty-five nautical miles off Delaware bay.

She's heading south at a speed of twenty knots." He plotted the location on the battle tracker screen.

Pershing was standing at the back of the room dressed in slacks, a golf shirt, and a floppy broad-brim hat. He was about to deploy to Brazil. "OK good, we've got a location, now we need intercept options."

"Can't we leave this to the Coast Guard?" asked Howard.

"Negative, they can't be trusted."

"Sir," one of the GES staff called out from his terminal. "We've got a vetted maritime services provider based in Charleston, South Carolina. We've used them before, they're called MAROPS."

"Get me the number."

Pershing waited at the analyst's shoulder, grabbed the note with the number, and strode back to his office.

Why is this boat so important wondered Howard as he turned back to his terminal. The intelligence team had dropped all work on Objective Yankee to locate it. Pershing had given them nothing other than the boat's registration and known movements. That annoyed him. If it was linked to the operation then he should have all of the information. He had already worked out the owner was a MVI director but was not privy to any further details.

Pershing reappeared a moment later with his bag slung over one shoulder. "Howard, Charles King will be arriving in a few hours to personally oversee the operation. Till then I want you to keep the team focused on Objectives Red Sox and Yankee."

"Dude, what about the boat?"

"Keep an eye on it. If anything changes give me a call."

"That all?"

"Yeah, our priority is locating the terrorists. Hell, that's what the CIA are paying us for." He turned and made for the door.

Howard waited till Pershing had left the SCIF then turned to the other analysts. "OK, team." The room went quiet. "We've got the boat under control now so let's refocus on Objective Red Sox down in Brazil. We've got a general location but I want fidelity. Mr. Pershing hits the ground in twelve hours. We've got till then to come up with the goods." He sat back in his chair and reached for the can of energy drink on his desk. It was empty. He rose and waddled from his desk to the door, swiped his pass, and entered the reception area. Rather than visit the kitchenette he grabbed his phone from its cubbyhole. He checked the screen. He had three missed calls from a number he didn't recognize as well as a text message.

Call me - Larkin

Larkin? The only Larkin he knew was Thomas Larkin, the CIA director responsible for outsourcing contracts. He bummed a cigarette from the guard behind the desk and walked out of the bunker. As he reached the perimeter fence he saw Pershing driving away in one of the buggies. He watched him disappear then dialed the missed number.

It connected after one ring. "Larkin. Speak."

Howard was caught off guard and bumbled his way through an introduction.

"Listen Terrance, before we get started, I want you to know I've pulled your file. I've also spoken to your boss, Everest. Now that man truly is an uninspiring gentleman."

"OK."

"I can see real potential in you. You've got what others don't have, smarts. Most CIA employees are ladder-climbing assclowns. Those people don't find their way into my directorate. Now, you're probably wondering why I wanted to talk to you."

"Ah, yes sir."

"I'll cut to the chase. It's about GES. You're currently working for them?"

"Yes sir, I'm working the Mexico terrorist attack."

Larkin grunted. "Is that what they're calling it. Between you and me, Terry, I've got serious doubts about GES. My gut feeling is they're neck deep in activities that are diametrically opposed to the CIA's interests and… I want you to find out what they are."

Howard swallowed. "Yes, sir."

"You do well, son, and you'll soon realize working for me is extremely beneficial to your career." The call terminated.

He slid the phone back in his pocket and lit the cigarette as he contemplated what just happened. He knew Larkin was in charge of the contractors the CIA used for security and basic intelligence work. As far as manpower went he was only a small player. However, when it came to budget, well, he controlled close to a third of the CIA's money and that was real power. Howard finished his cigarette, dropped the butt and ground it into the grass with his shoe.

THE EUROCOPTER TOUCHED down on the grass pad behind the GES administration buildings. King grabbed his bag and when the pilot opened the door he jumped out. He strode across to where a tall attractive woman was waiting next to one of the camp's buggies. "Is the team ready?"

"Yes sir, they're waiting for you in the holding area."

He climbed into the ATV. "Let's get going then."

She drove him out to a road that led to the huge sheds of the HA, or holding area. They stopped just inside the doors. Two black SUVs were parked in the middle of the open space. Team 2 and Pershing were waiting next to the cars.

"Gather round, boys," said King as he strode across to meet them. He gave Pershing a nod as the team formed a half-circle in front of him. "I don't have to tell you all how important your mission is. You came up against these fuckers in Mexico and they got the drop on you."

To a man they wore a look of anger.

King continued, "This is your chance to hit back. Get down there, capture Objective Red Sox, and make him talk. Team 1 has been crushing it in Venezuela, now it's your turn." He eyeballed each of the men stopping when he got to Matt, who'd just returned from Germany with Shrek. Matt had a swollen jaw and one eye was bloodshot. "Shrek, what's wrong with your boy?"

"He had a run in with a wrecking ball."

"You been to see a medic?"

Matt shook his head.

"Jesus man, can you even talk? Your jaw could be broken. Shrek, he's off the team. I can't get you a replacement so you'll have to run one man down."

The team leader nodded. "Not a problem. Matt, unpack your kit."

The injured operator looked crestfallen. He grabbed his bags from the vehicle.

"Dump them in the buggy. I'll have my assistant take you to the hospital." King turned back to the rest of the team. "Good luck, gentlemen."

Team 2, minus Matt, climbed into the SUVs.

King pointed at Pershing. "Don't fuck this up, or Pollard will have both our heads." He turned on his heel and strode back to the ATV where his assistant was waiting with Matt. "Drop me at the SCIF then take him to the doctor."

The two SUVs followed them out the shed and turned right toward the main gate.

His assistant dropped him at the gate to the SCIF and he swiped his way into the underground facility. The guard at the desk gave him a nod as he strode through to the intelligence facility floor. He opened the door and scanned the room. The analysts were all behind their desks working at their terminals. An overweight man locked eyes with him and stood.

"Terrance Howard, I presume?"

"Yes sir, you're Charles King aren't you?"

"That's correct." He lifted his chin toward the screens bolted to the wall above them. They displayed a tracking map and the intelligence log. "So where are we at, Mr. Howard?"

Chapter Thirteen

CARACAS, VENEZUELA

ANTONIO HADN'T RETURNED to Camilla's apartment since the incident. As he walked up the stairs his pulse quickened and he hesitated. Then a hand on his shoulder reassured him and he unlocked the newly repaired door and stepped inside. "This is where they attacked us." He fought back the panic that assailed him.

"It's OK, Antonio. We're here to make sure this won't happen to anyone else," said Ivan.

He breathed deeply and watched as the Russian inspected the living room. The coffee table was upturned and the carpet still stained with blood. He went to the kitchen and found a cloth and a container of water. On his hands and knees he scrubbed at the carpet. Tears welled in his eyes as the blood refused to budge.

"Leave that." Ivan took the bucket and helped him to his feet. "I need you to tell me exactly what happened here."

They sat in the kitchen and Antonio told his story. It felt good to tell someone, to get the weight off his shoulders. He felt like Igor really wanted to help. The Russian was a good listener.

"Do you mind if I ask some questions?"

Antonio sighed. "No. It's fine."

"You said all the ringleaders were here. How did they know when and where to meet?"

"I told them."

"In person?"

"Some, but others I confirmed with a Twitter message. Are you wondering how they found us?"

Igor nodded. "The *colectivo* would not have the capability to find a small well organized group like yours."

"Then who else could it be? The police would not do this. The risk is too great. If Voluntad found out they would use it against them."

"Do you know of any other groups who have been attacked?"

"Yes, there have been a number of attacks, all against the students who organize the demonstrations."

Igor pulled out a small notepad. "Tell me everything you remember from the attack."

ATLANTIC OCEAN

The angular bow of the *Nemesis* sliced through the choppy seas with ease as she cruised south with Saneh at the helm. It was an hour till sunset but the low cloud almost completely blocked the sun giving the horizon a dull glow. She was impressed with how easily the craft handled the degrading conditions. The waves had gained in size but the carbon composite hull was as stable as ever. It barely rocked as they plowed forward at a steady twenty-five knots.

She checked the navigation system and made a quick calculation in her head. Fuel consumption had increased slightly with the choppy seas. When they were further south, clear of the US mainland, then they would have to drop back to about fifteen knots if they were to make it all the way to Jamaica. If not they would have to abandon the boat. She pursed her lips; that would be a real shame. She pulled her iPRIMAL from her pocket and sent a short update to Chua. He might be able to work out a way to get them more fuel.

"You ready for a shift change, Mr. Ebadi?" Mirza asked from behind her.

Saneh laughed. She was dressed in some of Wesley's clothes. Surprisingly they fit well thanks to his slight frame and penchant for tight jeans.

Mirza handed her a mug of hot chocolate.

"No green tea?"

"I thought you might want to sleep."

"True, I should probably get my head down, but I still need to have a few words with our friend below."

"Do you want me to bring him up?"

"Yes, please."

Saneh waited for Mirza to fetch Wesley and sit him on a couch. Then when Mirza took over the helm she headed aft to speak to the banker.

"What happened to the prick that tried to kill me?" he asked as she sat facing him.

"He went for a swim."

"Oh, OK, good." Wesley glanced nervously around the cabin then back to Saneh. "So what happens now?"

"Well, that depends on you. Answer my questions and you'll find we are very generous and take care of our friends. But, tell me lies and you too can go swimming."

Wesley swallowed. "Who are you?"

"We're contentious objectors."

"To what?"

"Organizations that get rich by making other people's lives miserable. You know, like Manhattan Ventures Investments."

He shook his head. "You have no idea what you're up against. Jordan Pollard isn't some run-of-the-mill banker. He's connected, he's powerful, and he's got money to burn. The bastard tried to have me killed. Even the goddamn CIA outsources their dirty work to him."

Saneh smiled. "That's a good start. What do you know about his CIA contracts?"

He shrugged. "Not much, I wasn't trusted with that information. All I know is King and his goons subcontract to the Agency. I'm not sure what they do, I just know it pays well. With Mexico screwed it's the only thing keeping the security guys afloat."

"What about Venezuela?"

"Jesus, is there anything you guys don't know? Look, Pollard needed a cool half a billion for what could only be an energy deal. There's nothing else down there. I helped raise the capital but wasn't privy to any of the planning or anything like that."

"But you were briefed in for Mexico?"

"Yeah, but that was more legit. Although the shit they were doing to the locals was messed up."

"You didn't do anything about it though."

"What was I supposed to do? You've seen what these people are capable of. They would have killed me."

Saneh arched one of her eyebrows. "They've already tried to kill you, Wesley, and they're not going to stop till you're dead. You won't be safe until King and Pollard are neutralized and we're the only ones that can do that."

She decided that was enough for the time being. She would let Wesley dwell on the thought overnight and start again in the morning. "Mirza, I'm going to take Wesley back to his room then I'm going to get some sleep."

"Roger."

A moment later, having secured their prisoner in his cabin, she lay on her back in one of the spare bedrooms. As the pulsing of the engines lulled her to sleep her thoughts turned to Bishop. She finally felt like she'd escaped the debt she owed him for saving her life and recruiting her into PRIMAL. The playing field between them was now level. The funny thing was that it only made her think of him even more.

RIO DE JANEIRO

The sun had just dropped below the horizon when the gray DC-9 touched down at Alfonsos Air Force Base on the outskirts of Rio. It taxied to a private hangar where three SUVs were parked under fluorescent lights.

Pershing was first out when the stairs dropped. He made a beeline to the man waiting in front of the vehicles and extended his hand. "Danny, good to see you again."

Danny Harper, an officer from the local CIA station, shook his hand. "You too bud, been too long. We haven't touched base since you moved over to the dark side."

He gave a wry smile. "Hey, like I said when I left. Any time you need a job you just ask."

"I appreciate that. Now, I got you the vehicles you need and we've organized a safe house in town. You need anything else you just holler." He glanced over Pershing's shoulder at the GES operatives unloading their equipment from the jet. "Seems you've got quite the team. What's your mission?"

"Rendition of a terrorist."

"Islamist?"

Pershing shook his head.

Harper knew not to inquire further and handed him the keys for two of the SUVs. "We've got you a nice little place in Gavea. They're going to knock it down in a few weeks to build a condo so it was cheap. It's a bit of a drive from here so we should get going."

It took Pershing and Team 2 a minute to load their equipment. Then they followed Harper's vehicle out of the airbase and across the sprawling city. Pershing was familiar with the city as was most of the GES team. He paid little attention to the highways and dark streets as they flashed past. He watched the screen of his phone, tracking their movement on a command and control app.

Forty-five minutes later the convoy pulled over to the side of the road and Harper jumped out, unlocked a gate, and waved them in.

The two-story home was hidden from the road by a sheet metal fence and construction signage.

"Electricity is on, plumbing works, and we dropped some bedding and water inside." Harper tossed Pershing a set of keys. "You get any problems with the locals just give me a call." He winked. "Have fun and try not to blow anything up."

"No problems, and don't worry, we'll keep this real low key."

Harper drove away leaving them standing in the dark outside the house. Pershing unlocked the front door and flicked on the lights. In the middle of the empty living room was a pile of bottled water, stretchers, and sleeping bags. He turned to Shrek. "Set up your gear in here. I'll give orders in half an hour."

Pershing took a few minutes to assemble one of the stretchers as the men worked around him. He sat on the cot, opened his laptop, and plugged in his phone. Browsing through his emails he found one from Howard. A smile crossed his lips as he read. The team had tied down Objective Red Sox's historic location to an internet café two kilometers from their current position. He could have men there within the hour. Unplugging his phone, he dialed King.

"Henry, I take it you're in country?"

"Yes sir, what's our ETA on the recovery of the *Nemesis*?"

"They'll be passing through the interdiction box in the morning."

"Roger, I'll have my people out on the ground within the next hour or so."

"Good, let me know when you've got him."

"Will do."

"So you know, I'm staying with the intel team until this Major League Network is dealt with."

"I trust Howard has been keeping you informed regarding Red Sox?"

"Yes he has. I've got to run. Good hunting." The call terminated.

Pershing smiled as he slipped the phone into his pocket.

Within a matter of hours Objective Red Sox would be in his grasp. Then the German was going to spill everything he knew and Pershing was going to hunt down every other member of his team. He was looking forward to making them pay for Mexico.

MIAMI

Bishop relaxed in the co-pilot seat as Mitch brought the Gulfstream down at Miami International airport. "Nice one, mate," he said as they touched down gently.

The Brit made to reply but instead yawned.

"Hey, you're not going to fly to Jamaica tonight are you?"

Mitch shook his head and yawned again. "Negative, I'm going bunk down here and fly first thing in the morning."

"Good, the last thing we need is you falling asleep at the wheel."

"Hello, it's called a yoke."

"Whatever."

As they taxied across to the General Aviation Center Bishop unbuckled and moved back to the cabin to grab his daypack. He'd managed to clean the camouflage cream from his face in the tiny bathroom and had changed into a clean T-shirt and a pair of jeans. Inside his pack were a spare shirt, cash, and toiletries.

The jet came to a halt and the turbines powered down as he double-checked he had his passport, wallet, and iPRIMAL. He slipped the valuables into his pockets. "Give my best to the others when you see them."

"Will do."

"That refueling plan all sorted?"

"Yep, the CAT is flying to Jamaica with everything we need."

"OK, catch you later." Bishop lowered the aircraft stairs. He walked down, squinting at the bright lights that illuminated the tarmac. As he made his way to the terminal he glanced at his watch. His flight to Rio De Janeiro left from the other side of the airport in less than an hour. Ten hours later he would be on the ground in a foreign city of six million searching for a man who hated him and didn't want to be found. A man who he had to find before GES did. If he failed the outcome for both Kurtz and all of them would be terminal. The German was tough but Bishop knew even he would crack in the hands of professionals, and Kurtz knew everything there was to know about PRIMAL.

Chapter Fourteen

KINGSTON, JAMAICA

FLASH YAWNED as he studied the link analysis chart the team back in the Bunker had sent him. It showed all the intel they'd gathered on MVI and GES, including the tenuous links to the CIA. He expanded the dollar bill icon that represented MVI's activities in Venezuela. The icon had no links other than the few emails they had pulled off the security company's network. The emails hinted GES may have some involvement in the anti-government movement but there were no specifics.

He grunted with frustration and left his desk to stand in front of the fan that was spinning in the corner of the makeshift office. The air conditioning unit installed in the hangar had failed and the place was hotter than hell. What he wouldn't give to be back in the Bunker with his own desk space and a fridge filled with cold drinks and chocolate bars. Not to mention the chance to take his motorbike for a blast down the runway.

He'd spent the better part of the day trying to hack Kurtz's Skype account and identify the IP address of the computer he had used to access it. With it he could pinpoint the exact location and vector Bishop in when he arrived. He was very close, a matter of a few more hours work. But he needed a break, hence the sidebar with the Venezuelan link-analysis chart.

The trill of the secure phone on Chua's desk pulled him out of his thoughts and he reluctantly dragged himself away from the fan to answer it. "Hey."

"Hello."

"Hey, it's Flash, who's this?"

"Is Chen there?"

"No, he's getting some sleep. Do you want to leave a message?" Flash glanced at the screen of the phone. There was a key flashing in the corner. It was secure, which meant whoever was on the other end of the line was part of PRIMAL, possibly a source.

"Perhaps you can help me." The voice sounded English and very proper.

"Sure, but I'm going to need your name first."

"My name is Ivan."

Flash almost dropped the phone. Ivan was one of Chua's Blades; a deep cover operative who frequently laid the groundwork for PRIMAL operations. The former FSB operative was almost legendary within the intelligence team.

"What can I do for you, Ivan?"

"I've made contact with a member of the Venezuelan student resistance. He says his group was attacked by the *colectivo* last week. His girlfriend was raped and a member of the opposition party was murdered. I want to know if it's possible for them to be tracked through social media. It's the only way they communicate."

"Who are the *colectivo*?"

"Gangs, thugs, criminals hired by the government to break up the demonstrations."

"Got ya. Yeah, possibly, but it would be a little sophisticated for regular thugs. I mean, they could probably pull metadata off photos but if they've disabled those functions then we're talking cell phone triangulation and that takes serious resources. I don't even think the Venezuelan security forces have the gear to do it."

"So they may have help."

"Yeah, someone else could be providing the tech and the skill."

"I'm sending you through a sketch. It's a tattoo worn by one of the attackers. I need you to find who it belongs to."

"Right, that could be a long shot."

"The tattoo belongs to an American, no doubt in my mind. Let Chua know. I don't think GES are trying to take down the government. I think they're helping the government target the students."

"OK, so… hello?" The call was dead.

Flash walked back to his computer and sat down. Ivan's information, if it was accurate, could have unlocked what GES and MVI were doing in Venezuela. Had Jordan Pollard traded specialist counter-revolutionary capability for an energy deal?

Chua's phone beeped and Flash glanced down at the message. It was a file. He sent it via encrypted Wi-Fi to his computer and opened it. It was a photo of a sketch. Whoever had drawn the dragon clutching a trident was skilled. It was clearly based on the SEAL insignia but a dragon had replaced the usual eagle. He'd seen the SEAL trident plastered all over books and movies ever since the Bin Laden raid had brought the group into the limelight.

That by itself wasn't much though. He had no way of searching for the owner of the tattoo. There was no database of military ink.

Flash slumped back in his chair and sighed. Then it hit him; he had the personnel files of a significant number of GES employees. Less than a week ago Mitch had used a drone to enable him to hack an isolated server and download a bucket-load of information. It had all been dumped in a custom database. He opened it and typed in the words tattoo and SEAL. Five files matched. Two of them were emails containing nothing of value. The other three were personnel files. He opened the first one and scrolled down to the identifying features component.

Member has sleeve tattoos on both upper arms and shoulders that include Gaelic patterns and Sanskrit text.

He opened the next file.

Member has a tattoo of a dragon clutching a trident.

Jackpot! Flash read the rest of the document. James 'Jimmy' Scott was a former DEVGRU team leader who'd left the SEALs after ten years of service and twelve operational deployments. His specialist skills included counter-terrorism, counter-insurgency, close protection, and advanced force operations. They finally had a lead in Venezuela.

CARACAS, VENEZUELA

The Venezuelan hadn't offered a name and Jimmy knew better than to ask. The bearded official had arrived at the old sugar warehouse with an entourage of heavy hitters at exactly the time agreed. The man refused to do business over the phone. Smart, thought Jimmy, considering the NSA was all over the country's communications like Fox News on a government conspiracy.

"I trust your accommodation has been suitable for your needs," said the security operative.

Jimmy assumed the man was an officer from the government's top intelligence service, or maybe a private security contractor. Either way he was the government representative who had provided them with the warehouse and their operational mandate. This was the first time they had seen him since King had made the introduction.

"It does the job."

"Yes, you've been very successful so far. We've seen a steady decrease in both the intensity and regularity of the demonstrations." The man scanned the warehouse as he spoke. His eyes lingered on Pete's computer setup in the corner.

"Thanks."

"Is there anything else you need?"

Jimmy coughed. "Hey bud, you going cut to the chase or are we just gonna keep finger banging?"

The man frowned. "An interesting choice of phrase."

"I'm not here to fuck around. You got something to say, spit it out."

The Venezuelan nodded. "There's someone that needs to disappear."

"That I can do. What's the name?"

"Dante, Dante Otero."

Jimmy took a notebook from his pocket and scribbled the name down. "You got a phone number? It would make this a hell of a lot easier."

"Yes, I have a cell number." He turned to one of his assistants who wrote the number on a piece of paper and handed it to him. He passed it to Jimmy. "This needs to be unattributable."

"Do I look like a fucking moron? It'll be clean and it'll be blamed on the *colectivo* dead shits. What's the time frame?"

"As soon as possible."

He stroked his mustache. "That'll cost extra."

"I will take it into consideration with Mr. King."

Jimmy spat on the concrete. "No, you'll take it into consideration with me. Mr. King isn't the one putting his life on the line. I want twenty-K US each. All six of us. Cash."

The intelligence operative's eyes narrowed.

"Or, get one of your people to do it." He gestured to the heavies standing by the door. "But, they look a little simple. They'll probably screw the pooch."

"The terms are acceptable. Get it done." The man turned and made for the exit.

"Nice doing business with you, cockbreath," muttered Jimmy as he paced across to Pete's intel setup. He dropped the two scraps of paper on the desk. "New target, numb-nuts! Find this fucker ASAP."

Chapter Fifteen

LASCAR ISLAND

VANCE STOOD under the rusted roof of the dilapidated hangar that butted against the cliff. The doors were wide open and a cool breeze caressed his face as he watched a Lascar Logistics C-130 pivot on the tarmac. The back blast from the four turboprops replaced the breeze as it stopped with the ramp facing him. The reek of jet fuel filled the hangar and he grimaced as a final blast of exhaust and prop wash nearly tore his Hawaiian shirt from his bulky frame. If he had hair it would be streaming out behind him like a windsock.

Kruger, the massive blonde-haired South African, and the two other operators from the Critical Assault Team were waiting with him. Dressed in civilian clothing, they stood alongside a pallet stacked with black nylon drag bags and rugged Pelican cases. Next to it were another two pallets. Each had a huge black bladder of fuel strapped to it along with what looked like a bulky green backpack. Another of the PRIMAL team was sitting on a forklift behind the pallets.

The white C-130's ramp lowered with a whine. The transporter was one of four in the Lascar Logistics fleet and the only one piloted by a Priority Movements Airlift crew. The veteran pilots usually flew missions in support of aid workers, however they occasionally flew contracts for discrete government agencies. Today they knew they were supporting a clandestine operation but had no idea who PRIMAL was or that Lascar Island wasn't just a transit location. The false cliff face to the rear of the hangar was shut to maintain the deception.

Vance approached the loadmaster with a broad smile. "Yo, these cats arrived this morning. Glad you made it on time because we're kind of limited for accommodation." Vance was playing the part of an ignorant caretaker, as opposed to his actual role as Director of Operations.

The loadmaster gestured inside the cargo bay of the aircraft. "I've got a crate here for you. Once it's off we can load up and get going."

Vance thrust the manifest he was holding into the loadmaster's hands. "I'll get my boy to take care of it."

The loadmaster gave him thumbs-up and Vance waved at Frank, who was operating the forklift. He watched as Frank unloaded the single crate then loaded the three pallets. When it was done he walked over to where Kruger was waiting with the others. "Give 'em hell, bud."

Kruger gave a solemn nod. "We will." Then the three-man team walked up the ramp and disappeared inside. Vance gave the loadmaster a nod and the ramp whined shut. The four turboprops increased power with a roar and the aircraft lumbered onto the runway.

Vance walked out of the hangar and watched as the C-130 accelerated along the tarmac and lifted off.

Frank pulled the forklift alongside. "Kinda like sending your kids off on their first day of school."

His brow furrowed. "Do you even have kids, Frank?"

"No. But if I did, I think you'd run a great daddy daycare."

He laughed. "What's in the crate?" He reached inside his pocket and activated a remote control. At the back of the hangar the rock wall split and a gap appeared.

"Well, judging by the manifest it's the spare parts Mitch needs for the Pain Train."

Vance strolled inside as Frank drove the forklift beside him. He sighed, now he had most of his force deployed forward to Jamaica. Perhaps it was time he too got back in the field.

ATLANTIC OCEAN

Torrential rain buffeted the two nine-meter Rigid Hulled Inflatable Boats that bobbed in the choppy swell. The early morning sun wasn't visible through the storm clouds that had gathered overhead.

The rain would not impact the mission. The RHIBs were purpose-built and equipped for all-weather maritime interdiction. They had a center console with a canopy that housed a radar dome, twin three-hundred horsepower engines, and a forward mounting for a medium machine gun. Four contractors manned each high-powered vessel, all of them wearing personal floatation devices and carrying side arms.

"The Coast Guard aircraft has just gone off station, Mike," the man behind the console of the lead boat yelled over the wind.

"OK, let's lock and load." Mike Peters was a middle-aged former Navy Warrant who ran MAROPS, a private firm that occasionally subcontracted to GES. Average height with sandy blonde hair, he'd spent his entire military career operating SWCC boats for SOCOM. The heavy rain and the poor conditions didn't faze him.

At the bow of each boat a crewmember unsnapped an equipment case and hefted a M60E machine gun onto the pintle mount. Once slotted in place, they loaded a belt of ammunition from another crate.

Mike stood next to the helmsmen of his boat and studied the radar screen. A single blip appeared at the far edge. He grabbed the radio mike and transmitted, "Contact. Let's get rolling."

The machine gunners grasped their weapons and slid their feet into the loops attached to the floor. The other men, the boarding party, grabbed the handholds on the gunwales and braced themselves.

Each boat's six hundred horses roared as the helmsmen pushed forward on the throttles and the two boats accelerated crashing through the waves leaving a violent wake behind them.

Mike grinned as he gripped the side of the console. He lived for this.

KINGSTON, JAMAICA

Mitch unlocked the rusted door on the hangar and was hit by a blast of humidity and musty stench. "Bloody hell." He'd parked the Gulfstream in front of the hangar in Jamaica, having arrived from Miami International mid-morning. Once he pulled back the main doors he would move the business jet inside.

He dropped his backpack next to his stretcher and strode across to the industrial air conditioner he'd fitted in the far corner. He tried powering it up but nothing happened. Suspecting an electrical fault he traced the power cable back to the wall where it was plugged into an old three-phase point. He disconnected it and pried the rubber cover from the plug. Sure enough one of the wires was loose. A single twist with a multi-tool resolved the issue and soon the unit was humming again. Happy the system was fixed he walked across to the office that was functioning as PRIMAL's forward headquarters. "When did the aircon blitz out?" he asked as he pushed open the door.

"Thank god you're back," exclaimed Flash from behind his desk. The portly intelligence specialist's T-shirt was drenched in sweat. "Please tell me you've fixed it."

"Yeah mate, she's humming along nicely." He gave Chua a nod. Unlike Flash, PRIMAL's Asian American chief of intelligence didn't seem fazed by the heat.

"Mitch, welcome back," Chua said. "Good work on the intel grab at King's residence. Did Bishop get away OK?"

Mitch dropped into a chair. "Yeah, no problems. How are Saneh and Mirza going?"

Chua checked his watch. "We've got a morning call with them in a few minutes. If you hang around you'll find out. Fuel is still an issue."

"Was Vance able to put together what I need?"

"Yes, the CAT and the fuel will arrive this afternoon. I'm planning to deploy the boys to Brazil so they can respond rapidly if Bishop needs them. Aleks was due to fly in around the same time but his flight out of Hamburg has been delayed by heavy snow."

"Any updates on Kurtz?"

"No, Aleks left him a message but there's been no response. There's a chance GES or the CIA have got to him first."

Mitch shook his head. "Nah mate, that slippery kraut's way too good for them."

"I hope you're right."

A ringing sound emanated from Chua's laptop.

"It's Saneh and Mirza." He activated the secure call and kept it on speaker. "How's it going, team?"

It was Saneh who replied. "Hello Chen, things are tracking well. The boat is running smoothly and Wesley has been very cooperative."

"Good news. How's your fuel situation?"

"Not bad, we've backed off to twenty knots. The onboard computer is telling me that's the optimal speed."

"Hey Saneh, it's Mitch here. Do you have enough fuel to get all the way to Jamaica?"

"At this stage it's going to be tight but I think we'll make it. Worse case scenario we can refuel at an outlying island. Maybe Cuba."

Mitch glanced at Chua who shook his head vigorously. "Chua is telling me that's not workable. But don't worry, good old Mitch has a redundancy plan in place should the need arise."

"That's good to know..." Her voice trailed off. "That's weird."

"What's up?" asked Mitch.

"I've got two contacts ahead of us. They're closing fast. I'm going to change our course."

Chua frowned. "Has anyone hailed you?"

"Negative, I'm going to push further offshore."

Seconds passed and everyone in the command center was deathly quiet.

"Damn, they're tracking right for us."

Chapter Sixteen

ATLANTIC OCEAN

"MIRZA, get Wesley up here. We're going to need his help." Saneh angled the nose of the *Nemesis* away from the approaching vessels and pushed the throttles for the diesels to the stops. The bow was slicing through the heavy swell at almost thirty knots as rain battered the cabin.

"Right away." Behind her Mirza disappeared down the stairs into the hull.

She watched the radar screen. Each time the band swept around the approaching contacts were closer. "Damn it." The boats were less than half a mile to their front heading directly for them.

"What's up?" Wesley appeared with Mirza.

"We've got trouble."

"What sort of trouble?"

The radio crackled to life. "*Nemesis*, heave to immediately or you will be fired upon."

"That sort of trouble."

"Hey, this boat can outrun anything afloat. We just need to start the turbines," said Wesley.

"OK, how do we do that?" Saneh stepped aside and allowed Wesley access to the control panel.

His fingers danced over the engineering screen activating the three 5,600 horsepower jet turbines.

Saneh felt the deck vibrate as they turned over. She glanced at the radar screen; the contacts were almost on them. She squinted through the rain-streaked windshield, trying to see through the frantically sweeping wipers. "Mirza, can you get up front and see if you can spot them?"

"I'm on it." He grabbed a spray jacket and checked the pistol he had taken from the dead guard.

As he made his way out to the deck Saneh watched Wesley frantically stabbing at buttons on the engineering screen. "What's wrong?"

"I can only get one turbine up."

The radio crackled again. "*Nemesis*, I have visual on you. Heave to immediately or I will fire."

Mirza's voice came in over her earpiece, "I've got eyes on two RHIBs directly ahead."

"OK, hold on." She spun the wheel and pushed on the throttle of the one running turbine. The massive motor-yacht spun away from the two boats, the sleek hull crashing in the swell. She glanced down at the console; they were pulling thirty-five knots.

The sound of a machine gun roared over the engines and a line of tracers zipped across their bow.

"Holy shit!" screamed Wesley as he gripped the side of the cabin.

"We're past them," reported Mirza. "We need to go full throttle."

"We already are," replied Saneh as she banked the boat from side to side to throw off the gunner's aim.

"They're coming around," Mirza said as he ran to the stern of the boat.

Two more lines of tracer lashed past either side. The smaller craft were easily keeping pace.

She turned to the white-faced banker. "Wesley, if we don't get those engines going we're dead."

He stared at her blankly.

She slapped him. "Wesley, what the hell's wrong with the engines?"

"The safety systems are stopping them from starting."

"*Nemesis*, heave to now or we will destroy you!" blared the radio.

"How do we fix it?"

"In the engine room. There's a panel."

Saneh flinched as the hull shuddered. Their pursuers had decided to engage to disable the boat. She grasped his arm. "I need you to get down there and sort it out."

She heard Mirza's pistol bark.

Wesley dashed down the stairs and disappeared as more bullets lashed the side of the boat. Saneh spun them in the opposite direction. "Mirza are you OK?"

He took a moment to reply. "Yes, but they've dropped back. I can't hit anything."

"*Nemesis*, you are outgunned. Heave to immediately."

Saneh knew if she kept evading someone was going to get killed. She grabbed the radio mike. "OK, OK, we're stopping." She eased back on the throttles bringing the engines to an idle. "Mirza, tell me when they're close."

At the stern Mirza crouched and watched one of the RHIBs pull in behind them. The other stood off, about fifty yards away.

Inside, Saneh stood behind the console watching the engineering display intently. One of the turbines was green. The other two were red. "Come on, Wesley," she murmured.

"They're going to be onboard in seconds," reported Mirza.

The two red engines went green. "Hold on!" She pushed all three throttles to their stops and looked back.

At the stern of *Nemesis* the three turbines screamed, launching torrents of water out of the jets. The wall of water hit the side of the closest RHIB and flipped it, knocking the crew into the ocean. Mirza rose and fired two shots at the other RHIB. The gunner ducked for cover as the *Nemesis* surged forward, rapidly gaining speed.

Saneh clung to the side of the cabin as the boat tipped back and the RHIBs disappeared behind them. Like a howling banshee the *Nemesis* tore through the ocean at nearly seventy knots, launching over the stormy seas, spray exploding off the bow.

Mirza staggered back into the cabin. He slid the doors shut behind him blocking the torrent of noise. "Good work, skipper!"

She shot him a grin from the console. "Well done, Wesley."

Wesley appeared from below decks and managed a grin.

"I'm guessing we're going to need Mitch's fuel contingency," she said.

GES FACILITY, VIRGINIA

Howard sat at his desk fighting the urge to scream in frustration. He felt like he'd been working on Objective Yankee and Red Sox for weeks and was no closer to finding out who they worked for. The team had checked every connection, scoured every database, investigated every loose end, and still nothing.

They had good fidelity on Wilhelm Jager from when he was in the police force but nothing after he left. There had been the incident with the rapists then nothing. What incensed him even more was he wasn't being given all the information. He knew the boat was owned by one of the MVI directors but had no idea why it was significant. He glanced across at Pershing's office. Charles King, the CEO of GES had commandeered it.

Howard contemplated going outside for a cigarette but instead headed for the office. He knocked on the door.

"Come in."

Charles King directed him to the seat in front of his desk. "How can I help you, Terrance?"

He noticed there was an open bottle of scotch whiskey on the desk next to a glass tumbler. "Mr. King, I'm concerned I'm not getting all the information I need to do my job."

"What do you mean?"

"I mean, I think Pershing and you are holding back information that may assist the CIA in locating and neutralizing Objective Yankee and his supporters."

King's eyes narrowed. "What information do you think we have?"

"For a start this boat you had me track down, the *Nemesis*. Why is it significant?"

King reached for the bottle. "You're pretty sharp aren't you?" He sloshed whiskey in the glass and handed it to him. Then he took a swig from the bottle. "The boat belongs to one of the directors of MVI. You know what that is?"

He sipped from the glass. "The parent company to GES, a private equity firm based out of New York."

"Correct. Well it's possible the same bastards who trashed the mine in Mexico have abducted one of our people and stolen his boat."

"You're kidding me."

"There's more. A little over an hour ago one of our contractors attempted to intercept the boat and failed. It's now heading south at break neck speed."

"Dude, why didn't you let me know? I can get assets on it. We can track it and find out where they're based."

"I just did." King leaned in close. "Between you and me, I think someone is trying to shut down my boss."

"Jordan Pollard?"

King nodded.

"Do we have a list of his enemies?"

He shrugged. "There are a lot of them."

"Yes, but if I can tie any of them to the intel we already have it might help."

"I'll see what I can do." He took another swig. "Do we have anything more on Objective Yankee? This Aden guy."

Howard shook his head. "No, Red Sox is the key. Once Pershing bags him in Rio we'll know more."

"That'd better be the case or I'm going to be out of a job." He screwed the cap back on the bottle. "Now, how about you see what additional surveillance you can whistle up."

"Will do, sir." Howard left the office and walked back to

his desk. King was completely different to Pershing, he reflected. He valued information but didn't hoard it. The sort of man he could work with in the future. He grabbed his phone from his desk. Larkin would want an update and would have to approve the surveillance assets he needed.

Chapter Seventeen

RIO DE JANEIRO, BRAZIL

BISHOP WAS STILL tired after flying from Miami to Rio. A screaming child had kept him awake for most of the trip. Not even his noise-cancelling headphones had been able to deal with the infant's wailing.

The only upside was he didn't have to wait for his bags. Without the burden of checked luggage it only took him twenty minutes to clear customs and find a cab in the rank outside Rio de Janeiro International Airport. His Portuguese was limited to a few phrases so he showed the driver where he wanted to go on the map he'd taken from a stand in front of a hire car desk.

Rio was a city he'd always wanted to visit and as the cab traveled along the dual lane highway he found himself wondering what Saneh was doing. He pushed the thought from his mind. He needed to focus on finding Kurtz before GES did.

The cab dropped him in the popular beachside suburb

of Leblon, Kurtz's last known location. Flash had given him the address of an internet café the German had used to check his Skype account. It was two blocks over. First things first, he needed to find accommodation.

He walked down a tree-lined street with multi-story buildings on each side. The lower levels housed shops and businesses; everything from language schools to juice bars and eateries. The area had a similar feel to Waikiki, Hawaii; tropical and very touristy. It surprised Bishop that Kurtz would choose to come here, unless he'd found a sinister underbelly to the area. Walking past a bank he stopped in the shade of a tall tree and inspected a sign advertising cheap rooms. The hostel looked clean and tidy so he walked in.

Fifteen minutes later he was back on the street having dumped his backpack in his new room. As he walked down the street he took note of what people were wearing, what sort of cars they were driving, and how they interacted with each other. It was something Ivan had taught him, counter-surveillance 101. By benchmarking what was normal for an area he would be more likely to spot something out of the ordinary.

He turned down the street where the internet café was located and started scanning. There was a restaurant across the road and he found an empty table just inside. The establishment had large open windows giving a clear view across the street to the café.

As he devoured a breakfast platter of meats and cheeses, washed down with a banana smoothie, he noticed a tourist who seemed to be paying a little too much attention to the internet café. In the half-hour he'd been in the restaurant the well-built sightseer had walked past twice. Considering the man's athletic build and military bearing it set alarm bells ringing.

Bishop slurped down the last of his smoothie and spotted another well-built man sitting at a bus stop. No less than three buses had passed and he hadn't moved. The hairs on Bishop's neck prickled. The internet café was under surveillance. He casually rose, left some money on the table, and departed the restaurant.

Strolling along the street, he turned down a side alley, keen to put buildings between him and what had to be a surveillance team. He spotted a white SUV parked against the curb and as he walked past he glanced through the tinted glass directly into the face of George Henry Pershing; the man who'd killed two of his friends in Mexico and destroyed the lives of dozens of farmers.

They locked eyes. Bishop had seen the former-CIA officer twice before, once on the streets of Chihuahua, and once at the now destroyed gold mine. He sprinted away as the car door flung open and Pershing screamed into his radio. "Objective Yankee is here! He's here!"

Bishop only made it forty yards when a volley of gunfire shattered the windows in a shop front opposite him. He dived to the ground taking cover behind a metal dumpster. Bullets hit the steel with a clang as a car screeched to a halt.

He sprinted out from behind the dumpster, narrowly avoided a bus, and took off down the opposite side of the street. His legs were burning and his lungs heaving as he skidded around a corner and down a one-way lane. The traffic was flowing against his pursuers. He glanced back and saw the SUV jump the curb and chase him along the sidewalk.

Pedestrians screamed and ran for safety as the truck behind him screeched to a halt just short of an outdoor restaurant. Tires squealed as it reversed, the driver searching for a way around.

He bolted through the heavy traffic into a park filled with people. Slowing to a walking pace, he sucked air into his lungs as he strode through the crowd scanning for more GES contractors.

He spotted a line of motor scooters on the opposite side of the park and headed toward them. A teenager was sitting on one of the bikes with a helmet on his lap. Bishop pulled all the cash he had from his pocket. "How much for the scooter?"

"Not for sale."

Bishop slipped the Omega watch from his wrist. "Swap?"

The kid took the watch and felt its weight in his hand.

Down the street Bishop caught a glimpse of the white SUV driving around the park. He had seconds not minutes. "It's a good deal." Grabbing the helmet, he shoved the youth off the bike, donned the helmet, and turned the ignition. He gunned the two-stroke engine and the nimble scooter bolted forward.

Glancing over his shoulder he spotted the SUV rapidly approaching. As he looked back another truck skidded to a halt in front of him. Bishop gunned the scooter and slid it sideways. It cleared the curb, nearly bucking him off, and he raced back through the park. He weaved between pedestrians, blaring the bike's shrill horn.

Reaching the far side of the park he merged with the traffic and sped down a four-lane road between backed-up cars. He raced up a sweeping ramp and found himself on a highway overpass.

Pershing smiled as his vehicle hit the on-ramp to the highway. The SUV had kept up by traveling along the sidewalk. Now the game had changed; the scooter's strength, its agility, was diminished as the traffic flowed freely on the highway. Its small size and engine were now a liability. "We need to take him down before the next exit."

"Not a problem. We nudge him off and he's done," said Chris.

"I want him alive."

"Just a little nudge then."

The other SUV had caught up and was alongside them.

Pershing thumbed the radio mike. "Shrek, push forward and block. We're going to ram him from behind."

"Wilco, boss."

Bishop kept glancing in his mirrors, wishing the scooter had an extra fifty horsepower. The two SUVs were maneuvering front and rear and he had an eighteen-wheeler boxing him in against the barrier. He had the throttle maxed out but the little scooter had nothing more to give. "Now this is a shit sandwich."

He spotted a gap in the concrete barrier fifty yards out, right as the lead SUV slammed on the brakes and tried to hit him. He jerked the bars up, bounced over the drain at the edge of the highway, and shot through the two-foot gap. "Oh crap." The opposite side was a drop into thick green vegetation. The scooter dove nose first. Vines and branches whipped his face and tore at his clothes. Unable to hold on he let go of the bike. The vines arrested his fall but the scooter crashed through to the bottom of the hill.

"This is why real men don't ride scooters." Bishop struggled out of the leafy clutches and slid down to the scooter. It seemed undamaged but when he thumbed the starter it refused to turn over. The screech of tires caught his attention and he tried again. The pursuers had taken the next exit and he could see them curving around the off ramp.

"Come on girl." The engine finally caught and he strangled the throttle, smoking the back wheel. He took off down a narrow winding road that led to the favela.

Despite the crash, the scooter performed well on the narrow road. He dodged cars, trash cans, children, and dogs as he sped at full throttle, leaving the SUVs behind. The road snaked past apartment buildings and townhouses before the ramshackle dwellings of the favela began appearing.

He rode past rows of vans and cars, not noticing they were all brightly emblazoned with sponsorship logos. He skidded up a narrow laneway and caught a glimpse of a Red Bull banner strung between buildings as he flew beneath it. "What the hell?" As he reached the top of the hill he realized he had scootered into the middle of a sporting event. A crowd of bystanders was blocking the street.

Glancing over his shoulder he saw the two SUVs screech to a halt and GES operators dismount. He eyeballed Pershing and revved the scooter. Tooting the horn he pushed his way through the crowd. A marshal in an orange shirt tried to stop him from shoving his way through a row of hay bales. He forced the man aside and zoomed into a marshaling area filled with helmeted downhill mountain bikers. Looking back, he spotted his pursuers barging their way through the crowd. Frantically searching for an exit he spotted the only way out; underneath another Red Bull banner and down a flight of stairs.

"Fuck it." The crowd cheered as he smoked the rear tire and launched the scooter down the stairs.

Pershing watched in disbelief as his target disappeared. He turned to Shrek. "Get someone after him."

The brawny operator snatched a downhill bike from one of the riders.

"Hey bro, that's..." The youth shut his mouth when Shrek glared at him.

He thrust the bike at Chris, his 2IC. "Get after him."

Chris examined the bike for a moment before throwing a leg over and pedaling down the stairs.

"Should wear a helmet," yelled the bike's owner who was dressed in full protective armor.

"Shut your mouth," snapped Shrek.

"Where does the track end?" Pershing asked a clipboard carrying official.

"All the way to the bottom of the hill. You'll have to drive around."

He turned and pushed his way through the crowd. "You heard him, Shrek. Let's roll."

Bishop's teeth jarred as the scooter bounced down another flight of stairs. He hit the bottom and more locals cheered as he accelerated along a straight section of road. Checking the wing mirror he spotted one of the GES guys in hot pursuit, riding a downhill mountain bike. He swerved around a ramp that would have launched him up a wall, and skidded down another set of stairs. His plan was to ditch the scooter and disappear into the favela but the guy on the bike was on his heels.

As he rode he tried to remember what Chua had taught him on their one ride back on the island. Not that much of it mattered, the scooter's suspension was useless compared to the downhill bike following him. He rode around another jump and the crowd booed. Bouncing across an open courtyard he followed the track as it wound under an arch, around a tight corner, and along a footpath. He glanced over his shoulder; the GES rider was gaining on him. They sped down another set of stairs, along a street, then under another arch.

"Fuuuck!" The scooter launched off a two-yard drop onto a wooden ramp. It hit hard and almost bucked him off. Ahead he spotted another ramp. With nowhere else to go he accelerated toward it. The scooter seemed to hang in the air before it cleared the gap and slammed down on top of a shipping container. Bishop jammed on the brakes and skidded to a halt inches from a huge drop.

He leaped off the scooter and spun around ready for the GES operative.

The other rider hadn't made the first jump. His front tire had washed out slamming him to the ground and knocking him unconscious. From the top of the container Bishop could see a pair of paramedics already on the scene. He climbed down from the container, handed his helmet to a wide-eyed youth, and slipped into the crowd.

At the bottom of the hill Pershing and his men were waiting. They'd fanned out and were searching the crowd. The GES operative checked his watch. It had been fifteen minutes since they arrived at the bottom and there was still no sign of their man or Aden. He grabbed an official by the shoulder. "What's going on?"

The official raised an eyebrow questioningly. "Accident. They're bringing him down now."

There were four men carrying the litter. Pershing pushed through the crowd with Shrek. "Shit, it's Chris," said the team leader.

An ambulance arrived and they loaded the casualty inside.

"Shrek, send one of your boys with the ambulance."

"Roger, do you want us to start searching the favela?"

He shook his head. "No. We'll go back to the internet

café and find out what we can." Pershing glanced up the hill at the shantytown. They were on the right trail now. It was only a matter of time till they had Yankee or Red Sox in the bag.

FOZ DO IGUACU, BRAZIL

Kurtz stepped off the bus and groaned as he stretched his legs and scanned the surroundings. He had been onboard the smelly rattling bus for almost twenty-four hours and was in desperate need of some food, a shower, and a drink. It was mid-afternoon and he hadn't even had breakfast yet.

Grabbing his bag from where the driver dumped it on the curb, he walked down the dusty street. From what he could see Foz do Iguacu was a bit of a dump. His research had led him to believe it was a mecca for tourists keen to see the nearby Iguacu falls. In reality it looked run down, filthy, and industrial. There were a couple of people on the street, a few cars, and a mangy dog that started following him.

He walked past a tire repair shop and stopped in front of the Hotel Nacional. The five-story square building was painted a bright shade of flamingo pink with blue bars over the lower level windows. It took him a few minutes to arrange a room. After a quick shower and a bite to eat he purchased a new mobile phone from a shop across the road.

He rang the local number he'd scribbled on a piece of paper. The man who answered gave him directions to another location not far away. He hailed a passing cab and within a few minutes was standing out the front of a rented house that the Escape not-for-profit was using as an operating base.

He knocked and a young guy opened the door. Kurtz immediately summed him up as ex-military. He wore a thick beard, scruffy hair, a tank top, and a pair of cut-off cargo pants as shorts.

"I'm Arnie," he said with a British accent.

"Kurtz." He shook his hand and followed him to the living room where three other men were sitting on couches and drinking beer.

"Lads, this is Kurtz," said Arnie. "He's joining us after working in Rio with Break Away."

The men introduced themselves and he took a seat. One of them offered him a beer and he savored the first taste of the ice-cold amber liquid.

"You just get in, mate?" one of the men asked. Like Arnie he had a British accent.

"Yes, caught the bus from Rio."

"Ripper innit?"

"No, it was most unpleasant."

The men laughed as Kurtz swigged from his bottle. Arnie picked up a remote control and switched on a flat screen TV that had a laptop plugged into it.

"Kurtz, we've been working on this one for quite a while so I wanted to take the opportunity to brief you in." He pressed a remote button and a map appeared. "This is the location of a brothel on the outskirts of town that deals mainly in underage girls."

As Arnie ran through what essentially was a detailed set of orders Kurtz found himself smiling. This was more like the team environment he missed. A close-knit group of professionals, who planned in detail, rehearsed, then executed their raid with efficiency. Finally, he had found somewhere he could forget PRIMAL and make a difference.

"OK," concluded Arnie at the end of the briefing. "That's the lowdown on what we're facing."

He nodded. "When are we going to rescue the girls?"

"Well, I thought we could run a few rehearsals tomorrow morning then hit them at dusk the next day, before things start to get busy."

The other three men nodded in agreement. It was clear to Kurtz that everyone in the room had prior military service. Judging by their ages it was probable they had all served in either Afghanistan or Iraq, or both.

"We've got a recce car we'll use tomorrow and hire two vans for the actual job."

"And what happens with the girls?"

"There's a women's and children's rescue shelter in Medianeira run by the Red Cross. We've taken girls to them before and they've been able to get them back to their relatives."

Kurtz took another swig from his beer. "I'm very impressed. You've done a really good job planning this."

Arnie grinned. "Well, coming from a Kraut that's a pretty big compliment."

Chapter Eighteen

KINGSTON, JAMAICA

MITCH WAS WAITING outside the hangar when the Lascar Logistics C-130 taxied along the apron and powered down. The big transporter had completed the flight from Lascar Island to Jamaica with an hour to spare thanks to a roaring tailwind. The side door of the aircraft popped open and Kruger's six-foot-five frame appeared. He stepped down the stairs with a dive bag under each arm. The other two CAT operators, Miklos and Pavel, followed him.

"Welcome to Jamaica, chaps."

"Not exactly what I was expecting, *ja*." Kruger scowled.

"Sorry mate, you looking for a Pina Colada and a beach?" said Mitch.

A broad smile replaced the scowl. "That's exactly what I want."

"From one tropical prison to another," said Miklos as he dumped his gear on the ground. "Do we know when Aleks is getting in?"

"His flight was delayed, he'll arrive first thing tomorrow." He jerked his thumb in the direction of the side door to the hangar. "You lads get inside and make yourselves comfortable. I need to check a few things with the crew."

Mitch left the three men and climbed into the C-130. He was greeted by the American loadmaster. "Are you Mitch?"

"Yeah that's me."

"Then these belong to you." He pointed to the two fuel bladders sitting on pallets at the rear of the aircraft. "Anytime you want to get them off my aircraft, feel free. Flying around with a shit-ton of flammable gas makes me a little nervous."

"What do you mean? You've got this again in your tanks. What's another eight thousand liters going to matter?"

The loadmaster shook his head.

Mitch gave the pallets a once over then left the aircrew to their post-flight maintenance. Once they were finished they would move to a hotel in town for some rest. He strode across to the hangar and rejoined Kruger and the boys inside. They had already identified their bed spaces and were pulling their gear out and laying it on the floor. Chua was talking to Kruger and seemed stressed. "What's up?"

"It's Bishop. He ran into Pershing in Rio," said Chua.

"Literally?"

"Yes, at least five of the contractors were casing the internet café that Kurtz used. Bishop saw them first but they spotted him and gave chase."

"Is he OK?"

"Yes, he's found somewhere to stay in a favela. The main concern now is whether Pershing will find Kurtz first."

"Do you need us to head to Brazil now?" asked Kruger.

"No, Bishop's in the clear, for now. He needs a location and that's something we don't have yet," replied Chua.

"What about Mirza and Saneh?" Mitch said. "Maybe we should refuel them now while we've got a chance."

"The only problem is it leaves us down a pilot which limits exfil options from this location."

"You think that might be a requirement?"

Chua nodded. "With the interdiction of the *Nemesis* and Pershing tracking Kurtz it's hard to assess how much they know."

"That might be something you need to talk through with Vance," said Mitch.

"You're probably right. One thing is clear though, we need to go on the offensive and we need to do it ASAP."

RIO DE JANEIRO, BRAZIL

Pershing stepped up to the counter in the internet café and showed the woman a photo of Wilhelm Jager. He saw the instant recognition in her face. "You know him, don't you?"

She swallowed and glanced at Shrek for the third time in as many seconds. "I have seen him here a few times." Her English was broken.

"Where is he now?"

"He left two days ago. There was another man here, who followed him."

"Do you know where this other man is now?" Pershing's pulse quickened. Could the man be Aden?

She nodded. "Yes, he stays at Leblon Castle Hostel. It is just around the corner."

Pershing broke into a broad smile and reached in his

pocket for his wallet. He took out a few US hundred dollar bills and handed them over. "Thank you so much, ma'am. You've been very helpful."

He left with Shrek in tow. They walked around the corner and he spotted the sign to the backpacker hostel. He pushed open the doors and strode to the counter. There was no one there so he stabbed the bell with his finger. An elderly gentleman with a gray droopy mustache walked in from a back room.

"Hello sir, by chance do you speak English?"

The mustache bobbed as he nodded.

"Excellent." He pulled out the photo. "I'd like to know if this man was staying here with some other guests."

The caretaker glanced at the photo, then at Pershing, and then Shrek.

"Yes, his name is Kurtz. He was staying in Room 203 but has disappeared."

"Kurtz, huh. Is he still using the room?"

"No, he disappeared. But his friend, Mr. Brian, is in Room 305." Pershing flashed him a smile and handed him fifty dollars. "Thank you, sir."

"Why do you keep giving these people money after they've already told you what they know?" asked Shrek as they climbed the worn carpet to the third floor.

"Didn't your mamma ever tell you? You catch more flies with honey." Pershing went to pull open the door to the corridor and the knob came off in his hand. "Son of a bitch." He grabbed hold of the shaft and managed to open it.

Cockroaches scurried across the corridor floor as he counted the doors. When he got to 305 he stopped. "Shrek, pass me your pistol." Pershing had left his in the car. He found it uncomfortable and difficult to conceal in just a shirt. Shrek on the other hand could hide a bazooka in his belt and handed over a full-size double-stack .45.

Pershing checked the weapon was chambered and knocked on the door. A moment later the door opened a crack.

"What do you want?"

"Information," said Pershing calmly as he pointed the pistol through the gap. The man wasn't Aden.

Shrek shoulder-charged the door and knocked the startled man onto his rear. He was an older guy with gray hair, no shirt, and a belly that hung over his shorts.

They stormed into the small room as the man cowered on the floor.

"Get up." Pershing tossed him the shirt that was hanging on a chair. Then he spun the chair and sat on it cowboy style. "Are you Brian?"

The man nodded as he put on his shirt.

"American?"

"Yes."

"OK, good." Pershing handed back Shrek's pistol. "We're trying to find this gentleman." He passed the photo to Shrek who showed it to Brian. "You might know him as Kurtz. His real name is Wilhelm Jager. He's wanted by US agencies for a series of attacks against abortion clinics in Alabama, Texas, and Missouri."

Brian frowned. "Do they even have clinics in those states?"

"Don't get smart, hot shot. Right now I have evidence you've been consorting with an enemy of the United States of America. Unless you want to be put on a no-fly list and have your passport canceled, I'd start talking. Now, Jager. Where's he at?"

"Who are you people?"

"We're representatives of the US government." Pershing flicked open a cardholder and showed the man his CIA contractor ID. "We've been given the task of bringing Wilhelm Jager in for questioning."

"OK, OK, he helped us out with one of our jobs. Then he ran off, caught a bus across to the tri-border area."

"Jobs? What do you mean by jobs?"

"I run a non-profit. We get young girls out of brothels and back to their families. Kurtz, I mean Wilhelm, helped us with our last job. The guy's messed up, PTSD to the hilt. Didn't like the way we do business."

Pershing almost felt a level of admiration for the overweight retiree. He was out there making a difference in the world when he could have been drinking beers on his porch. "When did he leave?"

"Yesterday. No, no, actually it was the day before. He left in a hurry, more stressed than usual. So I followed him. Saw him get on a bus to Foz do Iguacu."

"OK, thank you. Is there anything else we should know?"

Brian shook his head.

"Do you mind giving my buddy Shrek here your number in case we need to talk to you again?"

Brian put his number into Shrek's phone.

"I apologize for the inconvenience." Pershing took his wallet from his pocket and counted out five hundred dollars. "Here, I want make a contribution to what you're doing."

"No, that's not necessary."

Pershing placed the cash on top of an old box TV. "I insist." He turned and left the room with Shrek in tow. By the time they reached the lobby he was already on the phone to Howard in the SCIF.

"I need you to get me the names and locations of every

not-for-profit based in the tri-border region. Focus on anyone linked to sex trafficking." He terminated the call as they strode back to the SUVs. "Shrek, I want the gear packed and us on the road inside thirty minutes."

"Roger, boss."

Pershing dialed his local CIA contact's number. He knew there were a number of CIA safe houses in the tri-border area. He needed one configured for interrogation and rendition.

LASCAR ISLAND

Vance stared at the Kindle sitting on the coffee table in the corner of his office. He contemplated leaving his desk, laying on the full-length couch and reading another book. Anything to keep his mind off the current operation. With most of his assets deployed forward he felt a little redundant.

There were still personnel in the base: intelligence staff, watchkeepers, and a handful of maintenance workers. That wasn't the problem. The issue was he was usually up to his neck wheeling and dealing everything from drones to field operatives and intelligence assets. The nature of this operation had pushed that control forward to Chua, his chief of intel, and the second-in-command of PRIMAL. It wasn't that he doubted Chen's decision-making or ability, he just found it hard to step back and take a supporting role.

The communicator app on the tablet in front of him flashed and he stabbed the screen with his finger. Chua's ears must have been burning because his face appeared on the screen. "Hey bud, how's things?" Vance noticed dark circles under Chua's eyes.

"You read my latest report?"

He nodded. "Yeah, there's no doubt. GES is hunting Kurtz to get to us. How's Flash going tracking him down?"

"No luck. He's dropped off the grid completely. We're relying on Bishop to find him."

"And now he's one step behind the GES crew."

"Yes, and what's more I've got Mirza and Saneh at sea with limited fuel. They've got our best chance at shutting down MVI, GES, and the whole show, Mr. Wesley Chambers."

"That's our priority then. Get Mirza, Saneh, and Chambers to a secure location. Bishop can look after himself and we've got the CAT on standby if he needs assistance."

Chua shook his head. "That's the dilemma, Mitch can't effect a refuel and be on stand-by to fly in the CAT."

"Then get the refuel done ASAP and get him back on dry land."

"You're right." Chua sighed. "I'm exhausted. Maybe you should come forward and take over."

Vance shook his head. "Negative, you're doing just fine. I think it's wise for us not to have all our eggs in one basket at the moment."

"I agree, in fact I wanted to talk to you about shutting Jamaica down. With the attempted interdiction of the *Nemesis*, and Pershing going after Kurtz, I'm worried GES may have the assets to locate us."

"Your call. Once the CAT deploys to Brazil it makes sense to move."

"Can you get the team in the Bunker to investigate the options?"

"Can do, buddy."

"Cool, have you heard anything else from Ivan?"

"Yeah, he's established a safe house and contacted a local asset. Hasn't been able to dig up any more information on the SEAL Flash identified. Have you guys got anything new, like what exactly they're doing down there?"

"No, but Chambers thinks it's an oil project."

"Isn't Venezuela closed to US investment?"

Chua nodded. "It is. But if MVI are providing counter-revolutionary services to the government through GES they may have been able to strike a deal. I've done a little research on the oil market. By all indications Venezuela is struggling to get its industry off the ground. With the plummeting oil prices and uptick in US production, MVI have probably got themselves a bargain."

"Risky, but makes sense. See if you can get any more information from Chambers when you bring him in." He paused. "Tell Saneh not to let Mitch interrogate him. We don't want the kid freaking out on us."

Chua finally smiled. "OK, I'll brief Mitch now and get him out the door for the refuel."

"OK, you're doing good, junior. I'm proud."

"Thanks, old man." Chua laughed as he signed off.

Vance's knees creaked as he leveraged himself out of his chair. Chua wasn't wrong, he was getting to be an old man. First it was glasses and next it would be arthritis. The years of abuse to his body were catching up. It seemed like a lifetime ago that he and Ice were running around Kosovo together. On his way out he paused at the bookshelf behind the door. He pulled a book out and opened it to a well-thumbed page. There pressed between the pages was a picture of him and James 'Ice' Castle, his best friend and the man who had helped him establish PRIMAL.

CARACAS, VENEZUELA

"Pete, SITREP on the target," Jimmy Scott said thumbing the transmit button on his radio. He was sitting in the front of their battered van outside a large house on the outskirts of Caracas. It was late evening and his team had been waiting in the van for four hours.

Pete's voice came through tinny and distorted. "I still haven't got another hit. The phone could be off."

High above the van and a few hundred meters away the Schiebel Camcopter was hovering, its high-resolution infrared camera focused on the building. The video feed transmitted directly to the van where one of Jimmy's teammates was monitoring it. "There's no sign of guards or dogs, boss. We should wrap this up now and get back for some shut-eye."

Jimmy pulled his balaclava down over his face. "Alright, let's do this. Remember this is a break and enter turned violent. I want to be in and out in under two minutes."

Hank started the van and they drove alongside the metal front gates that protected the estate. When they stopped one of the operators slid open the door, jumped out with a Halligan bar and wrenched open the door to the side of the main gate. Jimmy led the team through the ornate entrance across the lawn to the front door of the two-story mansion.

"This guy's got some money," said one of the men who was carrying a sledgehammer. He stood alongside the door and lined up his swing.

"OK, go."

The hammer smashed the lock and the four men stormed inside. The lights were still on and a figure appeared from the living room. Jimmy punched him in the gut, knocking him to the ground.

Someone else yelled and one of the other operators silenced him with a flurry of blows from a baton.

Jimmy stood over the man he'd knocked down. "What's your name?" he asked in Spanish.

The man glared defiantly and adjusted his black-rimmed glasses. "I'm not afraid of you," he said hoarsely.

"You want me to kill your friend? Or do you want to tell me your fucking name?" Jimmy brandished a cheap carving knife. The sort of weapon a petty thief would use.

"Dante, my name is Dante."

"Well Dante, today is not your day, is it." He knelt down and plunged the carving knife into the bookish political leader's stomach. Blood spilled from his mouth as Jimmy jerked the blade up, slicing a huge rent in the man's lungs and heart.

A blood-curdling scream filled the house and Jimmy looked up. Standing at the top of the staircase was a middle-aged woman dressed in a nightgown. She wore a look of utter horror.

"Shut her up, Hank," growled Jimmy.

The heavy-set operator sprinted up the stairs and grabbed the hysterical woman, pressing a gloved hand over her mouth.

"Trash the house, take anything of value," Jimmy ordered the others. He glanced up at Hank. "You OK to take care of her?"

The operator shook his head. "I don't do women, Jimmy."

"For fuck's sake." He pulled the knife from Dante's chest and strode up the stairs. The woman struggled vainly against Hank. Jimmy dragged her into the bathroom. He held the knife against her throat and reached inside her nightgown with his free hand. She cursed and spat, oblivious to the blade that nicked her skin.

"Feisty bitch." Jimmy dropped the knife and slammed her head against the sink with a clunk. She collapsed on the tiles moaning. Her nightgown fell open revealing a firm body and ample breasts. As he fumbled with his pants the radio on his belt crackled.

"Jimmy, this is Pete."

He grabbed the radio. "What?"

"You've got red and blues inbound. Better high-tail it out of there."

"Damn it." He grabbed a fist full of the woman's hair and smacked her head against the tiles until she was out cold.

"OK boys, let's roll."

Loaded up with jewelry, cash, and some liquor, they piled into their van and drove off. As they turned the corner two police cars screamed past them with lights flashing.

"Job done."

Chapter Nineteen

CARIBBEAN SEA

SANEH STOOD at the bow of the *Nemesis* and let the breeze flow through her long brown hair. She rubbed her eyes and drew a deep breath. The last twenty-four hours had taken their toll and she longed to roll out a yoga mat on the wooden deck and stretch away her stiffness.

At least the weather had improved; the storm front had passed during the night. It left behind clear blue skies and a tranquil ocean that hissed under the bow as they cruised at a comfortable twenty knots.

The fuel situation was critical, they had burned thousands of gallons evading the two RHIBs. She glanced at her watch, it was 0655. Mitch was five minutes late. She double-checked the GPS map on her iPRIMAL. They were halfway between the Bahamas and Cuba, in international waters.

She heard the drone of an aircraft a moment before she spotted the speck on the horizon. Lifting the powerful binoculars that hung around her neck she focused them on the aircraft. The magnification allowed her to make out the distinctive four-engine, high tail design of a C-130 transporter. For a split second she feared it was a US Coast Guard aircraft. Then her earpiece crackled and Mirza spoke.

"Saneh, Mitch is inbound."

Relief washed over her as she lowered the binoculars and watched the aircraft grow in size. It roared overhead. She padded down the side and watched the aircraft bank around for another pass. It waggled its wings as it lined up a few hundred yards off the side. Saneh stepped down onto the swimming platform that extended from the back of the boat. Tied to the railing and bobbing in the water was the *Nemesis'* tender. Wesley had helped her unload the compact RHIB from the stowage point under the foredeck.

Inside the aircraft Mitch stood behind the two fuel bladders. He was dressed in a wetsuit with an MC-6 steerable parachute strapped to his back and a reserve attached to his front. His heart was pounding but he wore a broad grin.

"You're good to go." The loadmaster finished checking his chute and gave him a thumbs-up.

Mitch had only jumped with a parachute once before. That time he'd been strapped to the front of Kruger. This time he was on his own.

The loadmaster dropped the ramp and Mitch's heart leaped as the ocean raced past a thousand feet below.

"OK, standby." The loadmaster gave his static line a reassuring tug. Then he hit a button and the two bundled fuel bladders slid to the edge of the ramp.

Mitch's heart was beating as fast as it did when he pulled out a 1:35 split on the rowing machine. His legs felt wobbly and he had the urge to puke.

"OK, go." The loadmaster hit the trigger for the bundles and they disappeared over the ramp.

Mitch walked forward, sliding his static line along the wire. He stared straight ahead and stepped out into nothing. There was a roar of engines as he fell through the slipstream then silence as his parachute unfurled above him. He glanced around and spotted the *Nemesis* off to one side. In front of him the second fuel bladder hit the water with a splash, its parachute collapsing and drifting down on top of it. He remembered to glance up and check his chute; all good. He searched the back of the risers in front of him for the steering toggles. Locating them he pulled the left one down turning the chute toward the fuel bundles.

Fighting the urge to howl with delight he located the releases for the parachute. Then, right as he was about to hit the water, he pulled the wire loops and dropped away from the chute. He plunged into the clear blue water. Bobbing to the surface he spent a few seconds fitting his fins before kicking his way over to the bladders. He heard a high-powered engine off to one side as he grabbed the floats that kept the thousands of gallons of fuel afloat and turned his head to see Saneh at the helm of a small boat.

"Ahoy there," she yelled as she brought the craft alongside.

Mitch grabbed the hand line on the rubber gunwale and hauled himself out of the water. "Permission to come aboard, skipper."

"You are already ya land lubber." Saneh clipped a line onto a fuel bladder. She already had the first bladder attached.

As they slowly tugged the fuel Mitch got his first real look at *Nemesis*. "My god Saneh, she's beautiful."

"She's alright."

They pulled up at the back of the motor-yacht where Mirza was waiting. He grabbed hold of the boat and tied it to the rear deck. Grasping Mitch's hand, he helped him aboard. "Welcome to the *Nemesis*, Mitch."

The Brit dashed up the steps and peeked inside the cabin. "This thing is awesome!"

"There's plenty of time for you to check her out after we pump this fuel into the tanks," yelled Saneh from the tender.

Mitch spun around, snapped his heels together, and gave a crisp salute. "Yes, Skipper. First things first, let's get the bladders tied off. Then we can run the fuel lines into the tanks."

GES FACILITY, VIRGINIA

Howard watched as King poured two glasses of whiskey from the bottle on his desk. The CEO had gone to the effort of finding another glass so he didn't have to drink from the bottle. King handed him one of the tumblers. "OK, so we're hot on the trail of Red Sox. We still don't know where Yankee is but we have to assume the two of them are working together."

Howard raised his glass. "We're getting closer."

"OK, so what have we got on the boat?"

Howard nodded at the printed map he'd placed on the desk. "I had one of the analysts do some modeling on the vessel, her route, rate of fuel consumption, and likely destinations. According to the marina she was full when she left New York. Running on her most economic speed she would have made it all the way down as far as Miami by now."

"That's what she was doing when the Coast Guard was tracking her?"

"Correct. However, our dudes down in South Carolina forced her to burn literally thousands of gallons of fuel to get away. Which means she would have to be either making for the shore, berthing at one of the islands of the Bahamas, or refueling somewhere in here." There was a red zone marked on the map between Florida and Cuba.

"Well we know she hasn't come near the shore. The Coast Guard would have spotted her."

"Yep, which is why I requested surveillance support from a special access program down south."

"Mayan Panther?"

Howard frowned. "Yes, how do you know about—"

"You're not the only one with connections. Go on."

"Well a JSTARS picked up a contact in this area, dead in the water. What's weird is it was stationary for almost two hours and no other vessels came near it. Then it started moving again, heading south at thirty knots."

"They managed to refuel." King placed his glass on the desk. "But how? It's not like they could have submarine support." He paused. "We're not dealing with the Russians are we?"

Howard shook his head. "No, it's much simpler than that. I asked for a pull of all the air traffic feeds and when I layered them on top of the position I found this." He placed another map on the table. This one had the route and refuel location overlaid with flight tracks.

"Those sneaky bastards."

"Yep, at 0700 someone dropped fuel for them from a cargo plane out of Jamaica."

"Jamaica?"

"The flight originated from Norman Manley

International airport and that's where I think the boat is heading based off its trajectory."

"Where is the aircraft now?"

"Miami International. I've already spoken to the local authorities. They searched it and found nothing out of the ordinary."

"Whose plane is it?"

"It was a contracted flight. Lascar Logistics. Just another global air freight outfit."

King jumped out of his chair and grabbed his jacket. "Good job."

"Yeah, now we just have to work out how to target them in Jamaica."

King headed for the door. "That part's easy. I'm going down there on the next flight. Call the Chief of Station and tell him I'm coming. See if you can arrange surveillance on the port facilities and airport."

"Do you want me to come with?"

"No, I need you to stay here and run the SCIF. We still need to find the rest of the network."

King stormed out of the office and left Howard sitting by himself sipping the glass of whiskey. He grinned as he leaned back in the chair. Larkin was going to be impressed.

CARACAS, VENEZUELA

The nurse behind the counter gave Antonio a nod as he carried a fresh bunch of flowers into his girlfriend's ward. He paused outside Camilla's room and forced a smile. Pushing open the door he found her exactly as he had left her the day before.

The bed was angled so she was sitting rather than lying. Her gaze was fixed on a point on the wall, face expressionless. In the corner of the room sat her father. He was watching her with a forlorn look of his own.

"Hello, Camilla." He changed the flowers in the vase in the corner of the room. "How are you today?" He didn't expect a response. She hadn't spoken since the incident.

"Still no change," her father said. "She just stares into space like she's not really there."

"Why don't you stretch your legs, Mr. Hernandez. I will watch her for a bit."

Her father nodded and pried himself from the chair. Since he had arrived in town he'd sat by his daughter's side, never leaving for fear she would be alone when she finally decided to speak.

Antonio waited till he left before leaning forward to talk to her. "I've got help, Camilla. I've found people who can help me make them pay."

She turned to face him with eyes glassy with tears and nodded.

He felt his heart soar; it was the first sign of life he'd seen from her since she was admitted to hospital.

A knock sounded. He turned to see his friend Chabi at the door. "Hello, good of you to come by."

The student walked in and sat in the chair Camilla's father had vacated. "Has she said anything?"

"No, but she's moving."

Chabi nodded and dropped his eyes to the floor. "So I guess you heard what happened to Dante?"

"No, what?"

"He was murdered last night."

"What, how?"

"A break and enter when he was visiting his friend. They

stabbed him so they could steal a handful of trinkets. Well, at least that's what the police are saying."

He clenched his jaw. Then he leaned forward and kissed Camilla on the forehead. "They'll pay. For everything," he whispered before making for the door.

"Where are you going?" asked his friend.

Antonio ignored him as he strode from the room and down the hospital corridor, heels ringing on the freshly polished floor. He dialed Igor on the cell phone the Russian had given him. "We need to meet. There's been another attack."

BAHAMAS, CARIBBEAN SEA

Mitch stood at the console of the *Nemesis* with a skipper's cap sitting jauntily on his head. "This thing's amazing." The motor-yacht was doing nearly forty knots as they blasted through the clear waters of the Bahamas.

"Yeah we know, Wesley told us all about it." Saneh was sitting at the table eating a sandwich. Mirza was downstairs fetching the banker who'd slept in.

"No seriously, you have no idea how cutting edge this is. We're talking the sort of tech they use in naval hardware. You throw a couple of Exocet launchers on this and a 25mm and you've got yourself a serious surface combatant."

Saneh finished the sandwich. "It's pretty and it goes fast. That's all I care about."

"Who the hell is this guy and where the hell did he come from?" Wesley was standing on the bottom deck staring at Mitch. "We're in the middle of nowhere."

She smiled sweetly. "Wesley meet Mitch. He's the one who solved our fuel problem. Mitch, this is Wesley, the former owner of the *Nemesis*."

"Former owner?"

She cocked an eyebrow. "Yes, you got a problem with that?"

He shook his head. "No."

"Now be a good boy and take a seat."

Wesley sat next to Mirza on the opposite side of the table to Saneh. "Look, I've been thinking about what you said about hurting MVI and I know how we can do it."

"Go on."

"I want some assurances first. I'm going to have to disappear and I'm not going to spend the rest of my life living cheap on a beach in Thailand. You guys are resourceful; I want a new identity and I want fifteen million dollars."

Saneh turned to Mirza. "What do you think?"

He shrugged. "It sounds reasonable. But, I'm interested to know the details before we commit."

She nodded in agreement. "Start talking, Wesley."

"Fine. As you know MVI has raised a shitload of capital for the project in Venezuela. Assets have been liquidated, investments sold off, and now there's half a billion dollars in cash sitting in a number of corporate accounts."

"Yes."

"Well, I think we can steal it."

Saneh leaned forward. "Go on."

"OK, MVI has three directors and a chairman. Each of us has a ten digit code that allows us to authorize the transfer of funds from the corporate accounts. You need three codes to move money."

"So we need to find two of the others," said Saneh.

Wesley shook his head. "Thing is, if you have the chairman's code you only need one other."

"All we need to do is work out where the chairman will be."

The banker smiled. "That's the easy bit. In two day's time he's going to be in Venezuela."

"That's good to know," said Mirza.

Wesley clapped his hands. "So do we have a deal?"

Saneh lifted her chin. "We'll think about it."

RIO DE JANEIRO, BRAZIL

Bishop spent the night in a tiny hostel in the favela. In the morning he caught a cab back to Leblon and staked out his hotel. After two hours he hadn't spotted any sign of Pershing, his men, or their SUVs. Confident he was in the clear he grabbed his bag, checked out, and destroyed the fake passport he'd used as identification to book the room. He bought new clothes down by the beach and changed in a public restroom. Dressed in shorts, a T-shirt, sandals, and a floppy hat, he looked like a regular tourist.

Wandering along the street that housed the internet café he scanned for the GES crew. Unable to spot anyone of interest, he picked a location on a bench and sat down with an ice-cream watching people come and go. After thirty minutes he walked into the café.

"Excuse me."

The girl behind the counter glanced up from her computer and smiled.

"I'm looking for my friend. I was wondering if you've seen him." He held out his phone with a photo of Kurtz on the screen. The German wore a broad smile and had his arm around Bishop's shoulders.

The woman frowned. "Why is everyone trying to find him?"

He glanced around. "When were the other men here?"

"Yesterday afternoon. I told them he was staying at the Leblon Castle hotel with his friends." She lowered her voice. "I think they were police. They went and talked to his friends at the hotel."

"Where is that?"

"Up the road, but you don't have to go there. One of his friends is over there in the corner, the American."

Bishop looked in the direction she pointed expecting to see one of Pershing's men. Instead he spotted an old guy hunched over one of the terminals.

"He's in here every day. Your friend was working with him on something."

Bishop walked over and sat at the terminal next to the man. "Excuse me."

The man turned to him. "Yes?"

"I'm trying to find a friend of mine. I think you might be able to help me." Bishop showed him his phone.

The man shook his head. "Hey, I don't want any trouble. I already told the other guys what I know."

"Other guys?"

"Yes, the CIA contractors. They said your friend was a terrorist."

Bishop laughed. "A terrorist? Kurtz isn't a terrorist. He's just a former soldier with some issues. I need to find him before he hurts someone, or himself."

The American studied Bishop's face. "You're a soldier too aren't you?" He didn't wait for Bishop to reply. "Find Kurtz, he's a good man but he needs help. I told the others where he went. I'm not sure if it was the right thing to do."

"Where did he go?"

"Foz do Iguacu, the tri-border area. He'll be working with one of the counter sex trafficking teams. Probably Escape, they're all ex-military guys. You need to hurry, they've got a big head start."

"Escape, eh? Do the contractors know about Escape?"

"No, I only told them Kurtz was heading to Foz."

He contemplated the information before standing up. "Thank you." He left the shop and used his phone to search for a car hire place. There was one nearby in Barra De Tijuca. Flagging a cab, he gave the driver the address and a one hundred dollar note. "I need you to drive as fast as you can."

Chapter Twenty

FOZ DO IGUACU, BRAZIL

KURTZ WAS IMPRESSED. The team from Escape were thoroughly prepared for the raid. He was standing in a field five miles out of town inspecting a tape mock-up of the target building. Using Google Earth and knowledge obtained from a ground recce the four-man team had constructed a full-scale replica including a basic floor layout. Arnie was talking them through the entire operation in what was essentially a Rehearsal Of Concept or ROC drill. It was a procedure they used in PRIMAL.

"So you happy with how it's going to go down?" asked Arnie.

"*Ja*, my job is easy."

"Yeah mate, sorry. We needed another driver and you're the new guy. We'll get you more involved on the next job."

He nodded. "It's fine. I understand."

"Awesome, well if everyone is happy we'll pack up and head back to the house."

It didn't take them long to pull the sticks from the ground and bundle the tape into the back of their battered sedan.

"Lads, I'm going to take Kurtz for a final recce then I'll drop him back at his hotel," said Arnie as they drove through town. The three others got out of the vehicle leaving Arnie and Kurtz inside. "The route's pretty easy, mate," he said as they drove through the suburbs. "The brothel's down near the lake. It gets a constant stream of locals and tourists. Some of them just shag the regular hookers but a lot are there for the very young girls."

They followed the road along the river, past resorts and hotels. It was a part of the city Kurtz was yet to see and he understood now why it was a popular tourist destination. The pockets of jungle between the golf courses and swimming pools were lush and green.

"We're not going to stop but I'll slow down a little." Arnie nodded out the window as they passed a villa with a jetty that extended out onto the river. There was a parking lot in front of it filled with sedans and pickups.

Kurtz took a mental snapshot as they continued down the road. The mock-up they had rehearsed with was perfect as far as he could see. "So, no guns?"

"No, not that we've seen. But the guys that run these things aren't nice guys, you know what I mean? They've probably got guns but don't carry them around. We're going to be in and out before they know what's going on." Arnie turned the car around and they headed back toward town. "Hey, if you're not confident about this no one's going to think less of you for sitting it out."

"No, you've planned everything well. I am perfectly comfortable with it."

Arnie grinned. "Good, because tomorrow morning we're going to change these girls' lives."

Kurtz couldn't help but feed off his energy. "*Ja*, this is going to be good."

"Better than good, mate, it's going to be epic. Just wait till you see their faces when they realize they're finally going to be free."

Arnie pulled up outside Kurtz's hotel. "So we'll be here at 0700 tomorrow morning with the vans. Make sure you've got your game face on."

"I will." Kurtz hopped out and closed the door.

As the car drove off he decided to go to the corner store across the street. He would get some dinner then hit the sack. There was no way he was going to drink; he didn't want to let Arnie and his team down.

THE TWO SUVS stopped at the CIA safe house fifteen miles from Foz do Iguacu. The former farm had been converted to a CIA facility in the mid-90's following an increase in operations in the tri-border area. It had a twelve hundred yard grass airstrip, a hardened farmhouse with all the security trappings, a barn filled with vehicles and maintenance equipment, a boathouse on the estuary of the Lago Itaipu, and a caretaker staff of three.

Surrounded by dense jungle it took considerable effort to maintain both the grass runway strip and give the impression the farm was functioning. Pershing happened to know it was a backwater posting where the CIA's screw-ups and non-swimmers were often sent to contemplate their future.

"Sir, welcome to Camp Cayman." The caretaker that

greeted them at the steps to the safe house was young, bookish, and female.

"I'm not a sir, I'm a mister," Pershing drawled. "My men are going to need somewhere to put their gear and then we're going to need local vehicles."

"Yes, Mr. Pershing. There are vehicles in the barn. You should be able to find something that suits your needs." She directed him to the porch. "The upper level of the facility is configured to accommodate twelve. I've set aside two bunk rooms for your men and a master bedroom for yourself."

Pershing stepped inside and glanced around the living room and the kitchen. The place was basic but functional. "I was under the impression this was a rendition facility."

"It is, if you'll follow me." She opened a door in the hallway and led him down a flight of stairs.

The basement was a workshop complete with a bench and tools hanging on the wall. He turned to the caretaker with a frown.

She winked and slid a shelving unit sideways to reveal a steel door. She punched a code into the digital lock and it opened with a clunk. "We've got a completely self-contained operations room along with an interrogation cell and more accommodation." She led him down the single corridor that had doors off to each side. He glanced inside one and saw it was an observation room for the interrogation cell.

She finished the tour at the operations room. "There are remote cameras around the perimeter along with ground sensors. On top of the house we've got a high-resolution thermal camera and a comms array."

"OK, I'm impressed..." He raised his eyebrows.

"Clare."

"OK, Clare, I'm impressed. Where are your colleagues?"

"One of them has gone to town for food. We didn't expect another five mouths to feed. The other is out mowing the runway."

"Once my people are ready I'm going to need your help to track someone down."

Clare smiled. "It would be my pleasure. I don't get much of a chance to practice my fieldcraft."

"Well then today's your lucky day." As they climbed back upstairs Pershing had another thought. "Clare, by chance are you a coffee drinker?"

"Yes, Mr. Pershing, I am. There's a French press in the kitchen."

"Excellent, can you make a pot and bring it down to the ops room. We've got some planning to do."

Thirty minutes later Pershing had Shrek and his team gathered around a map of Foz do Iguacu. Clare was standing at the back of the room watching with one of her colleagues. Pershing had marked the location Howard had provided him for the two counter sex trafficking operations located in the vicinity of the area. Fortunately they were situated less than a kilometer apart.

"The plan is simple. We have a snatch team loitering on the outer perimeter and two surveillance operatives in close. When we identify Objective Red Sox the surveillance team will maintain observation. Once he goes firm in a location the snatch team will move."

"What if he makes a run for it?" asked Shrek.

"Then we've got the surveillance guys on the ground to block or pursue. I'll be coordinating the operation with the snatch team."

"OK, but what about the river? Both locations are close to the river and if he gets onto it we're up shit creek," continued Shrek.

"We've got a boat," said Clare from the back of the room.

"Good, Clare, you're on the river. Shrek, send one of your boys with her. It'll be just the three of us in the snatch team so we need to stay flexible," said Pershing. "OK, gear on, comms check, and let's roll."

KINGSTON, JAMAICA

The US embassy in Jamaica was a modern three-story complex surrounded by sweeping lawns and tall palms. King doubted the CIA contingent had much on its plate. Jamaica was hardly the frontline when it came to espionage and counter-terrorism operations. He waited at the security checkpoint until a staffer arrived to escort him to see the Chief of Station. As he entered the man's plush office he noticed numerous photos and plaques adorning the wall. It told him something about the chief. He was all about show.

"Mr. King, it's a pleasure to have you here. My name's Adrian."

King shook his hand firmly and sat at the desk. "Pleasure is mine, Adrian." The senior CIA officer was slightly overweight with collar length blonde hair and blue eyes. King had him pegged as a career officer; the type who played the game and never stepped on any toes.

"I just got off the phone with Thomas Larkin. He asked me to do everything I can to help you."

King was a little lost for words. How the hell did Larkin know about Jamaica and why was he getting involved? There was only one answer, Howard.

Adrian continued, "As you requested, I've had the port

facilities monitored and the airport under surveillance for the last few hours."

"And the C-130?"

"Inquiries indicate it spent time at one of the air freight hangars. A logistics company have hired it but there's nothing out of the ordinary."

"The terrorists we're dealing with are very capable. They'll have strict operational security."

"Yes, well I guess the only way to find out is to send people in."

"When's the earliest we can do that?"

"I've spoken with the Deputy Commissioner of the Constabulary. It's taken a few favors but we've arranged for a raid at dawn tomorrow."

King nodded. "Perfect, have you coordinated with the Coast Guard regarding the vessel of interest?"

"Already done. They have a base opposite the airport." Adrian rose from his desk. "Everything is well in hand, Mr. King. We may not handle many counter-terrorism operations here but that doesn't mean we're not capable. Now, if you don't mind I've got some other matters to attend to. One of my people will take you down to the armory and have you kitted out. I'm guessing from your background you'll want to observe the raid."

He rose. "Greatly appreciated."

Adrian shook his hand again. "Just be sure to tell Mr. Larkin how helpful we were."

"I will certainly do that."

As he followed a staffer through the building he tried to work out why Larkin was helping GES, when he'd made it clear he was watching Pollard like a hawk. Was he trying to muscle his way into the company or did he want leverage?

One thing was sure; he needed to deal with this problem quickly and effectively.

CARACAS, VENEZUELA

Antonio knocked on the door of the two-story mansion and waited. The area was one of Caracas's most affluent. It was a part of town that, until now, he'd never visited. He ran his fingers along the door jamb and noted that like Camilla's place it had been recently repaired. A minute passed before someone spoke from behind the heavy wood.

"Who is it?"

He cleared his throat. "I was a friend of Dante. I want to talk to you about what happened."

There was a pause. "I don't know what you are talking about. Go away."

Igor had told him this may happen. "I was attacked by the same men. I just want to ask you some questions."

"Go away!"

He took a deep breath. "If you were a friend of Dante, I know you are a friend of the people. I want to help stop the men that killed him. I want to give him and so many others the justice they deserve."

Ten seconds passed before the voice spoke. "What is your name?"

"Antonio, I'm a member of the *Movimiento*."

"Dante spoke of your group. Caitlin Bracho was with you when she was taken."

"Yes, they murdered her. They beat me and they raped my girlfriend."

The door opened. "Come inside," said a middle-aged man.

Antonio winced as he spotted the bruising on his face.

"It looks worse than it is."

He took the seat he was offered in the kitchen as the man poured him a cup of tea. "Can you tell me what happened?"

The man shrugged. "They burst in through the front door. It was just after dinner. Half a dozen thugs, maybe more. I don't remember much after they hit me. They killed Dante and assaulted my wife. Then they stole some of our things and left."

"Can you describe any of them?"

"They were big, muscly men, and wearing balaclavas. Americans, I think."

"Why do you say they were Americans?"

"One of them spoke English, sounded American. I don't know what he said but he used the name Jimmy."

"Did you tell the police this?"

He shook his head. "No, you can't trust the police. They said it was a robbery. An unfortunate accident according to the detective. Liars."

Antonio finished the tea. "Thank you for your time."

"Be careful, my friend," said the man as he walked with him to the door. "These men are brutal animals. They killed Dante without the slightest hesitation."

"Why do you think they left the rest of you alive?"

"I don't know. But they were definitely here to kill Dante. The poor man, he didn't stand a chance."

"How would they have known he was here? Did he visit you often?"

"No, that's what worries me the most. He never even

told me he was coming. He just arrived at my doorstep last night. He was scared of something but wouldn't talk."

Antonio shook his hand and walked along the gravel driveway, through the unlocked gate, to the street where Igor was waiting in his car.

"How did it go?" asked the Russian.

"It was the same people. But I don't think they're the *colectivo*. They spoke English. One of them was called Jimmy."

GULF OF GONAVE, CARIBBEAN SEA

Saneh checked the fuel readings as the *Nemesis* cut its way through the Gulf of Gonave between Cuba and Haiti. She had been running the engines at around forty knots ever since they refueled. They had burnt over half the resupply but also made excellent time. At this speed they were only five hours from Kingston and the rest of the team.

Her iPRIMAL vibrated on the console. She picked up the Bluetooth headset that was next to it and pushed it in her ear.

"Saneh, it's Chen, how are you tracking?"

"Good, if the weather holds we should make Kingston by 2100 tonight."

"Excellent, that'll give us a few hours to refuel and cross-load before we move on to the next phase of the operation."

"And that is?"

"We're going to take the fight direct to GES."

"What's going to happen to Wesley?"

"He'll need to work with Flash on the banking transactions."

"We're going to honor the deal he offered?"

"If Wesley gets us what he's promised, I'll deliver what we agreed to."

"Good, any news on Kurtz?"

"No, Bishop's just outside the tri-border area. Aleks is inbound. When he arrives, we'll move the CAT to Brazil."

"Do you need Mirza and me to back him up?"

"No, I've got a job for you in Venezuela. You've given us one piece of the financial puzzle, now I need the other. You've got lead on Pollard."

Saneh smiled. "Look forward to it."

"I'll give you a detailed briefing when I see you tonight."

"OK."

"Oh and Saneh."

"Yes."

"Vance and I are very impressed with how you've handled your part of the mission. I'll see you soon." Chua ended the call.

Her lips parted in a half-smile as she stared out through the windshield at the clear blue waters of the gulf. It had taken almost two years but finally she felt like she'd broken out from Bishop's shadow. Now, they could operate as a team on equal footing.

BRAZIL

Bishop was struggling not to fall asleep at the wheel of his hired Hyundai sedan. He'd been driving for fifteen hours straight and the pile of energy drink cans in the passenger footwell was testament to how much caffeine he had consumed. His gut churned and his eyelids felt like they were filled with sand. He rubbed them and checked the clock on the dash. It was 0450.

He was impressed with the little car. The Korean-made sedan had been the only vehicle left at the rental agency. He had taken it reluctantly but soon realized it was more than capable of speeding across Brazil on what was a reasonably well-maintained network of roads and highways.

He didn't slow as he drove through the city of Cascavel. The streets were empty. His iPRIMAL rang, startling him. The device was hooked up to the Bluetooth system in the speakers.

"Hello."

"Bish, it's Chen. How you doing, buddy?"

"I feel like I've been on a month long tequila bender, passed out in a gutter, and had a donkey crap in my mouth. But, apart from that, I'm great."

"Good. I just wanted to let you know we're shutting down the Jamaican FOB in the next few hours. By mid-morning we'll be mobile."

"Why? What's going on?"

"A precaution. GES attempted to intercept the *Nemesis* in addition to tracking Kurtz."

"The *Nemesis*? Is Saneh OK?"

"Yeah, they escaped. They've just arrived here."

Bishop exhaled a breath he didn't realize he was holding.

"They're going to be heading to Venezuela and meeting with Ivan," continued Chua.

"OK, well I'll arrive in Foz in a few hours. If I can find Kurtz before Pershing I'm going to try to convince him to drive with me back to Medianeira. There's an airport there. We can get a flight to Rio."

"Copy that. We're going to forward base the CAT at an

airfield closer to you. As soon as you have any intel I can get them to your location ASAP. Hey, I've got to run. I'll check in once we're out of Jamaica."

"OK, good luck."

"You too."

Bishop tilted his head sideways to stretch the muscles in his neck. Glancing at the clock he did a quick calculation in his head. Pershing would have had nearly a full six hours on the ground by now. However, Bishop had an advantage. He knew the group the former PRIMAL operative was working with. He hoped like hell that would be enough.

Chapter Twenty-One

KINGSTON, JAMAICA

CHUA SHUT down his laptop and slid it inside his backpack. It was the last of the PRIMAL equipment left in the hangar. Kruger and the boys were loading the rest of the gear into the Gulfstream. All that he and Flash were going to take on the boat were their laptops, a secure satellite bearer, and some personal effects.

Kruger stuck his head around the office door. "Chua, we're good to go as soon as Aleks gets here. We'll wait on onboard Sleek."

"Right, his flight just landed so he won't be long." He shouldered his backpack and joined the rest of the team in the hangar. Saneh and Mirza were waiting with Flash.

"You sure about this?" asked Saneh.

Chua nodded. "Yeah, I've got plenty of experience on boats. We'll be fine."

"Speak for yourself, bro. I want to go in the jet," said Flash.

Saneh laughed. "Mirza will take you both down to the tender. I'm going to head over and meet Aleks. Stay safe."

"I will. OK, let's go."

"Look after him, Flash," said Saneh.

The overweight analyst shrugged. "Who's going to look after me?"

Mirza helped Flash with one of his bags. "Wesley is already onboard," he said as he led the two intel guys through the darkness to the beach. "I secured him in one of the cabins, even though he's well and truly on-team. He knows if he screws this he's done for."

Mirza pulled up the wire fence and helped them slide their bags under it. As Chua shimmied under he spotted the *Nemesis'* RHIB tethered on the beach.

"The boat's only a few hundred meters offshore. You can just see it."

Chua searched out to sea and in the faint glow of first light he could just make out the dark shape of a hull. "Thanks, Mirza."

"Good luck." With that he disappeared into the darkness.

"This is a pretty wild plan, man," said Flash as he dropped his bags in the boat. "Surely we could have jumped a flight back to Hawaii or something."

Chua helped him push the tender out past the surf and jumped in. "We can't take Wesley back to the island. What's more, staying mobile makes sense when GES are looking for us." He started the engine and waited for the analyst to climb onboard.

"Yeah, but seriously, bro. Two intel geeks and a banker in a boat. It sounds like the start of a bad joke."

Chua laughed as he spun the wheel and jockeyed the throttle, launching them out of the surf. The sun was starting to peek over the horizon spreading an orange hue over the clear water. It was a beautiful time to be on the sea. For a moment he relaxed and the tension of commanding a multi-faceted covert operation washed away.

FOZ DO IGUACU, BRAZIL

Kurtz woke at six having slept like a log. His lumpy mattress at the hotel in Foz Do Iguacu hadn't bothered him. For the first time since leaving PRIMAL he felt like he was part of a team again. The work in Rio had been satisfying but was nothing like this. Arnie and his boys were warriors like him and they planned and rehearsed just as professionals should. He dressed, pulled on his boots, and downed the protein shake he'd bought the night before. Grabbing his backpack, he headed downstairs to wait.

At 0700 sharp two vans, one white and one red, stopped outside the hotel. Arnie got out of the second vehicle and tossed him the keys. "You pumped, mate?"

Kurtz grinned as he caught them. "*Ja*, let's do this." He got in and turned the ignition. Arnie buckled himself into the seat next to him. Two of the other team members were in the back.

They crossed town and drove onto the road that led to the brothel. As they passed one of the resorts Kurtz noticed a compact white sedan following them. Thinking nothing of it he concentrated on keeping pace with the lead vehicle. As they slowed to turn off the road the car overtook them. Kurtz gave it a cursory glance as it shot past. As the white car disappeared around a corner he parked out the front of the brothel alongside the lead van.

"OK lads, two minutes in and out." Arnie pulled a balaclava over his face and leaped out. Kurtz waited with the engine running and watched as the two men in the back followed Arnie. One of them carried a sledgehammer but the front door was open and they streamed in.

He glanced in the rear-vision mirror and thought he saw the same car that was following them pass by again. He shook his head. White sedans were common with tourists.

True to his word it only took Arnie two minutes. He and the others reappeared with six terrified young girls and bundled them into the vans. Arnie climbed back in and slammed the door. "OK, let's get the hell out of here."

An SUV screamed into the parking lot and skidded to a halt in a cloud of dust, blocking the way out. A second vehicle pulled in behind the first, armed gunmen pouring from it as it stopped. Within seconds there were surrounded, with assault rifles pointed at them.

"What the hell?" Arnie reached inside his backpack and pulled out an extendable baton.

"No, you can't fight them," said Kurtz.

"Get out of the vehicles!" screamed one of the gunmen in a US accent.

"We need to do as they say," Kurtz said calmly.

"Fuck that, they're probably one of the sex-trafficking gangs. We get out and they'll kill us."

Kurtz shook his head. "No, they're Americans."

"Get out of the cars!" The gunman repeated. To reinforce his point he fired a single round into one of the tires of the lead van.

Suddenly Aleks's message made complete sense. His former partner wasn't trying to find him for PRIMAL. He had been trying to warn him he was being tracked. Kurtz pulled his phone from his pocket and punched in the number he had committed to memory. He didn't dare lift the phone to his ear so he held it low. "It's me, Kurtz. I'm in Foz Do Iguacu and I've been compromised."

Arnie frowned. "What the hell are you talking about?"

"You need to get out of the car now, Arnie. Get everyone out. These people won't hurt you, they're after me. Tell them you only just met me. Tell them you need to get the girls to safety." Kurtz left the phone connected and dropped it in his pocket.

There was another shot as the gunman blew out another tire on the van.

Arnie clenched his jaw and opened the door. "Mate, I hope you're right. OK, everyone get out."

Kurtz waited till they were all clear. Then he popped his own door, but instead of getting out, he dropped the shifter in reverse and stomped on the accelerator. The van shot backward, smashing a chunk out of the side of the brothel. Bullets hit the back of it as it scraped alongside the building and down toward the river. Kurtz thrust the door open and dived out as it gathered speed. He rolled once and sprung to his feet, sprinting behind the brothel. The van continued down the slope. Bullets shattered the windows as it dropped off the bank and splashed into the river.

Kurtz sprinted for the dock on the riverfront. A small wooden workboat with a large outboard motor was tethered alongside. He grabbed the line tying it to the railing and jerked it loose. There was yelling coming from the car park and he knew he had seconds before the gunmen were on him.

The engine started with a single pull. He twisted the throttle and sent the boat roaring along the river. Bullets snapped and hissed over his head, one striking the side of the hull as he crouched low. In a matter of seconds he was a hundred yards up the winding river and out of sight behind the leafy trees that lined the bank.

Kurtz took a deep breath and pulled the phone from his pocket as he kept the boat pointed up river. "Is anyone there?"

"Yes, it's Frank. Bishop isn't far away. Where are you?"

Bishop's name should have angered him but all he felt was relief. "OK, I'm heading north along the river. My point of departure was a small villa five miles north from the town center."

The roar of a powerful engine caught his attention and he glanced over his shoulder to see a silver aluminum-hulled boat gaining rapidly. Crouched in the front was one of the shooters.

Bullets lashed the water and snapped through the air. He slipped the phone back in his pocket and grabbed the side of the boat as he wrenched the tiller sideways. The little boat banked hard in a ninety-degree turn. The rifle barked again and Kurtz felt the round as it cracked past him. There was an almighty bang and the outboard motor exploded, spraying him with shards of hot metal. The little wooden boat washed off speed. The pursuers blasted past before circling back. A woman was at the helm. The armed man in the bow had his weapon aimed directly at him.

"Get your hands up!"

Kurtz felt the warm sensation of blood dripping down his arm. A splinter from the engine had nicked him. "I can't, you shot me," he snapped back.

The man slung his rifle as he moved to the back of the boat next to the woman. "You're going to get in this boat and kneel in the bow with your hands behind your back."

Kurtz glared at him.

"Do you understand?"

He nodded.

The helmswoman skillfully brought her vessel alongside. As he stepped across he feigned a fall and dropped face first into the aluminum boat. Shielding his hands with his body he slipped the phone under a pile of life jackets. Swearing he picked himself up and knelt.

A set of flexicuffs were drawn tight around his wrists and a hood was dropped over his head.

"We got him," reported the woman.

Kurtz felt a boot kick him between the shoulder-blades, knocking him face first into the hull. As he lay with his hands bound behind his back, panic and confusion assailed him. Who were these people and what did they want? What would happen if PRIMAL couldn't find him?

LASCAR ISLAND

Thousands of miles away in the operations room of the Bunker, Frank still had Kurtz's phone on speaker. The audio was muffled. "It's still on the boat." He glanced across to Vance who was sitting in his command chair.

As soon as the call had come in over the emergency contact line Frank had called for Vance. He'd managed to talk to Kurtz for a few seconds before the missing operative had gone silent. The audio feed was streaming on the Bunker's speakers capturing all of the gunshots, the yelling, and the roar of the engines. He had also sent the number of the incoming call to the intel team.

"OK, so what do we know?" asked Vance.

"He said he was just outside Foz at a villa five miles from

the town center." Frank placed a bubble on the overhead imagery displayed on the wall.

"There, right on the river." Vance used a laser pointer to identify a likely building.

"OK, let's say he entered the water at that point then went north in a boat. Judging by the noise I'm guessing at least a 150 horsepower outboard. At full throttle he would have been capable of 30 knots. The time from launch to the engine being shot would have taken him this far." Frank drew a line on the digital map. "That's when we hit a problem. He was intercepted and cross-loaded. We have no idea which direction he was taken."

The dull drone of the boat's engine coming in via Kurtz's phone stopped and there was a thud followed by the sound of people leaving the boat. Then there were footsteps and silence except for the sound of lapping water.

"They've offloaded him somewhere with a wooden dock," said Vance. "Work out the distance they could have traveled in either direction and start searching. Where the hell is Bishop in all this?"

Frank zoomed the map out. "He's about twenty minutes out of town."

"And where is the fix on the phone? Damn, I wish Chua or Flash were here."

He opened a comms line with the remainder of the intel team next door. "What have you got guys?"

"Sorry Frank, without assets on the ground the best we can do is a cell phone tower."

Frank recognized the voice as one of Chua's analysts, Nate. "Send us what you've got." A file came through and Flash dragged the overlay onto the digital map. A thick curved band appeared centered on a spot to the north of the city. The edge of it intersected the river for about a quarter of a mile.

"That's our search zone," said Vance.

Frank zoomed in. The banks of the river on the Brazilian side led to lush green fields. In the entire section there were only two piers reaching out into the water. One of them had a boat shed.

"That's it. Send the location to Bishop," bellowed Vance.

"Roger." Frank's fingers raced over his keyboard.

"How long till the CAT is airborne?"

"Aleks should be at the terminal now. They should be in the air in fifteen minutes."

"OK, and Chua, when will he be online?"

"He and Flash are onboard and underway. Chua has requested we manage all command and control from here. He's focusing on the MVI takedown."

Vance nodded. "Right, let's get some more staff in here. Things are about to get high speed."

Chapter Twenty-Two

KINGSTON, JAMAICA

ALEKS WAS the first to emerge from under the arrivals sign inside the terminal. He'd landed on the first flight of the day and had beaten the crowds by traveling light. He felt weary and his ribs still hurt from his battle with the American brute in Germany. Business class seats were never able to completely mitigate the jet lag from crossing time zones.

Saneh caught his eye and flashed him a smile. His mood instantly improved. He strode forward, wrapped his arms around her lithe frame, and lifted her high off the ground. "Saneh, how good it is to see a friendly face."

She laughed. "Put me down you big oaf." He placed her back on her feet and she punched him in the shoulder. "You've been missed, brother bear." She took a security pass out of her pocket and clipped it to his jacket. "We need to get moving, the others are waiting."

"Have you found Kurtz?"

"We're close. Bishop has tracked him to the tri-border area."

"When do we leave?"

"As soon as we're onboard Sleek."

She led him out the terminal, across the parking lot to the entrance of the general aviation section. As they walked along the access road Aleks noticed two dark-skinned men sitting in a parked car. To his trained eye they were out of place, like plain-clothes police on a sting.

"Are you OK?" asked Saneh.

He shook his head. "The two men in the car we passed. They look like police."

Saneh glanced back over her shoulder at the vehicle. "You're right. We need to hurry."

They showed their identification at the security gate and strode across the taxiway past a parked fuel truck toward a row of rusted hangars. Aleks discreetly glanced over his shoulder as they walked. The men in the car hadn't moved. Out the corner of his eye he spotted flashing blue lights. They were rapidly approaching.

"Saneh, run! Get the jet ready for takeoff." Aleks turned and sprinted back to the fuel truck. He wrenched open the door to the cabin and climbed inside. He found the keys in a folder in the center console and started the truck. The police vehicles were almost at the gate; a convoy led by a black armored vehicle.

Gunning the engine of the truck he accelerated, wrenching the wheel in the direction of the security checkpoint. The gates started to roll open. Aleks honked the horn as he planted his foot on the accelerator. As he was about to hit the gates he pushed open the cabin door and jumped clear.

The truck hit the gate with a deafening crash. Aleks

rolled and staggered to his feet. He sprinted away in the direction of the runway.

Behind him a megaphone blared. "Stop, stop, or we will shoot!"

He ignored the order and continued to run. Bullets snapped off the tarmac.

"We will shoot you!" echoed the voice.

He stopped with his hands in the air, looking for Saneh or the PRIMAL jet. The doors of one of the old hangars were wide open and the interior empty. He turned to face the police with his hands held over his head.

The fuel truck had jammed the gates stopping the police vehicles but a handful of black- clad SWAT operators had squeezed passed and were moving toward him with rifles raised.

He caught a glimpse of a small object sail over his head and strike the fuel truck. It detonated with a thump and the fuel tank blossomed in a huge explosion. The blast knocked the policemen off their feet and Aleks spun, shielding his face. He looked up to see Sleek taxiing along the tarmac with its boarding stairs down. The scream of jet engines rose in a crescendo as the jet turned onto the runway and prepared for takeoff. Saneh was crouching at the door holding a grenade launcher.

"Come on, Aleks!" she yelled.

He sprinted for the jet, ignoring the commotion behind him, and leaped onto the stairs.

"Nice of you to join us," said Kruger as he hauled him inside and slammed the door shut.

"Hold on!" yelled Mitch from the cockpit as they gathered speed with a roar.

Aleks strapped himself into a spare seat. He smiled

broadly as they screamed off the end of the runway. "It's good to be back!"

KING GOT out of the Jamaican police car and slammed the door. A hundred yards down the road the fuel tanker was still blazing as a pair of fire trucks doused it with foam. Adrian's local Special Operations Unit had completely bungled the job. Their surveillance had been compromised, they'd selected an obvious infiltration route, and they had no backup plan. They were about as special operations as a bunch of role-playing airsofters. In fact he had seen better tactics at his twelve-year-old son's paintball tournaments.

He pulled his phone out and rang Howard. "There's a business jet that just took off from Norman Manley Airport. Tell me you've got someone tracking it."

"Dude, of course. There's an AWACS on station in vicinity of the Cayman Islands. She's heading south and will be able to tell you exactly where the jet is going," replied Howard.

"Let me guess, arranged by our friend, Larkin?"

"Yes," he paused. "How did you know that?'

"He seems to be my guardian angel at the moment."

"Not a bad one to have. Hey, we just got a message from Pershing. They've got Red Sox."

"Finally, has he said anything yet? Do we know who Yankee is?"

"Not yet, they've only just got started. I'm sure they'll break him—"

"Mr. King! Mr. King!" a voice interrupted. It was the police commander. The tall Jamaican looked excited.

"OK, call me as soon as you hear anything on either Red Sox or the jet."

"Will do."

King hung up and turned to the police officer. "What can I do for you, Superintendent?" He tried his best to hide the contempt in his voice.

"We captured three men on the boat."

King was surprised. "On the *Nemesis*?"

"Yes, three men on the black boat. Do you want to go and see?"

"Definitely." King barely suppressed a grin as he followed the man to his four-wheel drive. They drove out to the public road and followed it behind the hangars that the escapees had probably used as a base. King shook his head. The fence was rusted with gaping holes in the wire. It would have been a simple job for the police to cut through and infiltrate under the cover of darkness. Fucking amateurs. At least they hadn't come out of this completely empty handed.

They skirted the airport security fence before driving off the road onto the sand where there was an inflatable boat waiting. King spotted the sleek lines of the *Nemesis* a few hundred yards out to sea where she was at anchor.

The inflatable took him and the Superintendent out to the boat. As they got closer King could see the bullet holes in the side of the superstructure, a result of the botched MAROPS interdiction. They bumped against the swim platform at the back and King climbed aboard. He strode up the stairs and walked into the cabin.

Inside half a dozen police officers were milling about. One of them was watching the three captives who were kneeling with black hoods over their heads and hands cuffed behind their backs.

"Show me their faces," King ordered. One by one the hoods were ripped off.

"Hey mon, what you doing? What the hell is going on?" screamed one of the dreadlocked fishermen. "This is our boat! We and I were given it fair and square."

"Shit!" King kicked the side of the cabin and stormed outside. He stood on the rear deck breathing through his teeth as he stared at the airport. One clusterfuck after another. He clenched a fist. At least they had Red Sox and he was going to talk. Pershing would make sure of that.

Chapter Twenty-Three

FOZ DO IGUACU, BRAZIL

BISHOP PARKED his Hyundai at the end of a dirt track and carried all the equipment he'd purchased down to the water's edge. He wore a fishing vest over his shirt and a floppy khaki broad-brim hat. Plugging a foot pump into the side of an inflatable kayak he worked furiously to fill it with air. Sweat dripped from his face and mosquitos attacked him despite the smothering of repellant he wore.

Two minutes later he launched the kayak and waded in after it. His eyes darted from the bank to the water and back again, searching for any predators. He'd watched enough Animal Planet to know South American waterways were filled with anacondas, piranhas, and caiman.

Once in the kayak, he checked his fishing rod was secure and paddled steadily. He stayed close to the heavily vegetated shoreline in an attempt to avoid the harsh midday sun and risk drawing attention.

According to the Bunker, Kurtz had been captured over

three hours ago. That meant Pershing could have moved him a significant distance. However, the location Bishop had been given was their only lead.

He continued paddling until he spotted the boatshed nestled in the jungle on the bank. A quick glance at his iPRIMAL confirmed it was the place he was searching for. Casually he flicked out his lure and reeled it back in.

For the better part of thirty minutes he pretended to fish, all the while actually watching the boatshed. The metal structure was squat and jutted out from the bank. Large sliding doors would allow a boat to enter without having to use a trailer and boat ramp. A wooden pier ran out from a side door. To its rear a path was cut through the jungle.

Feigning frustration he reeled in the lure for a final time and stowed the rod. Paddling gently he cruised to within a few hundred yards of his objective. He pushed the kayak under a low hanging tree and secured it to a branch. Slipping his iPRIMAL into a waterproof dry bag he secured it in his hip pocket before hanging a dive mask around his neck. Then he lowered himself over the side of the kayak into the water. Pushing thoughts of deadly predators from his mind he half waded, half swam under the trees. He stopped regularly to scan for movement.

The water was cool, refreshing compared to the oppressive humidity. Confident it was all clear he closed within ten yards of the boatshed's closed doors, slipped on the dive mask, took a deep breath, and submerged. Through the murky water he quickly made out the bottom of the boatshed doors. As he swam under them he almost hit a propeller. Sliding under the hull of the boat he surfaced slowly on the side away from the side door that joined the pier.

Allowing just his head to break the surface he scanned

the inside of the building. There was a wooden deck running around three of the walls. An aluminum-hulled boat sat in the gap in the middle. Jerry cans, rope, and other equipment lined the shelving on the walls. As his eyes adjusted to the dim light he spotted a security camera watching the door. If he avoided the other side of the boat he should remain well out of its field of view.

Working his way around to the stern of the boat, he grabbed the transom and pulled himself aboard. Lying below the sides, he searched the hull. His fingers found an empty casing. A few seconds later he found a mobile phone. Checking the screen, he saw it was still connected to one of the emergency numbers. He terminated the call and slipped it inside the dry bag. Pulling out his iPRIMAL he sent a message.

Touchdown on Kurtz's phone. In the boatshed.

The Bunker had already assessed the location was a probable CIA safe house. The manicured grass airstrip on the overhead imagery was a giveaway. Kurtz's phone was the final confirmation they needed. Now it was only a matter of time before Aleks and the CAT arrived. All he needed to do was keep eyes on the facility until then.

CARIBBEAN SEA

Mitch glanced out of the side window of the cockpit at the waves blasting past a few hundred feet below. Alongside him Mirza held the yoke as he monitored the radar-warning receiver on the multi-function screen and checked their route on a tablet. Sleek's Israeli-sourced avionics had detected the E-3 Sentry's powerful radar immediately after takeoff and Mitch had plotted a route to avoid it.

"We'll stay low and fast to avoid the AWACS then pop up just east of Caracas. We'll drop in on their air traffic radar as a private charter out of Grenada. It's going to burn a bit of fuel but we'll still be OK to make Brazil." Mitch stowed the tablet and grasped the yoke. "Hands on. Taking positive control."

"Control is yours. Hands off," Mirza said.

There was a knock at the cockpit door. "Come in," said Mitch.

Saneh appeared wearing a concerned expression. "Is there any reason we're sailing to Venezuela instead of flying?"

Mitch laughed as he adjusted the throttles. "We're evading the United States Air Force."

"OK, good to know. What's our ETA on Caracas?"

"About thirty minutes. Don't worry, we'll put on some altitude soon."

"As long as we get on the ground in one piece. Oh and Mirza, I just spoke to Vance. Ivan has set up a safe house for us and procured a couple of pistols."

"Good stuff." Mirza didn't take his eyes from the aircraft's instruments.

"OK, well, I'm going to leave you boys to it." Saneh closed the cabin door and returned to her rearward-facing seat. At the back of the aircraft the four members of the CAT were checking over their equipment. Their armor and weapons were the same mottled green camouflaged items used in their jungle training back on the island. The only difference was they now had their full-face CAT helmets, also camouflaged. The helmets provided essential protection in a close assault, in addition to enhancing aiming, night vision, hearing, and respiratory functions. Additionally each man had a black free-fall parachute and reserve. The Bunker had already warned them to be prepared for a parachute insertion and updated the team with the result of Bishop's close recon.

Aleks looked up and caught her eye. He left the others and sat in the seat next to her. "How are you?"

"I wish I was going with the rest of the team." Saneh knew she should be focusing on her own mission to Caracas, not the recovery of Kurtz.

"You wish you were with Bishop."

She had to admit he was on her mind. "There's so much that can go wrong with this op."

"He'll be OK. He did well to confirm Kurtz's location. We'll have both of them back by next morning."

FOZ DO IGUACU, BRAZIL

Kurtz knew he wasn't far from the boat where he had stashed his phone. That gave him hope; hope that PRIMAL would find him before it was too late. He didn't want to consider what 'too late' involved. He turned his head but couldn't see anything through the black hood.

"You're in some serious shit, Wilhelm Jager."

Kurtz turned to the southern accented voice. "I haven't done anything wrong," he said. "I came to Brazil to help save girls from sex slavery."

"Well then ain't you just Mr. Fucking Wonderful. Good cover for a terrorist."

Terrorist? What the hell were they talking about? thought Kurtz.

"We know all about your buddy, Aden. Were you in Mexico with him? Did you help him destroy the mine?"

Now Kurtz was really confused. The hood was ripped off and he squinted under bright lights.

"You can make this easy, Wilhelm. You tell us all about Aden, who he is, where we can find him, and then we might consider letting you go. We might even let your parents live."

A printout of a photo was held in front of him. The picture showed a bald-headed brute with a goatee on a couch between his parents. The thug wore a grin and had his arms around the elderly couple.

Kurtz strained against the restraints that held him to the chair.

"Steady there, cowboy. You're not going anywhere."

He jumped as the voice got closer to his ear. "I want you to know this isn't a government endorsed activity. We're not constrained by any Geneva conventions or any of that horseshit. So you either talk or I'm going to cause you more pain than you've ever felt in your life."

"*Lutsch meinen Schwanz du Arschloch!*"

A snicker told him someone else in the room understood German. He twisted his head but couldn't see past the dazzling bright lights.

"So it's going to be like that, is it? Shrek, he's all yours."

Kurtz braced himself for the punch that never came. Instead the lights dimmed and he found himself face to face with a grinning bald-headed giant who had little ears poking out from a Neanderthal-like skull. The man from the photo with his parents.

"Hey, got a chance to meet your mom, Wilhelm," grinned the behemoth.

"*Ja*, did she talk your ear off?"

"Oh, she did more than that. She sucked my cock like a real champion."

He laughed. "Your dick is too small to stop her talking." He didn't see the punch coming. It knocked him and the chair sideways. He tasted blood in his mouth as he lay on the floor.

JAMAICA, CARIBBEAN SEA

The fishing trawler made a steady fifteen knots as it cruised through the pristine waters south west of Jamaica. Its diesel engines throbbed beneath a weathered deck scattered with nets, floats, and crab pots. Chua was at the helm while Flash worked in the crew cabin below. The Asian American clutched the wooden wheel with both hands and had propped his iPRIMAL tablet in front as a navigation aid. "We've got at least a week of perfect weather," Chua yelled over his shoulder.

"Good," replied Flash. "Now if only I could get the bloody satellite comms to work. Wesley, try turning it a little further left."

The banker was at the rear of the boat standing over a laptop-sized satellite antenna. He nudged it with his foot.

"That's it, that's it!" screamed Flash. "Nope, gone again."

Chua shook his head. The two of them had been at it for the last hour and they really needed to get to work. To do that required data communications. He was also a little anxious being out of contact with Vance and the Bunker. A lot could have happened in the five hours since they left Kingston.

"Hey, stop what you're doing, Wes."

"I'm not touching it."

"Awesome, we've got comms."

"Great," said Chua. "Wesley, I need you to take the helm. Keep us on course."

He waited till the banker climbed the staircase into the wheelhouse. "The route is marked on the tablet."

"Bit of a step down from the *Nemesis*, dude."

"Low key is the name of the game." Chua climbed down the stairs to the tiny crew cabin that doubled as a galley. Flash had set up two laptops on a chipped and dented table that was bolted to the floor. "Wow, you can really smell the fish in here," he said as he sat at a computer and slipped on a headset.

Flash looked up from his screen. "Tell me about it. Saneh and Mirza get luxury and we get this old tub. Tell me again why we couldn't leave on the jet with everyone else?"

"Because, when you're about to steal nearly a billion dollars it's good to be mobile."

"The *Nemesis* was mobile."

"And subtle, very subtle." Chua logged onto the secure system.

"Bandwidth is shitty, video isn't going to work."

Chua scrolled to Vance's icon on the communications app and hit it. It connected in a couple of seconds.

"Chua, good to see you online. I was getting worried," Vance's voice boomed.

"Had a few problems with our satellite bearer. Did the team get away on Sleek?"

"You were right about GES. They made a play as

everyone was pulling out. Local police tried to raid the hangar. Aleks saved the day."

"Damn, how did they know we were there?"

"The *Nemesis* was heading south. They may have been able to track the refuel point with the C-130. I've got the team here looking into it."

"What about us here on the fishing boat?"

"There's nothing to suggest that they're on to you but we'll continue to monitor. The priority now is Venezuela and Brazil. Mitch just dropped Mirza and Saneh in Caracas to RV with Ivan."

"And Kurtz?"

"Bishop has located a probable CIA rendition facility just north of the tri-border area. The CAT will infiltrate tonight and if Kurtz is in location they'll recover him."

"And if he's not?"

"Then we might have to consider a hostage swap."

"They tried to kill Wesley. I don't think they're going to agree to swap him for Kurtz."

"I'm not talking about him. I'm talking about Jordan Pollard. As you know, we need him to facilitate the transaction and your boy says he'll be in Venezuela in twenty-four hours. If Mirza and Saneh can find a way to snatch him we'll be in business. Where are we at with the financial preparations?"

"Wesley and Flash have talked through the details. It's going to take some work but Flash is confident he can do the programming in time."

"It all hinges on Saneh and Mirza. If we can locate and neutralize the GES presence in Venezuela, we can secure Pollard. If not we've got to move to an alternate plan."

Chua contemplated the comment. "We could always go after the other two directors. Bishop and Mitch are familiar with King's place and we can track down the accountant."

"We have options but I don't want to fall back on them. I don't want to escalate ops in CONUS. Let me know when you've got the banking solution sorted. I'll give you a heads up if the situation changes."

"OK, Vance, will do."

"Stay safe salty sea dogs." The connection terminated.

Chua took off the headset and rubbed his eyes. "Alright, we've got some work to do."

"You sure we can trust Wesley?" asked Flash as his fingers danced over the keyboard. "I mean, he worked for the enemy."

"Yes, and they tried to kill him so now they're his enemy. And in times of war your enemy's—"

"Enemy is your friend. Yeah I get all that. I just think you're being a little trusting letting him drive the boat."

"Flash, he's got more experience than both of us and, just in case you needed another cliché, we're all in this boat together."

Chapter Twenty-Four

CARACAS, VENEZUELA

THE CAB CARRYING Saneh and Mirza pulled to the curb. She paid the fare and joined Mirza on the streets of Venezuela's capital. "Have you been here before?" she asked as they walked along the street.

"No. You?"

"Never. I've never even been to South America."

"A big day all round then," said Mirza.

"How so?"

"This will be the first time we've seen Ivan since Ukraine." The deep-cover operative had played a key role in the operation that had resulted in Saneh being recruited into PRIMAL. He was a legend among the vigilante team.

"True, I'm actually a little nervous." They turned the corner onto another street. Saneh glanced over her shoulder. None of the pedestrians paid them any attention.

Her iPRIMAL vibrated and she checked the screen. There was a message; a vehicle registration number.

"Mirza, we're looking for a car with this plate." She read out the number.

"Got it."

The car was parked at the curb thirty yards in front of them. A battered Toyota sedan with roof racks and a rusted trunk.

They climbed into the back of the car. Saneh looked at the rear vision mirror. The face of their driver was remarkably ordinary. It could have belonged to a cab driver in more than a dozen countries.

"Saneh, Mirza, it's a pleasure to see you again." The accent was neutral, almost British. "The bags at your feet are for you."

She reached down and opened one of the backpacks. Inside were a 9mm pistol, a holster, and two loaded magazines.

"Appreciated," said Mirza as he checked his own identical bag.

Ivan pulled the car away from the curb, drove through the city, and onto a highway. "We've got a safe house for you on the outskirts. It's large enough to accommodate additional operatives, should the need arise."

"Good," said Saneh. "What have you found out about GES's presence in Venezuela?"

"There's a death squad operating in the city. My investigations lead me to believe it's being led by this man." He passed a phone over his shoulder.

The photo on the screen showed a military man with a thick mustache. He was dressed in a naval dress uniform heavy with medals. She recognized the SEAL trident over his breast.

"His name is James Scott, and he's a GES contractor. I've

linked him to two killings; both victims were members of the opposition party. He and his team have also been intimidating students. They raped a young girl and put her in hospital. They also beat her boyfriend who was one of the protest organizers."

"They're here to quash the revolution," said Mirza.

"Targeting key leaders and influencers," added Saneh. "Doing all the government's dirty work and in return they get oil concessions."

Ivan nodded.

"So what are we going to do about it?" she asked as she handed back the phone.

"That, my dear girl, is your problem. My work here is done. Execution is not my forte. I'm a pen, a quill; a precise tool, not a blunt instrument."

"Well, then consider us a scalpel," said Saneh. "The hammer is yet to arrive, but when it falls Mr. James Scott is going to be under it."

"It pleases me immensely to hear that."

They left the highway and drove through a well-to-do area with leafy trees lining the roads and fenced estates. At the end of a cul-de-sac he turned down a driveway. The house was hidden from the road by a wooden fence and tall trees.

Ivan parked in front of a modern two-story residence with a double garage. He handed her two sets of keys. "One of these is for the house. The other is for the van that's in the garage. The Bunker has my report. They're adding additional analysis and information. You can expect it shortly. I've also identified a suitable infil location less than two hours drive from here. A disused airfield, it should be suitable for a small business jet."

She smiled. "You've thought of everything."

"One more point. There is a local contact. He has been very helpful so please ensure you take care of him."

"When will we meet him?"

"He's waiting inside. Now, if you have no more questions, I have a plane to catch."

Saneh watched the car as it left.

"He hasn't changed, has he," said Mirza.

"Not at all," said Saneh as she unlocked the front door.

Mirza had one hand inside his bag, grasping his pistol as he led the way. She followed him into the kitchen where a young man seated at a bench top greeted them with a grim smile.

"Hello, I am Antonio."

FOZ DO IGUACU, BRAZIL

Kurtz convulsed and lost control of his bladder as electricity coursed through his body. His muscles spasmed, his jaw clenching so hard he chipped a tooth. The pain was beyond anything he had ever felt. It was as if his entire body had been doused in fuel and set alight.

Then, as abruptly as it started the pain stopped. He let his head drop against his chest and moaned.

"It's a little clichéd," said the Texan. "I mean, Hollywood can be very creative and yet we still use waterboarding and electroshock. Probably because, as you just experienced, they're very effective. I like things that are effective. However, the reality is torture is a very personal thing. Some people don't respond well to waterboarding, others are all but immune to the sort of pain the electricity delivers. Others, like you I'm guessing, have been trained in the art of resistance."

Kurtz struggled to see through the tears streaming from his eyes.

"Yes, you've been trained, I can tell. We could probably tear all the fingernails from your hands and you'll never say a word. Isn't that right, Mr. Jager?"

Kurtz smiled grimly as he tried to focus on the blurry shape in front of him. "I told you. I used to be police. I came here to get girls away from creeps like your friend."

"Is that right? You think Shrek is a creep!"

He laughed. "Ogres are like onions." He put on his best impersonation of the cartoon character Shrek. He waited, expecting more pain but the blur moved away. A door opened then closed. He hung his head and closed his eyes.

A minute later he felt a hand on top of his, forcing his fingers flat. Pain exploded up his arm as a fingernail was torn off. He tried to stifle the scream but it came from deep within and couldn't be stopped. It echoed off the walls, a guttural wail from a man whose will had almost broken.

Behind the mirrored glass Pershing watched intently. Next to him Clare stood wide-eyed as Shrek tore another fingernail from the detainee's hand. The junior CIA officer dry-retched in her mouth and Pershing laughed. She glared at him.

"You think this is funny?" she asked.

"Not for him, it's not."

The door opened and Shrek stomped in. "He's a tough bastard, that's for sure. But he's ready to answer your questions." He caught Clare's look of disgust. "You don't approve?"

"You're breaking the law."

Pershing laughed. "I told you not to watch but you

insisted." He leaned in close to her face. "If you don't like what you see feel free to fuck off upstairs with your friends and leave the real work to the men."

Clare glared at him then left the room.

GES FACILITY, VIRGINIA

Howard knocked on King's office door and waited for a reply. The CEO had gone straight to his office in the SCIF after returning from Jamaica. He figured thirty minutes was enough time for him to check his emails.

"Terry, come in."

He pushed open the door and took a seat.

"Have you heard anything from Pershing?" King's eyes were bloodshot. He wore stubble on his face and usually clean-shaven scalp.

"No, he'll be working Red Sox over."

"I thought he would have broken him by now."

"Tough guy like that, probably taking a little longer than usual."

King sighed as he rubbed his temples with his fingers. "The AWACS came up dry?"

"Yeah, they were one step ahead of us. The tail number on the Gulfstream they escaped on was also a dead end. Dude, I think we're dealing with something much bigger than we initially anticipated."

"I concur."

"I mean, these guys started with horses and six shooters and now we're talking about twenty-two million dollar business jets, ship at sea refueling, electronic warfare…"

King nodded. "You think this is state sponsored?"

"It has to be. Who else can put together these sorts of resources? Someone is targeting GES and MVI and they're not messing around. You gotta come clean with me, man. Who the hell have you guys pissed off?"

King shrugged. "No one with the sort of clout you're talking about. We've pulled contracts for the CIA, MI6, other allies. All legit stuff."

"Well someone's pissed big time and they've got capability and intent. The threat to you guys is high and you don't have the resources to fight them."

"What are you saying?"

"You need the full resources of the CIA on this."

King shook his head.

Silence filled the room.

"You've got to come clean with me. What the hell are you guys doing in Venezuela?"

King fixed Howard with an icy stare.

Shit, he thought. I've overstepped the mark.

"We've got a contract with the Venezuelan government."

Howard's eyes widened. "No way."

"Pollard hooked it up. We're providing discreet capabilities to mitigate the demonstrations and minimize the potential of an uprising. In return we get exclusive access to the oil fields."

"Jesus, you guys have fucked up."

"Why?"

"The CIA is sponsoring the uprisings. It's one of Larkin's projects."

Chapter Twenty-Five

TRI-BORDER AREA, BRAZIL

BISHOP WOKE when his iPRIMAL vibrated against his chest. He swore as he pulled it from his vest. He hadn't meant to drift off but lack of sleep had left him exhausted. The message was from Mitch. The assault team was fifteen minutes out.

He was lying at the edge of the open field watching the CIA safe house five hundred yards away. He'd been there all day and was yet to spot anything suspicious. One man had mowed the airstrip but there was no sign of Pershing, Kurtz, or the GES team. Now darkness had fallen a number of rooms were illuminated from inside and he could see only one or two figures moving around. The lack of activity was concerning. Kurtz could have been moved to another location prior to his arrival.

He crawled back through the thick jungle and climbed to his feet. Moving along a track he'd previously reconnoitered he walked to the edge of another field that belonged to a different farm. The entire field was covered with succulent knee-high corn stalks; a perfect drop zone.

His phone buzzed again and he checked the battle-tracking map. The CAT was only minutes out. They would jump from 20,000 feet, pop canopies low, and glide silently to where he was waiting. He'd kept communications to a minimum in case the CIA safe house was equipped with interception technology. He knew this wasn't going to be a run of the mill job on poorly equipped criminals. He was expecting highly trained professionals and state-of-the-art equipment.

As he crouched by the edge of the cornfield a faint hiss caught his attention. He glanced up in time to see a dark shape pass over him. It disappeared over the cornfield and impacted with a thump. In the space of thirty seconds another three wraiths descended from the night sky.

Bishop flashed a tiny flashlight. A red light from the field flashed in reply. A moment later a hulking figure appeared from the darkness and joined him in the thick jungle.

"Aleks, welcome to Brazil," said Bishop, recognizing the broad-shouldered silhouette. The big Russian dropped a gear bag at his feet.

"Where are they holding him?" Aleks grunted in reply. He was wearing a jungle camouflage version of PRIMAL's carbon nanotube armor. The lightweight rig was festooned with pouches and equipment. With his full-faced, sensor-integrated helmet, Bishop thought he looked like the Predator. He almost felt sorry for the men inside the house; Death was coming to visit and he wasn't happy.

"Not far, mate. I'll go over the plan once everyone is sorted." Bishop unzipped the bag and pulled out his armor, Tavor assault rifle, and helmet. As he geared up the other men who had landed in the corn gathered around him.

He activated the augmented sensors built into his helmet. The black jungle was replaced with a fused image displaying infrared and thermal feeds. Flashing icons told him who each of the PRIMAL operatives were. The men had gathered in a rough circle around him, facing outward, ready for anything.

Bishop gave the team a once over. Kruger was carrying a MK48. The belt-fed machine gun looked like a toy against his massive frame. Strapped to his back was a collapsible stretcher. Miklos, the team sniper was carrying a customized AS Val rifle, and Pavel and Aleks had Tavor assault rifles, the same as his. All the weapons had suppressors and infrared laser aiming devices.

"Bish, Mitch packed us a drone," said Miklos.

"Let's get it airborne then."

The sniper shrugged off his backpack and unstrapped the little quadcopter. The Parrot Bebop had been integrated into the iPRIMAL system. He programmed the little UAV's route and with a whirr it zoomed skyward, transmitting what it saw back to displays in their helmets.

"When are we expecting Mitch for extraction?" asked Bishop as the drone flew over the target house.

"He can loiter for a little over sixty minutes. Then he's going to need to refuel and that could take a few hours."

"Roger, we better get moving then." He activated his iPRIMAL and broadcast the plan he'd developed to the rest of the team. It appeared in the bottom left corner of their helmets.

"This is our target building. It's got open terrain on all sides. I think the safest approach is here using the barn as cover."

A red arrow marked the route from the jungle, behind the barn, then over the final forty yards to the house.

"Aleks, what do you reckon about this as a suitable fire support position." A flashing point appeared on the map at ninety degrees to their assault axis.

"You've seen the ground. I'll take your advice."

"Right, Miklos and Kruger, you'll cover us from there. The others will assault through the barn. Once we break into the house you guys switch to cut off. Once we are secure we'll consolidate in the house."

"Do we know how many men are inside?" asked Aleks.

"Pershing had a handful when he went after me in Brazil. Maybe five shooters in total. I don't think he would have brought in more but there could be a caretaker element."

"There's no sign of movement from the drone," added Miklos.

"ROE for identified CIA operatives?" asked Kruger.

"Weapons free for all hostiles. If they light us up we kill them."

"Are we sure Kurtz is in there?" asked Pavel.

"Assume that he is," Bishop said confidently.

Aleks nodded. "He's in there. Let's go and get him."

"Drone has not identified any guards," Miklos updated.

"Right, let's do this." Bishop led them to their positions. First he placed the assault team, orientating them toward the barn. Then he took Miklos and Kruger into the jungle and showed them the fire support position.

As he moved back through the jungle to the assault team he found himself constantly glancing at the lights of the farmhouse. He hoped like hell Kurtz was inside and still alive. He joined the rest of the men; they were lined up facing the distant barn.

"Let's go," transmitted Aleks over their headsets.

Bishop felt a surge of adrenalin as he shouldered his

assault rifle and rose. Through the green hue of the helmet's sensors the empty field was a barren desert. A hundred yards away the barn loomed out of the darkness, a foreboding presence behind which the house glowed.

KURTZ FOUGHT against the blackness as it pressed in on all sides. He felt it trying to fight its way inside his brain. Trying to rob him of his sanity, crack his will, and draw out all his secrets. In this world of sensory deprivation and sporadic agony, the only company he had was his thoughts. Thoughts that were being twisted and manipulated by the cocktail of drugs that had been injected into his system.

Nothing is real, nothing is real he told himself as Karla's death was replayed, over and over, in his mind. He watched in horror as Bishop's finger squeezed the trigger and a single bullet flashed from the barrel and buried itself in her chest. He was frozen, unable to help, and unable to save her life. All he could do was watch as she collapsed to the ground, her pretty gray eyes wide with shock.

"Wake the fuck up!" screamed a voice. Panic flashed through his brain and he opened his eyes. One of them was bruised to the point where he could only open it slightly. Not that it mattered; there was nothing to see other than the bright light blasting his face.

"You ready to talk you piece of shit?" the massive ogre who'd been overseeing his interrogation screamed.

Kurtz's lips were swollen and dry, his mouth filled with blood, and he was missing half his front teeth, but he managed a broken smile. "You beat me and I'm still better looking than you." He chuckled.

"Whatever, I can keep doing this all day, skinny Nazi fuck."

Kurtz screamed as a hot soldering iron was touched to his testicles. Searing pain shot from his manhood into the pit of his stomach. It felt as if his soul was on fire.

"How do you like your nuts? Roasted?"

The stench of burning flesh filled Kurtz's nose and he screamed, "I'll talk! I'll talk! I'll tell you everything!"

Pershing was watching the proceedings through the one-way mirrored glass. How the lanky German had held out this long was beyond him. They had pumped him full of pain enhancing drugs, torn his fingernails and toenails out, beaten him to a pulp, and still he hadn't cracked. He sighed; they should have started with his balls. The tough guys always cracked when you attacked their manhood.

The door to the observation room burst open and Clare stuck her head in. "Mr. Pershing, we've got trouble."

He followed her out to the corridor into the operations room. She stopped in front of a screen and pointed to the infrared image. It showed an extended line of gunmen approaching from the treeline.

"How many?"

"Three."

He pulled his phone out. "What's your backup?"

"Local police out of Foz. They're twenty minutes away."

Pershing frowned. "You're shitting me?"

"We're on our own out here."

"Make the call."

One of Shrek's men, Mikey, stuck his head into the room. "What's going on?"

"We're under attack. Get Shrek in here."

Mikey turned and ran down the corridor.

Pershing dialed King's number. It went straight to a

message bank. "Our location has been compromised," he recorded. "Aden and his people have found us." He terminated the call as Shrek entered the room. The team leader was fully decked out in his combat rig complete with short-barreled 7.62mm FN rifle. "Hostiles inbound, Shrek. Time to take these bastards down."

"I'll take care of it." He yelled orders to his men and they headed upstairs.

"What do you want me to do?" asked Clare.

"Guard the prisoner. If they breach the lower level put a bullet in his head." Pershing pulled open a locker in the corner of the room. He pulled on a vest and checked the magazine on an AR carbine. "Where are your people?"

"They're upstairs."

Pershing watched the screens as Shrek and his men climbed up from the basement and fanned out in the house. On the other screen he could see the three gunmen moving cautiously toward the barn. He grabbed the radio from the desk in front of him. "Shrek, they're at the barn. I'll turn the lights on and you hit them from the porch side. Catch them in the open."

"Roger, moving now."

"Clare, lock us down."

There was a loud clunk that echoed through the bunker as the vault door sealed. If Shrek didn't neutralize the attackers he would at least slow them down. Pershing turned his attention to the cameras. He was not going to underestimate Aden again.

Chapter Twenty-Six

BISHOP TURNED into the barn alongside Aleks. Pavel covered the rear as they swept the inside of the structure for hostiles. He spotted the two SUVs parked together. "Guys, those are Pershing's trucks. Kurtz is here."

They cleared the barn then directed their attention to the house.

"No sign of movement," reported Miklos from his position in the jungle.

Stepping out of the barn, they moved into a two forward one back formation. They had only advanced a few yards when a dazzling bank of lights on the house flashed on. Gunshots rang out and Bishop felt a bullet strike his armor. Another tugged his sleeve. Next to him Aleks dropped to a knee as he returned fire.

Tracer reached out from the jungle as Kruger hit the front of the house with a long burst.

"Multiple targets at the house," Miklos reported. "Two tangos down."

The sensors in Bishop's helmet adjusted for the bright

lights and revealed the muzzle blasts coming from the front porch. He sprinted to the house firing his Tavor.

Pavel got there first with Aleks right behind him.

"Everyone OK?" Bishop asked as they crouched under a window. "Aleks–" Bullets punched through the planking. He dropped to the ground as splinters of wood showered him.

Aleks pulled off his backpack and ripped out a collapsible frame charge. He unfolded the explosives, stood ignoring the bullets, and stuck it to the side of the house. "Fire in the hole!" He hit the deck as it detonated.

The explosion shuddered through Bishop's chest. Debris rained down on them as the wall imploded. He climbed to his feet as Aleks tossed a flash bang through the ragged breach. It detonated with a thump and the hulking Russian leaped through. Bishop climbed after him as gunfire erupted from inside.

They'd entered a kitchen. The blast had thrown the oven across the room. Aleks was kneeling behind it firing rapid shots at a target in another room. As Bishop moved alongside Aleks's head snapped back and he collapsed. Bishop responded with an automatic burst. Tearing a HE grenade from his rig he popped the handle and tossed it into the next room. It exploded and Pavel pushed past him clearing the room with a series of deliberate shots.

"Clear!" Pavel transmitted.

"Aleks, you OK?" Bishop asked.

There was no response. The bullet had torn away half the helmet's sensors damaging the radio.

Aleks ripped it off and threw it to the ground.

"Stay at the rear, mate. Pavel and I will handle the rest."

"*Nyet!*" the Russian exclaimed as he staggered to his feet. "Kurtz is MY partner."

Bishop shook his head and continued clearing the ground floor. There were a total of four dead men. Three of them were dressed in assault rigs with helmets and NVGs; probable GES contractors. The other guy was young, wearing soft armor and carrying an AR carbine.

"This one's probably CIA," said Pavel.

Aleks lumbered out of the room, Tavor against his shoulder. Bishop hurried after him. As they moved down a narrow corridor he caught up with the Russian. He spotted a door on the left and checked the handle. It was unlocked. He pushed it open and lobbed in a stun grenade. There was a scream as the room shook and Bishop kicked the door. He charged in and nearly tripped down a staircase. Slowing, he paced down the stairs, Pavel on his heels, opening the angle down into the cellar. There was a man sitting on the floor with his hands over his ears. "Stay down!" Bishop yelled, his voice distorted by the helmet. "I've got one prisoner in the basement. No sign of Kurtz." Pavel raced down and flexi-cuffed the man's wrists.

At the top of the stairs Aleks swore and decided to clear the final rooms in the building. Kurtz had to be in one of them. He stepped inside the first room sweeping it with the flashlight on his weapon. All clear.

As he moved to the next room shots rang out. He felt the muzzle blast as a bullet struck his Tavor, tearing it from his grasp. He rushed the shooter, grabbing the hot barrel of the weapon. He pushed it toward the ceiling and chopped at the gunman's wrist. As he met his attacker face to face he realized it was the same man who'd tried to abduct Kurtz's parents.

"You commie fuck!" snarled the American as he tried to wrestle control of his short-barreled FN. "Come for your skinny Nazi boyfriend?" He smashed Aleks's face with a savage headbutt, let go of the rifle with one hand and went for his sidearm.

The pistol went off twice striking Aleks's chest plate. The impact winded him but he managed to keep a grasp on the rifle.

The GES operative lowered his aim and fired at the gap between the chest plate and groin armor.

Aleks grunted as bullets penetrated flesh. With a superhuman effort he twisted the assault rifle from the ogre's grasp and smashed it into his face.

The American stumbled backward firing blindly. Another bullet struck Aleks but he ignored it, aiming the rifle and squeezing the trigger. The powerful 7.62mm round caught his attacker in the throat blowing his spinal cord across the wall in a splash of blood and gore.

Shrek died wearing an expression of disbelief. He slumped to the ground having lost all control of his limbs and convulsed in a rapidly expanding pool of his own bodily fluids.

Aleks lifted his combat shirt where the rounds had penetrated the gap in his armor. Blood was seeping from two half-inch holes in his abdomen. He slumped against the wall and felt for an exit hole. There wasn't one. He pulled a self-adhesive trauma bandage from a pouch on his vest, ripped it open, and pressed it against the wounds. Then he stabbed his thigh with a morphine auto-injector. He waited till the warm sensation swept through his body then staggered to his feet. As he re-entered the corridor Pavel appeared.

"You OK?"

"*Da*, I ran into an old friend. He's dead now. Have you found Kurtz?"

"Not yet. I've cleared the upper level. It's empty. There's one prisoner downstairs."

"He will know where."

As they reached the door to the basement they could hear Bishop's voice. "Where's Pershing and the man he brought in?" The PRIMAL team leader had his knee in the captured man's back and was pinning his head to the concrete floor.

"Behind the shelves," the prisoner whimpered.

"Can you open it?"

"I've already tried, they've locked it from the inside."

Bishop glanced at Aleks as he made his way down the stairs. The Russian was white-faced but gave a thumbs-up.

Pavel examined the shelving then slid it sideways revealing a heavy steel door. He checked the hinges and the keypad.

"What's your assessment?" asked Bishop.

"We might be able to crack the door lock if we patch Flash in," said Pavel.

"He's offline and we don't have time."

"There's not enough HE to breach the door."

Bishop looked around the room and spotted a tiny camera in the corner. "There might be another way."

He found a piece of paper on a workbench and scribbled a message on it. Then he held the sign up to the camera.

30 seconds to open the door or we kill your man.

He stood over the prisoner on the floor, aimed his Tavor at the back of his head, and waited. The door didn't open. He fired a single round at the concrete floor next to his face. Bishop knew he couldn't execute the unarmed man, especially since he was a CIA agent. He turned and shot out the camera in frustration.

"Go in through the wall," grunted Aleks. "In Chechnya we always use the mouse hole." He dumped his backpack on the floor.

"Aleks, you hurt?" Bishop ran his eye over the Russian. Multiple bullet strikes had creased the camouflaged green armor. His nose looked broken and was bleeding.

"I'm fine," he snapped back. "Now let's get inside."

Pavel pushed aside a pile of boxes to reveal a section of concrete wall next to the steel door.

Bishop stripped the explosives out of Aleks's backpack along with a roll of cloth tape. "Ring cutting charge and a central punch."

Pavel helped him tape the explosives to the wall. They laid the cutting charges in a rough circle and then taped blocks of C4 in the middle. Bishop linked them with det cord and finished by taping a Bluetooth-activated detonator to the end of the cord. "Upstairs, go."

Pavel grabbed the prisoner and pushed him up to the ground floor. Bishop watched Aleks follow him. The big man walked stiffly.

When they were clear Bishop checked the iPRIMAL strapped to his wrist. The detonator app glowed green. "Aleks, stay here with the prisoner. Pavel and I will clear the basement."

The Russian shook his head. "*Nyet*, I need to go in."

"No, without your helmet, you're staying put." He thumbed the transmit button on his rifle's foregrip. "Miklos, Kruger, the ground and upper level of the house are clear. Aleks is here. I need you to move across and secure."

"Acknowledged."

Bishop turned to Pavel. "You ready?"

He tipped his helmet in response. "Let's do it."

Bishop tapped the iPRIMAL on his wrist.

The explosion was savage. A shockwave and fragments of concrete blew up the stairs. Dust billowed through the house and the lights flickered.

Bishop was down the stairs a moment later, his helmet protecting him from the dust. The integrated thermal sensors revealed an angry red hole had been blasted through the wall. The heavy steel door remained intact.

The breach was smaller than he anticipated. There was no way he was going to get through with all his gear on. He pulled the emergency bail handle on his armor and it fell to the ground with a thud. Placing his rifle down, he drew his pistol and dived headfirst into the breach. Molten reo-rod singed his fatigues as he wriggled through.

The charge had trashed what had been a storage room. The stench of explosives hung heavy in the air. A door from the room had been blown open. A grunt behind him signaled Pavel following him up.

He caught a glimpse of someone in the doorway. He pulled back as bullets furrowed the wall next to him. His pistol barked in reply and the target fled. The aiming laser emitting from his pistol failed to cut through the dust.

As he rounded the next doorway more shots rang out showering him in shards of concrete. He returned fire as a figure ran across the corridor through another side door. Giving chase, he crouched low, turning through the door into a small observation room. Another door slammed shut. He rose and looked through a large window. On the other side Kurtz was half-naked, tied to a chair. Behind him a woman held a pistol to his head.

As Pavel entered behind him a burst of automatic fire shattered the glass. Bishop ducked but one of the rounds hit the Russian's shoulder. Pavel spun, falling to the ground. He too had removed his armor.

Hunkered below the bottom of the window Bishop changed the magazine on his Beretta. The gunfire subsided and he returned fire blindly over the wall.

"Stand and face me like a man, you coward."

Bishop knew the Texan accent. It was Pershing. "Hey George, you still angry about Mexico?"

"I knew it was you. Stand the hell up, Aden, or I'll put a bullet in your buddy right now."

Bishop slowly got to his feet. Pershing was in the corner of the room with a carbine aimed at him. Only a few feet away Kurtz was tied to a metal chair. The German's face was battered and the floor under him was bloody. The groin of his pants had been sliced open and was drenched with fluid. The stench of scorched flesh hung in the air. He could only imagine the agony he'd been put through.

"Tables have turned, Pershing," he growled. "All your men are dead. Put the weapon down and I'll let you live."

"Oh, you're going to let me walk? After all we've been through?"

"I'm here for my guy. You hand him over and you and the girl live."

Pershing's eyes darted across to Kurtz and the woman. Bishop could see he was weighing his odds.

Pavel whispered over the comms, "Share me your camera feed."

"Let's talk about this man to man," said Bishop. He put his pistol down on the window ledge and removed his helmet. As he held it under his arm he activated the camera.

Kurtz groaned, trying to get words out as he raised his battered face from where it was resting against his chest. The female with the pistol was still pressing it firmly against the back of his head.

"Hang in there, buddy," Bishop murmured.

"Our backup is on its way, Aden. You might want to lay down your guns. I can cut you a deal."

"I don't think so."

"Suit yourself." Pershing raised his rifle.

Pavel didn't bother standing. He'd brought up Bishop's helmet camera feed on his own heads-up-display. He simply held his pistol over the wall, activated the laser, and using Bishop's helmet to aim, fired a single round. The bullet hit Pershing in the eye, tore through his brain, and punched a hole in the back of his head. His carbine clattered to the ground and he toppled sideways.

The woman threatening Kurtz screamed as Bishop snatched up his pistol and aimed it directly at her face. "Drop the weapon."

Kurtz jolted back in his chair. "No," he mumbled. "No!" His voice raised in intensity. "NOOOO!" Tears streamed down his face as he struggled against his bonds.

"Drop the gun," Bishop growled.

"You want me to do it?" asked Pavel. The Russian had his pistol aimed at the woman. "She's going to kill Kurtz."

The woman was frantic, her eyes darting from Bishop to Pavel and back again. He could see her hands trembling as she gripped the pistol.

"Stand down." He lowered his weapon, holstered it, and gestured for Pavel to do the same. "Hey, there's no threat here. We're just here for our friend, that's all. I know you didn't do this to him."

She sobbed hysterically and lowered the gun. Bishop pushed open the door separating the shattered observation room from the cell and walked slowly toward her.

"We don't hurt people like you," he said as she slumped to the ground. Pavel moved to Kurtz.

He relieved her of the pistol. "Hey, it's OK. You did the right thing."

She looked at him with eyes filled with tears. "I tried to stop them from torturing him, I tried."

Bishop grasped her hand. "Thank you."

"We're going to need a stretcher, morphine, and a blanket," said Pavel.

"How's your shoulder?" he asked.

"Just a scratch."

Bishop helped the woman to her feet. "Hey, I need you to open the vault door. Can you do that?"

She nodded. A minute later they had the door open and their full armor back on. He walked her upstairs and sat her down next to the other CIA officer they had spared. The rest of the team was waiting. Aleks was pale, slumped against the wall. "Miklos, find a blanket for Kurtz. Kruger, I need you downstairs with the stretcher."

"How's Aleks?" Bishop asked as they jogged downstairs through to the room where Pavel was attending to Kurtz.

"Not good." Kruger unfolded the stretcher. "He's been shot twice. I think he's got significant internal bleeding."

"Damn it, we can't carry them both."

"No, he can walk." Kruger helped Pavel move Kurtz onto the stretcher. The German moaned.

"These pricks messed him up good, bro." Kruger gave a low whistle.

"And they paid for it."

As they worked on the casualty Bishop rifled through Pershing's clothes. He found a cell phone and slipped it into his pocket. "OK, let's go."

They carried Kurtz out the cellar into the shattered living room. Aleks was still slumped against the wall but managed a grin when he saw Kurtz.

Bishop walked into the next room and dialed Mitch. "Sleek, this is Bish. We need extract immediately."

There was a hiss then the pilot's British accent cut through the airways. "Wilco, Bish, be aware you've got red and blues heading to your location. They're going to get there about the same time as me."

"Team, we've got hostiles inbound! We need to get to the strip, ASAP."

MITCH CHECKED the fuel gauge as he banked the business jet. He was down to the aircraft's reserve. Not optimal considering he was about to take off with a full load of gunslingers. He lined up with the grass strip and dropped flaps. Lowering the reinforced landing gear was next, increasing the jet's drag. He needed to bring her in as slow as possible. The strip was short and he knew it was going to offer little in the way of traction.

He was wearing a pair of augmented reality goggles that were transmitting a feed from the aircraft's suite of external cameras. Using the same technology as the CAT helmets they gave him an unprecedented view of the rapidly approaching runway.

As the rough surface raced up to meet him he tipped the nose and let the rear wheels kiss the grass. The engines roared as he reversed the thrust and punched a parachute release button. Behind the jet a single-shot parachute blossomed and Mitch was thrown forward against his harness as the jet slowed.

He spotted the team closing in carrying a stretcher. He released the parachute, braked one of the wheels and spun the jet in a tight circle before stopping. Grabbing his MP7 submachine gun he ran back, opened the door, and dropped the stairs.

The flashing blue lights of police vehicles reflected off the aircraft's white skin as the PRIMAL team shuffled across the airfield with the casualty. Behind them the convoy bounced across the field, closing fast. Mitch extended the MP7's stock and raised the weapon. Before he could fire a line of tracer reached out from Bishop's team and struck the cars. The PRIMAL team skidded to a halt as the stretcher-bearers reached the stairs.

Behind them a broad-shouldered figure with a machine gun continued to engage the police.

Mitch waved Kruger, Pavel, and Bishop up the stairs with the stretcher.

"Aleks, let's go!" Bishop fired his Tavor at the police cars. The two pickups were now reversing away from them.

The big Russian staggered out of the darkness with Kruger's machine gun slung across his chest. His face was pale, skin drenched in sweat. "Is Kurtz inside?"

"Yeah, mate." Mitch grabbed him as he collapsed and dragged him up the stairs. "Lads, I need a hand."

Bishop was at his shoulder and helped drag Aleks into the cabin. Mitch strode back to the cockpit and jumped in the pilot's seat. "Hold on, this is going to be rough." He threw on his goggles and hit the throttles.

The jet screamed as it fought against the brakes. Once the engines were generating enough thrust Mitch released them and pushed the throttle to the stops. Grass raced under the nose camera as they blasted down the short strip. He pulled back on the stick as their speed increased. "Come on, girl." The jet seemed to stick to the runway for a moment then with a shudder she lifted off with feet to spare. Thick jungle flashed underneath then inky black water as they banked over the estuary. "How we doing back there, lads?"

His question was met with deathly silence. He hit the autopilot and shrugged out of his harness. As soon as he entered the cabin he knew something was seriously wrong. Bishop was kneeling next to Aleks. The Russian's armor was stripped away. His abdomen was smeared in blood.

Bishop's eyes were misty. "We lost him, Mitch. Aleks is dead."

Chapter Twenty-Seven

GES FACILITY, VIRGINIA

HOWARD WATCHED as King stared at his tumbler of whiskey. The man was remarkably calm considering the events of the last twenty-four hours.

"Mr. King, I think we need to assume Pershing and his men are dead." Howard had received a message from the CIA station in Rio De Janeiro. A police unit had reported to the safe house outside of Foz do Iguacu and witnessed a business jet taking off.

"Same jet we lost out of Jamaica, right?"

"Probably. We haven't got much information other than the safe house was raided and there were two survivors."

"Pollard is going to lose his shit." King's eyes remained fixed on his drink.

"He doesn't know?"

King shook his head. "No, he's focused on the Venezuelan deal. Heads down there tomorrow." He took a sip from the glass. "You can bet Larkin knows all about it already. We can kiss our CIA contracts goodbye."

"I haven't spoken to him."

"You should, he's not a man you want to keep waiting." King finished the whiskey, placed the empty glass on the table and sat upright. "You had better report in. I'm going to call Pollard."

"Good luck, dude." Howard rose and made for the door.

"Pass on my regards, Terrance. I've got a feeling I might be needing a job soon."

Howard walked outside and grabbed his phone. He felt the slightest hint of sadness that Pershing was dead but it was quickly replaced with relief. If the former CIA agent had been neutralized there was no way his Mexico double-dealings were going to be revealed. On the other hand, it also meant he was back to relying on his measly CIA wage. He dialed Larkin; with any luck the contracting director would be able to offer him new opportunities.

LASCAR ISLAND

Vance was sitting at his desk when there was a soft knock at his door and Frank walked in. "What up? We get an update from Bishop and the boys?"

The watchkeeper cleared his throat. "Yeah, they've got Kurtz."

"Excellent." He caught Frank's grave expression and his voice lowered. "He OK?"

"Yeah he's OK. Vance... they lost Aleks."

He felt like he'd been punched in the gut. "When, how?"

"He took two rounds to the stomach, self-treated. The team didn't know till Kurtz was safe onboard the jet."

Vance swallowed as he tried to come to terms with the loss. "Is the rest of the team safe?"

"Yes, they're on their way to a Lascar facility in Panama. I've made arrangements for Aleks's body to be shipped from there on a flight to the UAE. Then he'll be transferred to his hometown."

"Yeah, OK." He swallowed hard. "What's happening with Kurtz?"

"He'll travel with Aleks's body back to the UAE. He'll be treated there."

"OK, when he's ready I guess he can make a decision on what he wants to do."

Frank nodded. "Bishop and the team are going to reorg in Panama, change the aircraft's markings, then RV with Saneh and Mirza in Venezuela. The intel shop has confirmed the runway Ivan identified is suitable."

He nodded. "Did they get Pershing?"

"Yes, the GES team was neutralized along with a CIA officer. The mission was a success."

"Hardly, we lost a good man."

"Aleks gave his life to get Kurtz out. In his mind the mission was a success," Frank said before leaving the office.

Vance glanced at his bookshelf. "To fallen brothers," he whispered and headed out the door back to the operations room. He needed to contact Chua and give him the news. Then he would get on to Mirza and Saneh. PRIMAL was going to make Jordan Pollard pay dearly for the loss of Aleks's life.

PANAMA

The Lascar Logistics terminal at Tocumen International Airport was one of the global company's largest. Three huge hangars housed a maintenance facility, freight forwarding warehouse, and offices for thirty staff. In the early hours of the morning the maintenance hangar usually bustled with activity as technicians prepared the Lascar aircraft for the day's work. However, today the hangar was empty of local staff and the doors closed. Inside, the C-130 that had dropped Mitch over the *Nemesis*, and Sleek, the business jet, were parked side by side under bright fluorescent lights.

Bishop, joined by Pavel, Miklos, and Kruger, carried their fallen brother solemnly up the C-130's ramp. Kurtz hobbled behind them with Mitch at his side. They laid the stretcher on the floor, said their farewells, and walked back out.

In the front of the cargo hold the Priority Movements Airlift crew waited a respectful distance. Bishop and Kurtz were the last to leave.

"He died because of me, Aden." Kurtz almost choked on the words.

"No mate, he gave his life to protect us all. If anyone's to blame it's me. I drove you away."

Kurtz turned to him with tears in his eyes. "This family means everything to me. You brought me back and he gave his life so I could live. I won't ever forget that."

Bishop wrapped his arm around the taller man's shoulder, fighting back his own tears. "You're my brother, Kurtz, that will never, ever change."

The German sobbed, hugging Bishop despite his wounded hands. When they separated he wiped tears from his face. "I want to destroy them, Aden. I want to help you kill them all."

Bishop shook his head. "You're all sorts of messed up, mate. We need to get you to a hospital."

"I'm fine. Nothing is broken, just a little singed." He managed a smile revealing the absence of his front teeth.

Bishop shot him a wry smile. "You sure?"

Kurtz nodded and they walked slowly down the ramp.

"OK, I'd just got a message from Saneh. She wants us in Caracas tonight. We're going to be rolling heavy so you'll have to stay onboard Sleek with Mitch. Once the mission's wrapped up we'll get you some serious medical attention. Maybe even some new teeth."

"*Ja*, I can live with that."

"OK, let's get loaded."

Bishop watched as Kurtz walked stiff-legged across to where the rest of the team was sorting their gear. He glanced back into the dark hold of the C-130. "Rest easy, brother."

CARACAS, VENEZUELA

Saneh's stomach was twisted with grief. Aleks had been her closest friend within the PRIMAL team. The big Russian had treated her like a sister and he was the brother she never had. She sat at the kitchen table in the Caracas safe house struggling to hold back tears.

Mirza placed a cup of green tea in front of her and placed a hand on her shoulder.

She wiped her eyes and grasped the warm mug with both hands. "Aleks died getting Kurtz back. We need to honor that and finish the people responsible."

"I agree." Mirza sat opposite. "We know Pollard is arriving tomorrow. That means we need to move on your plan tonight. Bishop and the team will have to infil just after dark."

"Yes, I already sent him a warning order."

They were interrupted by a knock at the front door. Mirza drew his pistol and moved to the entrance. Saneh readied her own weapon.

"It's Antonio." Mirza unlocked the door and exchanged greetings.

When the student walked into the kitchen he was carrying a backpack. "I've got them all," he said as he placed the bag on the table.

She nodded. "Good work."

He unzipped the bag and emptied a pile of mobile phones on the table. "I took all the batteries out just like you said."

"No one asked any questions?"

Antonio shook his head. "No, when I told them the police were listening they were happy to sell them to me."

"Great work. Do you want a hot drink?"

Antonio pulled out a chair and sat. "That would be nice."

Mirza made his way across to the kettle as Saneh inspected the phones.

"I don't see how this is going to help find the trident man. Or how this will make his men pay for what happened to my girlfriend, and the others."

She shot him a grim smile, her grief replaced by thoughts of retribution. "Trust me, he'll pay. They will all pay." She checked her watch. "In fact, Mirza, we need to get going to pick up the boys."

"Can I come?' asked Antonio.

"No, I've got a special job for you. I want you to organize a meeting."

Chapter Twenty-Eight

CARIBBEAN SEA

THE SUN REFLECTED BRIGHTLY off the calm seas but the mood on the fishing boat was dark. Chua and Flash had received the news of Aleks's death not long after the rest of the team. The two men mourned in separate ways. Chua spent an hour at the back of the boat silently staring out at the wake. Flash turned to his work, burying himself in the task of developing the program that would enable them to steal Pollard's funding. The other member of their tiny crew, Wesley Chambers, was left to keep them on course.

It was mid-morning when Chua finished his silent vigil and climbed down to the galley. "Hey, Flash, how are you doing?"

"Yeah I'm OK, bud. You?"

"As good as can be expected. So where are we at?"

Flash cracked his knuckles. "I think I've nailed it. The program I've written allows me to replicate the software the bank uses to authenticate. It needs two codes on two separate devices. They can't be in the same location and they need to be inputted within thirty seconds of each other. It's all part of the bank's anti-duress procedures. If you enter the wrong code the system automatically shuts you out. No second chances."

"So if Pollard or Wesley gives us the wrong code we're screwed?"

"Not quite. I've designed it so we can test the code with a spare device. OK, so we need both codes, a secure link, then once the transaction goes downrange we need to burn all the gear."

"We can go one better than that." Chua glanced at his watch. "I'm going to head up and replace Wesley. He's been at the helm for hours."

"Yeah, not a bad kid that one. Just got led astray."

"He's OK." Chua made his way up to the wheelhouse.

Wesley was whistling as he sat in the skipper's chair. He glanced sideways as Chua approached from the stairwell. "Hey."

"Wesley, how are we tracking?"

"On course and making good time."

"Thanks for looking after things. Flash and I just needed some time."

"No problem." He paused. "The guy who died, was he part of your team?"

"Yeah, hey, you don't need to worry about that. We'll come good on our deal if you play your part."

Wesley stepped away from the wheel. "I just wanted to say, I'm sorry. I don't know if anything I did contributed to your friend's death. But, I just never thought anyone was going to get hurt."

"It's OK, you're making up for it now. Get some rest. We're going to be busy later on."

The banker gave a nod and disappeared down the stairs leaving Chua alone at the helm. He confirmed the route, making small adjustments. As he gazed out over the blue waters his thoughts turned to Aleks. Chua felt the weight of the loss was on his shoulders. It was his first mission as the field commander and someone had been killed. That was going to weigh on his conscience for a long time. His only consolation was that vengeance was only hours away.

FALWELL AIRFIELD, VIRGINIA

King parked his sedan in front of the hangar at the small rural airfield. He had been summoned by Pollard and driven the fifty miles from the GES facility alone. The chairman's helicopter was already waiting on the tarmac.

His hands were clammy on the steering wheel. When he'd reported the loss in Brazil the night before Pollard had remained calm and softly spoken. Then in the morning the chairman had called and demanded King meet him here.

He left the car and walked across to the helicopter. The side door was open and Pollard was sitting in the luxurious cabin talking on the phone. When he spotted King he gestured for him to enter.

King sat in a leather chair opposite and waited.

Pollard pocketed his phone. "Your man Pershing let us down."

"The enemy we face is more formidable than anticipated."

"You don't say. So what are you going to do about it?"

King met his steely gaze. "The intelligence team will

locate the business jet. Once we do that we can cue CIA assets to destroy them."

"The Agency may not be so compliant." The roar of a jet caught Pollard's attention and he glanced out the window. "Well, I guess we're about to find out."

King stepped out of the helicopter and watched as a business jet touched down. It screamed along the runway, slowed, and turned toward them. The sleek Learjet taxied till it was alongside the helicopter then powered down.

"Our good friend, Larkin," snarled Pollard from behind him.

The stairs on the jet lowered and a moment later the barracuda-jawed CIA director appeared. He was dressed in a slim gray business suit, his dark hair slicked back against his head. "Gentlemen." He strode down the stairs and offered his hand to Pollard.

The chairman shook it with a grimace. "Thomas, to what do we owe the pleasure?"

Larkin's thin lips turned up on one side. "You know why I'm here. Had a little trouble down in Brazil did we?"

Pollard's grimace turned to a mask of rage. "You know exactly what happened."

"Yes, I do. I know your people failed to complete a simple task and as a result a CIA officer is dead. I'm canceling all of your CIA contracts. From henceforth you and your personnel are *persona non grata* as far as the Company and our associates are concerned."

"You can't do that. We've got millions of dollars worth of assets tied up in them."

"Yes and you are more than welcome to sell them to whoever takes over the contract. You've been found wanting, Jordan, and you'll pay the penalty."

"You flew all the way out here just to gloat didn't you, you piece of shit." The veins in Pollard's neck bulged.

Larkin smiled. "Don't be so dramatic. I was on my way through to DC. Bad news is always best delivered in person. CIA support to your SCIF will cease immediately. Terrance Howard will be reassigned. Mr. King, I trust you will facilitate his return."

King nodded.

"Don't worry, Jordan, my people will take over your little witch hunt. I'll make sure the problem is neutralized. Now, please excuse me, I have another appointment." He offered his hand to Pollard.

The chairman's gray eyes flashed with hatred. He turned and walked back to his helicopter.

Larkin nodded at King. "Some people just aren't cut out for this business." When Pollard was out of earshot he added, "I'll be in touch, Charles."

King followed Pollard back to the helicopter as the jet's engines screamed and it taxied onto the runway. Half a minute later it roared along the strip and lifted off.

"Fuck him, Charles. Venezuela is bigger than anything the CIA ever offered. Tomorrow we'll fly down there and finalize the deal."

"What about the legal case against the Mexican government?"

Pollard waved it off. "That's going to take years. Venezuela will start paying dividends as soon as we have the signed agreement. People will be falling over themselves to invest in the project." He signaled for the helicopter pilot to spool up the engines. "I'll meet you at Richmond airport tomorrow, 7 am sharp."

"Yes, sir." He waited for the chairman to get into the chopper, slammed the door shut, and walked back to his car.

The sound of the helicopter's engines rose in a crescendo then faded as it flew away. He sat in his car contemplating his future. Pollard was delusional if he thought they could survive this, he thought.

CARACAS, VENEZUELA

Pete yawned and rocked back in his chair. He'd spent the last three hours studying the social media feeds of half a dozen students, trying to hunt down the final elements of the *Movimiento*. Since the Dante raid things had gone quiet and Jimmy had become more and more irritable. The former SEAL was a psychopath, thought Pete. He glanced over to where the angry operator was beasting his way through another CrossFit circuit. He was jumping up and down on a box like a demented bullfrog.

A series of beeps drew his attention back to his monitors. A dozen social media accounts had begun broadcasting again. A single message was being retweeted over and over.

Rally tomorrow 0900 Altamira Square!

He checked the source of the tweet. It had originated from one of the devices the guys had raided earlier. "These morons never learn."

"What's that?"

Pete nearly leaped out of his skin. He glanced over his shoulder and saw Jimmy hunched over dripping sweat onto the dusty concrete. "Damn it, you scared the shit out of me!"

"Situational awareness, mother fucker. Get some! Now what have you got?"

"Twitter's going mental. They're planning another rally for tomorrow."

"Who?"

"One of the guys from the raid on Tuesday."

"You're shitting me."

Pete's fingers danced over the keyboard as he traced the first line of retweeters. "Actually, make that three of the guys who we raided."

"Didn't learn the first time, hey?"

"Clearly not."

"Can you get us a location?"

"Getting broad hits off a dozen cell towers, nothing concrete. If they start coming together I'll launch the bird and get a fix."

Jimmy grinned. "We'll do the job properly this time. Any luck they'll have another sweet piece of ass for the boys."

Pete tried not to frown.

"Let me know as soon as you get something. The guys are restless."

THE AIRFIELD IVAN had previously identified was a former military base, abandoned as a result of budget cuts. The tarmac was pitted, with weeds growing through the cracks. On all sides the dense jungle was slowly reclaiming the strip. Saneh and Mirza had arrived with over an hour to spare so they had walked the tarmac ensuring there were no obstructions.

The sun had set over an hour ago but visibility was still

good. There was a half moon and they were far enough from any urban areas that the sky was clear. Saneh leaned against the van at the end of the runway, while Mirza continued to explore the abandoned buildings of the derelict airbase.

"Tower, this is Sleek, I'm five from your location requesting fly by, over," Mitch's voice came in over her iPRIMAL.

She grinned. "Negative Sleek, the pattern is full."

"Damn. I take it the strip's all clear though?"

"Yes, you're good to go." Saneh winced as she used one of Bishop's favorite phrases.

"Coming in hot."

She heard the jet before she spotted it. Mitch was running total black out and would be using the onboard infrared cameras to land. Moonlight flashed on the white fuselage as it touched down at the end of the airstrip. Mitch bled off the speed and by the time the jet reached her it was moving at walking pace. He brought it to a complete halt with the wing only a couple yards from the van.

The stairs lowered and Kurtz appeared. He hobbled down the stairs and embraced her in a bear hug.

"I'm so sorry to hear about Aleks," she said, struggling to get her words out.

"He saved me," he mumbled.

They separated as the rest of the CAT began loading the van. Mirza appeared from the darkness and greeted them.

"I have to go," said Kurtz. "Mitch and I will be your guardian angels."

She flashed him a smile. "OK, I'll see you when it's done."

Kurtz retreated back inside the jet and the door closed. She gave the blacked out cockpit a wave.

"I see you, waving that hand," crooned Mitch over the communicator. She managed a smile and walked back to the van. Everyone was loaded and Mirza was in the driver's seat. Bishop stood next to the van and even in the moonlight she could see his face was haggard.

"CAT ready and reporting for duty ma'am," he said. "Brought the extra bang you requested."

"I'll give you a handover on the way to the target."

He shook his head. "Negative, this is your op, Saneh. I'm just here to make up numbers. You can give your mission orders to the whole team."

Chapter Twenty-Nine

CARACAS, VENEZUELA

PETE STUDIED his screen in disbelief, shaking his head. Five of the phones he was tracking were all pinging off the same tower. There was no way it was a coincidence. "Hey Jimmy, your buddies are having another meeting."

"Then let's get this show on the road. Hank, help cock lips get the drone airborne. The rest of you limp-dicked space cadets get geared up and ready to roll."

The old warehouse burst to life as Pete activated the software for the drone and the men raced to don their gear. He moved outside to where Hank was powering up the Schiebel Camcopter. Moments later its twin bladed disc was spinning furiously and it was ready to go to work. When he walked back to his desk Jimmy was waiting with a map.

"Where am I going?"

"They're all pinging off the tower near La Vega." He pointed out the area on the map. "Once you're in location I should have the address."

Jimmy slapped him on the shoulder. "Get to it, bro. It's time to shut these students up. I'll make sure they well and truly get the message this time."

The team piled inside their battered van as Pete plotted a route for the drone and uploaded the target handsets into the magic box. He glanced at the time on the screen. It was 2130. He frowned; the students didn't usually meet this late.

It took the helicopter a few minutes to transit to the suburb of La Vega. Once it was on station Pete set it to work. He programmed it to fly circuits over the area, searching like a bloodhound for the electronic scent. Forty seconds into the hunt the first two phones appeared together. A minute and a half later all five devices were pinging at a property on the outskirts of the city. Pete punched the address into his phone. He felt a tinge of guilt as he sent it to Jimmy.

MITCH HELD the Gulfstream in a circuit to the south of Caracas. Cruising at 30,000 feet he'd requested a holding pattern from Air Traffic Control at Maiquetia International Airport. He'd reported a difficulty with the landing gear that his engineer was attempting to rectify. In reality he was using Sleek's electronic warfare system to scan the area around the safe house.

"So Saneh thinks they're using signals intelligence to collect on the students?" asked Kurtz from the copilot's seat.

"That's right, mate. It's the only way they could track them. GES has the resources and the guys with the skills."

"These people are animals," hissed Kurtz. "What I wouldn't give to be on the ground with Bishop."

"I find that deeply offensive, Kurtz."

"*Nein*, that's not what I meant." A series of beeps emitted from the tablet Kurtz was holding.

"I know what you mean, mate. Now what's the system picked up?"

Kurtz held the device up. Squiggly lines danced on the screen.

"Holy crap."

"What?"

"Someone's running an encrypted command link and two data links."

Kurtz looked confused. "What does that mean?"

"It means there's a drone sniffing around out there." Mitch jabbed a button and opened a line of communications with the ground. "Saneh, this is Sleek."

Saneh's calm tone came in over his headset, "Saneh here, send."

"I've picked up data links for a drone. That's how they're locating the students. It'll have a SIGINT box onboard."

"Can you shut it down when we make contact?"

"I could but then, young lady, they would know we're onto them."

"True, can you jam the video link? I don't want the ground crew seeing anything."

"I can go one better. I can jam the signal and give you its origin."

There was a pause as Saneh considered the option. "Good, do it. I'll task Mirza and Miklos to hit the source. The rest of us will deal with the GES death squad."

"Roger, I'll send the grid as soon as we have it."

Mitch placed the aircraft on autopilot as he focused his attention on the tablet. His fingers danced on the screen as he instructed the aircraft's sensors to detect the drone's base station.

"Mike Whiskey One One, what is the status of your landing gear?" the tower asked over the aircraft's radio.

Kurtz keyed his mike. "This is Mike Whiskey One One, I've isolated the problem. Confident I can have it fixed in the next fifteen minutes. We have plenty of fuel, over."

"Acknowledged, maintain current circuit and report in once you're ready."

JIMMY'S PHONE pinged and he checked the address. "Fuck, yeah!" He flicked open his smartphone and used a navigation app to find it. Satellite imagery of the mansion showed it was isolated at the end of a cul-de-sac. Perfect. It was an expansive property with a landscaped front garden. The garden continued around the sides of the house to the rear that contained a swimming pool and backed onto numerous hectares of jungle. He smiled, not only would they be cleaning house but there would be plenty of good loot. "OK boys, we've got a target. It's a good one." He gave directions to Hank as they drove across town.

In the back of the van the team were dressed in their usual garb; dark T-shirts, jeans, and balaclavas rolled up on their heads. They were armed with batons and pistols; overkill for dealing with a handful of overzealous students.

It took fifteen minutes to cross town, find the cul-de-sac, and park the van. "Let's work them over properly this time," said Jimmy as they gathered at the entrance to the estate. The gate was unlocked and he pushed it open. A number of rooms on the bottom floor of the mansion had their lights on. It was a similar property to the one where they'd caught up with Dante. *Luxury compared to our stinking hovel,* thought Jimmy.

The five-man team strode across the lawns to the front of the house. Hank checked the door. "Locked, boss."

"Breach and sweep," whispered Jimmy.

Hank kicked the door savagely. The jamb tore off and he stormed inside the house.

Jimmy followed his men with his baton extended. They peeled off either side of the hallway.

He followed Hank into the living room.

"What the fuck." It was empty. Jimmy drew his pistol. Something was wrong.

"Boss, you're going to want to see this," one of the guys called out.

He strode into the kitchen with Hank on his heels. The other three men were standing in front of the refrigerator. They stepped aside when Jimmy arrived. There, stuck to the fridge, were pictures of Dante, the old chick they had accidentally killed, and the girl he'd raped.

"Fuck!" Jimmy turned and dove for the kitchen window, slashing with his baton as he crashed through.

The refrigerator exploded, tossing him into the garden bed outside. He hit the ground hard, his legs and back peppered with glass, metal shards, and splinters of wood.

He ignored the pain and scrambled to his feet. Gathering his wits he searched for his pistol. Shit, it was gone. He glanced back at the kitchen. There was no movement from the rest of his team, just smoldering wreckage. He gripped his baton and limped through the garden, heading for the thick jungle that bordered the back of the property.

The echo of the explosion was still rolling off the jungle-covered hills when Saneh ordered Kruger and Pavel forward to clear the house. The pair stepped out from the bushes, decked out in their CAT armor and helmets. They looked like terminators as they patrolled through the shattered front door and inside the devastated house.

Bishop scanned the house from his position on the other side of the manicured garden. He listened as others reported their movement through the building and confirmed the casualties in the kitchen. Through the CAT helmet he could see the orange glow of Saneh in the distance, monitoring her side of the perimeter.

Bishop advanced through the garden to get a better view of the back yard. Something caught his eye. Swiveling his head, his helmet's sensors revealed a man running. The figure disappeared into the jungle as Bishop snapped off a round. "We've got a squirter. In pursuit."

"I'm right behind you," transmitted Saneh.

He dashed through the garden and into the jungle. The thick vegetation minimized the effectiveness of the helmet's sensors. Visual range was reduced but the inbuilt sound amplifiers could give him an edge.

He pushed through the dense undergrowth and spotted the runner's footprints. The feet had kicked up a phosphorescent material on the jungle floor. The trail glowed faintly through his fused sensors, invisible to the human eye. He stepped up the pace, Tavor assault rifle held ready.

Ten yards on he saw splashes of warm liquid. His prey was wounded. "Saneh, I'm closing in on this guy."

He moved around a thick tree when a blow to the thigh caught him off balance. He staggered sideways as he was hit again with a baton, and lost his footing. Slipping backward he reached out and grabbed his attacker, holding on as he fell. He lost his grip on his assault rifle as they bounced down the slope.

Bishop's helmet slammed against a rock as he cartwheeled then splashed into a stream. The sensors became scrambled, the helmet useless. Pulling the quick release, he threw it off, and staggered to his feet. He searched frantically for his attacker as he drew his pistol.

There was a gut-wrenching scream as a figure shoulder-charged him. He fired, missing as he was knocked back. A fist hit him square on the jaw. He fell onto his butt, dropping the pistol as he landed in the water.

The attacker leaped on top of him, forcing his head under water and pinning him with his body.

Bishop fought frantically but his equipment weighed him down. He struggled to get his head above water.

"You're a dead fucker," snarled his attacker.

He sucked in air then was under again. This time the GES operative managed to get a forearm across his throat. His strength ebbed as he tried to punch the man. Slabs of muscle absorbed the blows. Desperation filled his mind as he tried to draw his combat knife from his armor. His gloved fingers refused to work as his lungs screamed for oxygen.

Just when he thought it was all over the attacker's body went limp. The arm on his throat released and he pushed the dead weight to the side. His head broke the surface and he gasped for air.

"Bishop!" Saneh's voice was frantic as she scrambled down the hill. She slid into the water and grabbed him, pulling his head up. "God, I thought I'd lost you."

He coughed and spluttered. "He got the drop on me."

"He sure did." She wiped his wet hair out of his face. "Are you OK?"

"Yeah."

"Good. Let's get back to the van."

Bishop recovered his pistol from the creek before inspecting the body of his attacker. Saneh had shot the stocky American clean through the skull. Bishop lifted the corpse's arm and inspected the tattoo, a dragon clutching a trident. "Saneh, you know this guy?"

She handed him his rifle. "Jimmy Scott, filthy little murdering rapist and employee of GES. She used her phone to snap a photo of the arm. "Come on, let's get out of here. Mirza and Miklos should be moving in on the support crew any moment now."

PETE BASHED his keyboard and swore. No matter what he did he couldn't get the video feed from the drone to come through. It was blocked by some kind of interference. At least he had control of the bird. The magic box on the aircraft was also working. The screen still showed the cluster of phones at the residence. He sighed. The students were probably all beaten half to death by now. Or raped by that maniac, Jimmy. Pushing the thought from his mind he sent a text message to the team leader telling him the drone was offline. Then he hit the return home function and leaned back in his chair.

The mission had been running for two months now and he'd had enough. Jimmy and the rest of the team treated him like a second-class citizen and his heart wasn't in the work. He hadn't signed on to help a bunch of thugs bash and murder students and politicians.

"Don't move."

The metallic voice nearly gave Pete a heart attack. He spun his chair around and was greeted by the most terrifying sight he'd ever seen. Two alien looking figures were pointing assault rifles directly at him.

"I said, don't move."

There was a crack and he felt the two probes from a Taser hit him in the chest. The barbs felt like red-hot spikes punching through his skin. Immediately, thousands of volts of electricity arced through his body and he convulsed in pain. He slid off the chair and collapsed to the floor. Warmth spread from his groin as he lost control of his bladder. Strong hands flipped him over and secured his hands behind his back.

Mirza ripped the taser probes out as Pavel slid a hood over the prisoner's head. Then they hauled him back onto his chair. The stench of urine filled the air.

He left Pavel to guard and called through to Saneh. "We've captured their intel guy."

"Just the one?" replied Saneh.

"Yes, he was flying the drone."

"Great work, can we use the location for the next phase?"

Mirza glanced around the abandoned warehouse. "Yeah, but I don't think we would want to stay for long."

"Plan is to be out in a matter of hours. Is the detainee talking yet?"

He glanced at the terrified analyst. "No, but he will."

"Good, we'll see you in a few minutes."

The buzz of an approaching rotorcraft filled the air.

Pavel tapped one of the computer screens the detainee had been monitoring. "It's the drone returning."

The throb of rotor blades grew louder then subsided. Mirza pushed open a side door. Sitting in the dark behind the building was a small black helicopter, the drone. He closed the door and turned his attention back to the drone's controller. "What's your name?" His voice sounded metallic and alien through the helmet's speakers.

"P, P, P, Pete."

"Listen Pete, you answer my questions, and you're going to be fine. We're not here for you, we just need information."

"O, O, OK. Look, I didn't kill anyone. I'm just the intel guy. The guy you want is Jimmy, he's the bad guy. I can tell you where he is."

"Jimmy's already dead!" hissed Mirza.

"Oh, god," wailed Pete.

Mirza almost smiled. This was going to be easier than he initially thought. "Tell me about your boss, Jordan Pollard."

"I don't know who that is. I work for King, Charles King. We're supposed to pick him up from the airport tomorrow morning. He's flying in with some big wig from the States for a meeting with the Venezuelans."

Chapter Thirty

CHESTERFIELD COUNTY, VIRGINIA

HOWARD READ the message on his phone for the third time.

0700 Chesterfield County Airport TL

He'd packed his gear and left the GES facility at five in the morning to make it to the airport on time. Now, at 0730, there was still no sign of Larkin. He shivered, crossed his arms, and stamped his feet. He glanced at the modest terminal, wishing to buy a hot mug of coffee. It didn't open until 0830. He was about to turn back to his car when the lights on the airfield flickered on. A light fog hung over the airport and the orange lights threw up an eerie glow.

A sleek business jet roared in under the cloud and touched down with a screech of rubber on tarmac. It raced toward him and slowed just short of the turn to the taxiway.

The Learjet was a beautiful aircraft, long and sleek with

a high tail and swept back wings. Howard wasn't a plane enthusiast but he guessed it was worth a small fortune. It stopped and the side door opened. He walked closer, tentatively, as a set of stairs unfolded. A figure in a suit appeared and waved him inside.

The interior was as he expected. Plush carpet, wooden paneling, leather recliners, a very attractive stewardess, and a security guy. He gave the stewardess a smile and spotted Larkin sitting at a table with his laptop in front of him and a phone pressed to his ear. The immaculately-dressed senior CIA director waved him to the chair opposite him.

"Would you like a coffee?" the stewardess asked.

He nodded his head vigorously. "Yes, please, sweetheart. Dark and sweet."

The coffee arrived a moment later, piping hot. Howard sipped it as Larkin finished his call.

"Terrance Howard, good to finally meet you, son."

"You too, sir."

"Sorry about the early meeting but I've got to be back at Langley by nine."

"No problem, sir."

Larkin fixed him with a stare then smiled broadly. "So you must be wondering why you're here."

Howard swallowed and nodded.

"I want to offer you a job, Terry. I can call you Terry, can't I?"

"It's fine, sir."

"Good, let me start from the beginning. When I was made Director of the Operational Support Program four years ago I wasn't particularly happy about it. I thought I was being sidelined. Pushed across to a program outside the core responsibilities of the Agency. But then everything changed. As you know, the CIA has been audited, investigated, and embarrassed by wave after wave of goody-two-shoes senators, lobby groups, and journalists. Classified operations were exposed, budgets slashed, capabilities compromised, and the game changed. Whistle-blowing rats sold out our darkest secrets and betrayed us. Our reputation among our allies was dragged through the dirt." Larkin wore a grave expression. "But, with change comes opportunity, great opportunity. A little over a year ago I pitched an idea to the boss that solved a lot of our problems. Do you know what that idea was Terry?"

He shook his head.

"Complete deniability. I proposed he let me develop a system of outsourcing the Agency's dirtiest work. It was to be a way of redeeming ourselves, a way of getting the job done without the threat of whistle-blowers and do-gooders. A system that lets us take the gloves off and fight our nation's enemies with both hands." Larkin's eyes narrowed and his jaw jutted out. "I call it the Redemption Network."

He ran his fingers through his dark hair. "Let me tell you how it works. I run a team of analysts who do the grind work. They work independently, plugged into a cloud-based network with priority access to feeds from our intelligence community. They put together target and mission packs then anonymously outsource the operation to a private contractor through a secure website. Only companies and individuals who have been vetted are able to bid for jobs. There is no contact between the CIA and the action arm. They're paid in digital currency from untraceable accounts. Regardless of whether the mission fails or succeeds, it is completely deniable."

Howard had placed his coffee down and was listening with complete focus. "That's brilliant. It's like eBay for Black Ops. How many analysts do you have?"

"That, you don't need to know. But I'm keen to add one more to the team."

"Dude, count me in."

Larkin smiled. "I thought as much. My people will be in touch with the details. You'll cut all ties with the CIA and work from anywhere you want. Base pay is twice what you're on now with bonuses for successful mission execution." He reached out and shook his hand. "Welcome to the Program."

Terrance couldn't help but grin. "Hey sir, I just need to know one thing. What's going to happen to Charles King and GES?"

Larkin nodded. "I've got plans for both."

"Good, King's a solid guy."

"I know, he just works for a greedy bastard."

CARACAS, VENEZUELA

MVI's business jet touched down just after 1300 hours at a private airstrip on the outskirts of Caracas. Pollard glanced out the window and spotted two black Suburban SUVs parked on the strip. He let King step out of the aircraft first. A door opened on the lead vehicle. A man wearing a baseball cap approached and shook his boss's hand. Pollard walked down the steps and joined them.

"Where's Jimmy?" King asked the man.

"He's in the truck, boss. He's worried about keeping a low profile."

Pollard ran an eye over the contractor and frowned. The man looked more like a computer programmer than a special operations veteran. "What's going on?" he demanded. "Charles, is this one of your men?"

"Yes, sir."

"Well then, let's get out of this damn heat and get on our way." Pollard strode across to the lead vehicle and allowed the GES man to open the door for him. King got in the other side.

The limousine interior of the armored Suburban was already chilly but Pollard reached up and cranked the air-conditioning to the max. "Damn this place is hot," he said as the convoy turned onto a narrow road bounded on both sides by thick jungle.

"How far is it to Caracas?"

King shrugged and tapped on the tinted glass that separated them from the driver. There was no response. "Hey, open up." He toggled the switch that lowered the glass but nothing happened. He tried the doors and the windows. Nothing worked. They were locked in.

"Charles, what the hell is going on?"

"I don't know."

They peered out the windows as the car continued into an industrial area. Traffic was light and they made rapid progress. After ten minutes they slowed and turned off the road. Pollard caught a glimpse of a warehouse as they passed through open doors and parked inside. Thirty seconds passed before one of the doors was pulled open.

"Gentlemen, if you would join us," a strange metallic voice said.

Pollard glared at King. "What the fuck have you led us into?"

"Me? This is your goddamn trip."

He stepped out of the vehicle and looked around. Masked gunmen surrounded him. They held their weapons with the sort of casual confidence that implied they were competent in the application of deadly force.

"Take a seat." The metallic voice emanated from a man wearing a full-face tactical helmet. The alien-like figure directed them to two folding metal chairs in the middle of the warehouse.

"Listen, if it's money you want."

"Sit!"

Pollard moved to the chair and sat down. King joined him.

"Look, we're powerful men. If you harm us the Government of the United States of America will find you and crush you."

The man in the hi-tech helmet laughed, a strange mechanical cackling. "Do you really think Uncle Sam gives two shits what happens to a retired Brigadier with a bent for beating students, killing politicians, and stealing land from farmers?"

The man leaned in so Pollard could see his own terrified reflection in the mirrored lenses of the helmet. "You're all alone, Mr. Jordan Pollard. The only person who can save you is... you."

"You work for Larkin, don't you? You work for that piece of shit Larkin!"

"Who I work for is irrelevant. What I want is imperative."

"And what do you want?"

"One simple thing. Your banking access code."

He laughed. "Not over my dead body."

"That can be arranged. Along with the bodies of your wife and your daughter. We are highly resourceful, Mr. Pollard. Don't underestimate us like your employee George Pershing did."

Realization passed over Pollard's features. "Aden, you're goddamn Aden."

The helmeted man shook his head. "My name is irrelevant. I need that number Jordan, and it's in your best interest to give it to me. Because, if you don't I'm going to get medieval on your ass. I'll start with your ears and I'll chop off every bit that protrudes as I work my way down your body."

"For fuck's sake, Jordan, give him the damn number," snapped King.

"Shut the hell up. You're fired, Charles."

The man in the helmet whipped out a wicked blade, leaned forward, grabbed him by the hair, and sliced his right ear off with a flick of his wrist. The scream echoed off the walls of the warehouse.

"I'm not fucking around. Give me the number." The man tossed the bloodied ear in his lap.

"Screw you!" he said defiantly as he picked up the ear and attempted to press it back onto the side of his head. Blood gushed through his fingers, running down his neck.

The man grabbed his hair again and wrenched back his head. He held the razor sharp blade over the bridge of his nose.

Pollard wavered. "OK, OK, I'll tell you... 8456783421."

"You sure? Because I'm going to check it and if it's wrong..."

His shoulders slumped.

"Tell him the correct number," said King. "These people will kill us."

Pollard continued to hold his severed ear on his head. "It is the correct number."

"Repeat it," ordered the voice.

"8456783421."

The man in the helmet turned and walked away from them. Pollard glared at the other gunmen. "You're all dead men walking," he snarled. "You know that don't you?"

"The number's good," were the last words he heard as a syringe was plunged into his neck. The room swam and he tried to stagger to his feet. Everything went black as he toppled over.

―――

CAYMAN ISLANDS, CARIBBEAN SEA

The fishing boat was at anchor a dozen nautical miles from the Cayman Islands. A flock of seagulls wheeled above searching for morsels of bait or tailings. Seeing nothing they flew into the distance in search of more lucrative pickings. Meanwhile inside the boat three men were sitting at the galley table waiting for a morsel of their own.

Flash had inputted the Chairman's code into his custom software and it had come back positive. Wesley's number also authenticated. However, that wasn't the tricky bit. The challenge was getting the banking system to allow non-proprietary software to handle the transaction of funds to over thirty different destinations. If it failed then even with the two codes they were sitting dead in the water, figuratively as well as literally.

"This is nerve-wracking," said Chua.

Wesley gave a nervous snort. "Even if it fails Pollard and King will track me down and kill me."

"You don't have to worry about them."

"Why?" His eyes went wide. "Oh shit you guys have waxed them haven't you? That's how you got his number."

"They've been neutralized."

Flash coughed. "All of the transactions have gone through. Roughly nine hundred and fifty million dollars is in our accounts. MVI is now a private equity firm with zero equity."

Wesley sighed and slumped forward in his seat.

"Good work, Flash," said Chua. "So we're done here?"

"Yes." Flash double-checked his computer. "We're good."

"I'll make the call."

An hour later a small workboat pulled alongside them. The three men climbed in with their bags. They were out of sight when the incendiary device inside the hull of the wooden fishing boat ignited. By the time they reached the wharf in Bodden Town the trawler and all their communications and IT equipment was burned to the water line. The husk of the old trawler sank beneath the sparkling blue waters in nearly eighteen hundred feet of sea.

When the workboat operator dropped them at the end of the wharf there was a cab waiting. Chua handed Wesley an envelope. "Everything you need is in there." He shook his hand. "Thanks for your help, Wes."

The banker gave him a nod and a wry smile. "I hope I've made up for at least a little bit of what MVI's done."

"Just remember. You never met any of us. This little boat trip never happened. I don't want to tell you what will happen if you talk."

"Understood." Wesley got into the cab. With a wave he disappeared down the road.

"Almost seems like a letdown, doesn't it," said Flash as they walked along the shorefront in search of a hotel.

"What do you mean?"

"All the tearing around, all the espionage, and the boat chases, and then click, we take everything they have."

"Hadn't thought of it like that."

"So what's going to happen to all the money?"

"We'll keep a lot of it. Use it to offset the cost of running PRIMAL. Some may be distributed to not-for-profits. Aleks's family will also receive a share."

"What about us?"

"Tariq, Vance, and I will discuss bonuses for the rest of the team."

"Nice, I've got a new bike I've had my eye on." They stopped in front of a white-walled double-story motel. "This alright?" asked Flash.

Chua yawned. "Yep, we'll get our heads down for a bit then catch a cab to the airport. Bishop and the crew will be heading through later tonight."

"I hate to say it," added Flash. "But I kind of miss the Bunker."

"I miss my own bed."

"Yeah, but any port in a storm."

Chua laughed. "I think we can finally ditch the nautical terms."

Chapter Thirty-One

CARACAS, VENEZUELA

IT WAS late afternoon when Saneh, Bishop, and the CAT reached the private terminal at Caracas International airport. Kurtz greeted them at the security gate with the required paperwork and they drove the two stolen Chevy Suburbans to the Gulfstream. They loaded their equipment, abandoned the SUVs, and in a minute the team was settling in, ready for takeoff.

Bishop slumped in one of the leather chairs.

"Is this seat taken?"

He glanced up to see Kurtz standing in the aisle. The German had relinquished his copilot seat to Mirza.

Bishop nodded. "It is now."

As Kurtz sat the aircraft rolled forward. Soon the engines screamed at full power and they gathered speed. They soared off the tarmac, climbed steadily, and banked toward the coast.

"I'm glad that's over," murmured Bishop as he watched the city shrink through the window.

"I wanted to thank you for finding me, Aden."

"You're my brother. I'd never abandon you." He swallowed hard. "Kurtz, can you ever forgive me for what happened with Karla? I made a snap decision, I never meant for it to happen."

Kurtz glanced away and rubbed an eye with a bandaged hand. "I forgive you, but can you forgive me for running?"

Bishop gripped the lanky German's forearm. "Mate, it goes without saying."

"Thank you." Kurtz pried himself out of the chair and moved to the back of the cabin to sit with Kruger and the boys.

Bishop gazed out the window at the clouds. Sadness washed over him as his thoughts turned to Aleks. The big Russian had been a close friend since the first day they'd met in Ukraine three years ago. He smiled as he remembered being driven at break-neck speed around the outskirts of Kiev. The day after, Aleks had risked his life to save Bishop.

"Everything seems to have worked out."

Saneh's voice pulled him back to reality. He gave her a smile. "You did a good job Team Leader. Mission is a resounding success."

She sat next to him. "I guess so. You did pretty well yourself."

He turned back to the window. "No, I didn't."

"You can't blame yourself for this one. Aleks knew exactly what he was doing. He put his life on the line to save Kurtz. You all did."

"Yeah, but he paid the price."

"You care too much sometimes, Aden Bishop. It's one of the reasons I like you."

He gave a slight smile. "Oh so now you like me?"

"Well, you've finally started to grow up."

Mitch's voice interrupted them. "Hello, this is your captain speaking. Just wanted to let you know we've got a flight time of one hour and thirty minutes. I anticipate clear skies so feel free to walk around the cabin. Please keep all firearms in the unload position and refrain from using any electronic countermeasure devices. I hope you enjoy your flight and thank you for traveling PRIMAL air."

He shook his head and chuckled. "I'm looking forward to a rest after this."

"How about we head down to the beach huts for a few days?" Saneh referred to the recreation area on Lascar Island. A place the two of them had enjoyed when they were together.

"I've got a better idea. Let's get away from it all. Take a trip, a real trip. Maybe Africa."

Her eyes lit up. "Africa, really? I've always wanted to go."

"I've got a friend working on a game reserve. I'd like you to meet her."

"A woman?"

He laughed. "It's not like that. She's helping us put the nails in Pollard's coffin."

"Christina Munoz, she's the journalist you saved in Mexico."

He snorted. "Have you been keeping tabs on me?"

She winked. "I keep tabs on all my men. So she's going to release an article?"

"She will once I've sent through the last of the facts. Chen is also prepping an intel pack to leak to the FBI."

"And now they're broke they won't be able to sue the Mexican government."

"Their world is definitely going to unravel very quickly." He paused. "Hey, who do you think this Larkin guy is?"

"Larkin?"

"Pollard asked if we were working for Larkin."

She shook her head. "No idea, that's one for Chua and his guys to figure out. You need to focus on resting and… fixing us."

"You mean you want there to be an us?"

She nodded. "No one else is going to put up with your antics."

He gave her hand a squeeze. "We make a good team."

"We make a killer team."

POLLARD'S EYES snapped open and he clutched his head. It was wrapped in bandages. He ignored the throbbing pain and looked around. Sitting in a chair at the end of his hospital bed, with his head resting in his hands, was Charles King. Next to him was the GES analyst who had led them into the ambush.

"Did they fix my ear?"

King snapped his head up. His shaved head nearly connected with the wall. "Yes, they managed to reattach it."

"Where the hell are my things?" he demanded.

"They're over here." He pointed to the folded clothes sitting on a table next to him.

Pollard staggered out of bed, grabbed his phone, and dialed Ian Macmillan, his Chief Financial Officer. "Have you checked our accounts?" he snapped when the call picked up.

"What? No."

"Well then fucking check them now."

He listened as the accountant fumbled with his computer. Then there was silence.

"Oh my God!" said the CFO.

"They're empty aren't they?" Pollard hissed through a clenched jaw.

"This doesn't make sense. How could this happen?"

"We've been robbed. Call the bank. Get their fraud team on it." He terminated the call and locked eyes with King. "We're going to find these people and we're going to kill them."

"Sir, the Venezuelans have been calling. We missed the meeting," replied King.

"That doesn't matter now we don't have the funds, does it."

Pollard grabbed his clothes and found the bathroom. As he dressed he caught his reflection in the mirror above the sink. The bandages wrapped around his head were stained with blood. "You're a dead man, Aden," he whispered.

He stormed out of the bathroom. "We're going." He made another call as he strode down the polished corridor. "Get the jet ready, we'll be there in ten minutes." As he pushed open the glass doors he nearly collided with a young man carrying a bunch of flowers. "Get out of the way," he snapped.

Antonio stood aside as the American barged his way through the doors and out onto the street with two other men in pursuit. So damn rude, the student thought as he walked down the corridor to Camilla's room. He knocked and her father opened the door.

"Antonio, it's good to see you."

"How is she?"

The smile melted from the elderly man's face. "No change."

Antonio walked across to the bed. "Hello Camilla, I brought you some fresh flowers." He laid them on her bedside table.

She stared at him with sad eyes. Her long brown hair had been freshly combed. Sitting on the edge of the bed he bent down and kissed her on the cheek. "It's all been taken care of," he said quietly, pulling out his phone. He held the screen so Camilla could see the photo the woman called Saneh had sent him. It was of a dead man who had been shot through the skull. Visible on one of the corpse's forearms was a tattoo of a dragon clutching a trident.

Tears formed in Camilla's eyes and ran down her cheeks. "Thank you."

Chapter Thirty-Two

LASCAR ISLAND

THEY GATHERED in front of a rocky outcrop high above the island. It was a favorite spot of Aleks's. A place where he would pause during one of his long hikes and gaze out over the Pacific Ocean. Many of the PRIMAL team had joined Aleks on his hikes but none had ever made the climb this early. They had commenced the ascent at four in the morning so they could be here at the crack of dawn.

Bishop had insisted on leading the service. He carried a box of candles to the escarpment in a backpack and handed them out to the others. One by one they were lit. Vance, Chua, Saneh, Kurtz, Mitch, Kruger, Pavel, Flash, Miklos, Frank, and nearly a dozen more of the support staff, were all there.

"We all know why we're here," said Bishop as the first hint of sunrise touched the horizon behind him. "We've lost a brother, a partner, a team leader, a warrior, but most of all, a loyal friend. Aleks Andreyev was a man who had no living enemies. He was a bear, with a big heart that had room for everyone."

Bishop took a deep breath trying not to choke up. "I first met him three years ago in the Ukraine, a contracted operative who thought he was working for the CIA. Within hours of meeting me he took me under his wing and saved my life. Months later when I invited him to join PRIMAL he leaped at the opportunity. You mean I get to help people, he said, and I get paid? This is amazing. That was Aleks. A man who would come to the aid of anyone in distress. A man who would stop to save a ladybug from being squashed on a footpath. A man who would give his life for any one of us at the drop of a hat. And, in the end, it's exactly what he did. He gave his life so others could live. Aleks left us a legacy to continue, a legacy of sacrifice, of commitment, of fighting for the little guy, and of loving your comrades regardless of the circumstances. I know each and every one of you will work hard to continue this legacy."

Behind him the horizon had taken on a soft glow that added to the solemnity of the moment. The jungle was silent and the only noise was the crash of waves hundreds of feet below.

Bishop dipped his head. "They shall not grow old, as we that are left grow old. Age shall not weary them, nor the years condemn. At the going down of the sun and in the morning, we will remember them. Lest we forget."

As they stood in silence watching the sunrise the team huddled closer together. Arms were thrown over shoulders and tears flowed freely. A wind rose up from the west and snuffed out their candles. It was almost as if Aleks had given them one last farewell.

BISHOP WALKED into the recreation room and spotted Chua sitting at a table reading a tablet. "Hey, mate, what's going on?" He opened the refrigerator and pulled out a bottle of sports drink. He was dressed in a gray gym shirt and a pair of loose fitting shorts. Sweat drenched the synthetic material from neck to groin.

"Hey Bish, you been hitting the gym?" Chua replied.

"No, Saneh's got me doing Bikram Yoga, bloody horrendous." He tipped his head back and downed two-thirds of the bottle.

Chua laughed. "You guys are all loved up again I see."

He gave a sideways glance.

"Well you should probably check this out." Chua nodded at the tablet.

He sat down. "What is it?"

"Christina's story, it made front page of the New York Times."

"No way, that's awesome."

Chua pushed the tablet across so he could see it.

He spent a few minutes reading the piece over. When he was done he handed it back. "It's a great article, compelling. Jordan Pollard will be fuming."

"I think the article is the least of his worries."

"Why? What's going on?"

"The intel pack's been leaked to the FBI. Pollard and King are going to have a nasty surprise when the Feds turn up."

"Nice!"

Bishop grabbed another bottle from the fridge. "Did you work out who this Larkin guy is?"

Chua shook his head. "Vance knew a Larkin when he was in the Agency, though. A preppy Ivy League guy with ties to all the right people. You know, one of those Skulls guys. Vance remembers him being a bit of high-flyer. He got caught up in a black op gone bad but didn't go down for it. Problem is I can't find anything recent on him. We've been sniffing around but without direct access to the CIA's personnel files it's a long shot."

"What if he's not CIA? Could be another private contractor."

"I've got the team researching but so far we've got zip."

He sat down again. "Hey, I think you did a good a job on this op, mate. We cleaned house on MVI and GES. They're not going to be hurting anyone else anytime soon. Or trying to track PRIMAL down for that matter."

"Thanks, Bish, that means a lot."

"Don't get too comfortable. I'm still going to mess with your plans as much as possible."

Chua laughed. "I wouldn't expect any less."

"So what's the plan from here? You and Vance finally going to take some time off?"

"Sure are. What about you?"

"Saneh and I are thinking of heading to Africa. I need to touch base with Christina Munoz and lady Ebadi wants to cuddle a leopard."

"Sounds good. So you two all good now?"

"We're getting there."

"You know everyone just wants you to hurry up, get married and start making babies. PRIMAL's going to need some new operatives eventually."

Bishop snorted in his sports drink. "What?"

Chua winked and stood up with his tablet. "Good luck with the Bikram, I'll catch you later."

NEW YORK CITY

The newspaper hit the polished wooden desk with a loud slap. "Have you read this crap?" Pollard screamed at the two men sitting in his office. He slumped in his chair and fought the urge to scratch at the bandage on his ear. "We've been completely exposed, robbed of all our capital, and had our tactical teams cut out from under us." The other men in the office, King and the CFO Ian Macmillan, looked as defeated as he was angry. "This Christina Munoz bitch has ruined us. There's no way we can recover from this with our reputation intact." He fixed King with an icy stare. "You were supposed to fix this."

King made to say something but stopped.

Ian Macmillan sighed, reached inside his jacket, and pulled out an envelope. "This might not be the best time, Jordan, but I wanted to do it in person." He rose and slid the envelope across the desk. "As of now I am tendering my resignation as CFO. All communication will need to happen through my attorney." He nodded and made a beeline for the door.

"Go fuck yourself, Ian. Get the hell out of my building." Pollard grabbed a pewter statue of a soldier from his desk and threw it. It smashed through the opaque glass door as it swung shut. He gripped his desk with both hands in an attempt to control his rage.

"Sir, GES is still in the black. We have enough capital to operate for at least a few months. The training facility will generate enough revenue to maintain itself."

"Shut the hell up, Charles."

King snapped his jaw shut.

"All we need to do is cover the costs of the legal team for Mexico. I'll finance the legal fees personally. We can sell the

Virginia facility for all I care. Then we're going to find the criminals that did this and destroy them."

King shook his head. "They've won, Jordan. Let it be, for now. Rebuild and get stronger. Then, and only then can, we find out who did this."

"No! I want Wesley found. I want Munoz found. I want Aden and his buddies found, and I want them all dead."

The intercom on Pollard's desk beeped. "Sir, there are men here—" The call was interrupted.

"What the hell?"

Two men stepped through the shattered glass door. They were wearing dark blue bulletproof vests emblazoned with the letters FBI. "Get your hands in the air!"

"Do you know who I am?" Pollard snarled at the pistol aimed at his face.

The agent smiled. "I know exactly who you are, you piece of shit. Jordan Pollard, you're under arrest for accessory to murder of Mexican and Venezuelan citizens, blackmail, and securities fraud. I could go on but I think you get the drift."

Strong hands hauled him from his desk and pressed him against the wall. Metal handcuffs restrained his hands behind his back.

"You're making a big mistake, gentlemen! I have powerful friends."

"So do we, ours is a Supreme Court judge. Maybe we should get them together sometime."

King had his head bowed and was fully compliant. He placed his hands in his lap and let the officer cuff him.

"Keep your mouth shut!" hissed Pollard as he was marched out. In the corridor a team of agents carried computers and files from MVI's offices. Rage burned in him as he was shoved past his secretary and thrust into the elevator. "I want my call."

"All in good time."

They reached the lobby and the doors opened. The agent led him out through the foyer. He skidded to a halt. Through the glass front of the building he spotted an army of camera crews.

"Keep walking."

He held his head high and jutted his chin as he was pushed through the throng. Journalists screamed out to him as the FBI agent rushed him to a waiting vehicle. He ducked his head inside and sat with his eyes to the front. The car pulled away from the curb with its siren wailing. Someone was going to die for this, he promised.

Chapter Thirty-Three

FBI DETENTION FACILITY, NEW YORK

KING SAT in an interrogation room barely three yards square. His hands were cuffed behind his back and he'd lost most of the feeling in his shoulders. There was no clock in the room but he guessed he'd been there for at least three hours.

He heard the door to the side open and turned to see who it was.

"Charles King, I told you I'd be in touch." Thomas Larkin strode into the room. "No need for the cuffs," he said to the FBI agent that accompanied him.

"Sir, that's against policy."

"Take them off and then get the hell out."

The man mumbled something, unshackled King, and left the room.

"Thanks." King rolled his shoulders in an attempt to get some feeling back.

"Not a problem. Don't worry about the CCTV." He

nodded at the camera in the corner of the room. "One of my boys has taken care of it."

"Are you here to get me out?"

Larkin smiled. "That's completely up to you." He sat in the chair opposite and crossed his legs. "I mean you and Pollard have been very naughty boys. The stuff you pulled down in Mexico was downright nasty and the Venezuelan piece, well, that was unconstitutional. I mean, working directly against the CIA. I think they call it treason?" He dropped a bundle of photos on the desk.

King looked at the pictures. They showed a burnt out church filled with charred bodies, a man who'd been stabbed in the chest, a young woman in a hospital bed, and a mangled corpse. "I didn't have a choice."

"Yes, you did. But, you chose money over morality. You've been sitting behind a desk with your head up your ass letting it all happen. I've got the records to prove it; emails, phone calls, the works. You and Pollard will be lucky not to get the death penalty."

He felt his gut twist. It had been so easy to distance himself from what the teams were doing. The photos brought it all home.

Larkin shot him a smile that reminded King of a shark. "But hey, I can't blame you. Who's going to go against Pollard? The guy's an inflexible power-mongering asshole."

"What do you need me to do?"

"Straight to the chase. That's what I like about you, Charles. There's no foreplay with you, no attempting to suck my dick, just a straight up question. It's pretty simple. I need you to continue to run GES."

King snorted. "GES is done. Pollard will dissolve the company to fund his legal fees."

"Don't worry about Pollard. I've arranged for him to…

retire. I just need to know you and GES are onboard. No more resource pilfering shenanigans, you work exclusively for OSP. I'll fund expansion, technology, and resources. You provide manpower when and where I need it, no questions asked. Oh, and there will be complete deniability. I've got a new contracting system that will give you anonymity."

"And what about the Major League Network?"

"You'll get your opportunity to deal with them."

He nodded. "And the charges against me?"

Larkin smirked. "What charges? You agree to work for me and they disappear."

King didn't need time to consider the offer. He rose and offered Larkin his hand. This was an opportunity to hit back at the Major League Network, except this time he would have the full support and assets of the CIA behind him. No more dodgy security contracts burning villages; he would be back protecting the nation's interests. "I'll do it."

JORDAN POLLARD STOOD in his cell staring at his reflection. The stainless steel mirror that hung over the sink was blurry but he could still make out the line of stitches that circled his right ear. He'd pulled off the bandages to check the damage. The pain from the wound only fueled the anger and hatred that had intensified during the twenty-four hours he had been in the cell. His life had collapsed around him and now he was going to focus everything on finding and killing the man called Aden and all his friends.

"Prisoner Pollard," said a voice from behind the heavy steel door. "You've got a visitor. Hands please."

A metal hatch slid open and he got off the bed, walked across, and thrust his hands through the opening. He was expecting a meeting with his lawyer. Cold metal snapped shut around his wrists and he pulled his hands back. The lock clunked open and two uniformed guards greeted him with smiles.

"After you," said one of them.

He shuffled down the long concrete walkway past the other cells. A mechanical door swung open and he followed the guard's directions into an interview room. They pushed him down onto a metal chair and chained his cuffs to a loop on the table in front of him. Pollard glared at them as they departed the tiny cell, slamming the door shut.

Five minutes passed before the cell door opened. "About fucking time."

The man who entered the room wasn't his lawyer. He was dressed like his lawyer and carried the same briefcase but it wasn't him. "Who the hell are you?"

A smile crossed the imposter's face as he reached inside his briefcase. "I'm your new defense attorney." He pulled out a suppressed pistol, pointed it directly at Pollard's face, and pulled the trigger.

LAS VEGAS

The knock at the door woke Howard. He checked the clock by the side of his hotel-room bed. It was ten in the morning. Way too early to be awake considering what he'd been through last night. He rolled over and gently shook the leather-clad Asian minx that lay next to him. "Hey, it's time to go."

She moaned and he poked her again.

One of her eyes opened, the eyebrow arching. "Poke me again you little bitch and I'll make you wish you didn't."

Howard felt the swell of an erection at the thought of it. Then he shook his head. "I'm sorry, Mistress Axera, I just have to get some work done."

She shook her hair and arched her back like a cat. "Fine, you didn't pay me for a full day anyway."

Howard rolled out of bed, threw on a robe, and watched her strut toward the door. She was petite but by god she knew how to handle a riding crop and handcuffs. "Thank you, Pershing," he mumbled as he watched her slip on a housecoat and grab her bag of tricks.

There was another thump on the door.

"OK, OK, I'm coming." He gave the dominatrix a smile. "Will you come back tonight? I'll make it worth your while."

She curled the corner of her lip. "I'll make it the most painful thing you've ever experienced."

He moaned in anticipation then made for the door. As he opened it he was confronted by a concierge holding a package. The young man wore an enthusiastic grin. Howard grabbed the package at the same time Axera slipped out past them. The concierge's jaw dropped.

"I will see you tonight, little piggy," she said.

He was about to slam the door when the young man coughed. "Oh yeah." He looked around and found his wallet. All he had was a twenty. He handed it to the man and slammed the door in his face.

Like a kid at Christmas he tore off the plastic wrapping and opened the box. Inside was a slim gray case made of carbon fiber. He turned it over examining it. On the front, under the folding handle, was a touch pad. He pressed his thumb against it. A green light flashed, there was a click, and it opened. Biometrically sealed. Very cool! thought Howard.

The computer inside was state-of-the-art. He powered it on and typed the log on details he had been texted earlier. The laptop booted up in seconds and displayed the main menu of the Redemption Network.

For the next hour he familiarized himself with what was by far the most sophisticated intelligence analysis platform he had ever used. He had access to all the CIA's databases as well as the FBI, NSA, TSA, and a number of other government agencies. Additionally, using a coalition gateway, he also could access the databases of over a dozen partner countries.

He was familiarizing himself with a powerful analytical tool when a message appeared on the screen. It was Larkin.

Welcome to Redemption Terry. I'm sending you a target pack that I want developed. I think you'll find it interesting. Once you're ready to execute I'll give you access to the tasking system. Good luck!

He hit accept on the file transfer and a moment later a folder appeared on his desktop. He opened it and commenced reading. Five hours, four energy drinks, and a burger from room service later, he was abreast of the information. Someone, maybe even Larkin, had been working on the intelligence deck since 2012. What had started as an investigation into the death of two CIA paramilitary officers in the UAE, Vance Durant and James Castle, had evolved into a witch-hunt come conspiracy theory that read like the plot from an action thriller.

The deaths occurred in 2004 but the case had evolved in 2012 when James Castle had turned up in Afghanistan. A special operations mission in eastern Afghanistan had recovered an unknown wounded Caucasian during a raid on a Taliban facilitation node. DNA testing had confirmed it was Castle.

Around the same time an ODA patrol reported being ambushed and effectively being rescued by someone using the call sign Ice. It was the same nickname Castle had previously been given in Kosovo.

The assessment made by the CIA analyst responsible for the intel deck was that Vance and Ice had faked their deaths in order to join an underground mercenary organization that recruited former special operations personnel. What Castle was doing in Afghanistan was an area of contention. The analyst believed he was part of a training team providing assistance to a Hazaran warlord. Another theory was that he was contracted by a Ukrainian arms dealer who was selling weapons to both sides and wanted the conflict to escalate.

Howard opened another can of energy drink as he considered the analysis. It actually made sense to him. The mine in Mexico had suffered at the hands of mercenaries with special ops training. He remembered the photo of Aden and the German, Wilhelm Jager. It was taken in Ukraine in 2012, the same time Castle was in Afghanistan. Could Aden and Castle be part of the same mercenary outfit? He made a note in the analytical program he was using; a dotted line now joined Aden and Kurtz to Castle and Vance. The big problem as he saw it was how to get to the next level. He had zero details on half the players and the others would have gone to ground using fake identities.

He smiled as he remembered he had two potential leads. The names of two associates: Christina Munoz and Wesley Chambers. Two civilians who might be able to fill in the intel gaps. He typed a message to Larkin.

I need additional assets to locate two persons of interest.

Larkin responded almost immediately with a link. Howard activated it and was taken to a secure website. He studied the site for a few seconds then grinned. It was the Redemption tasking tool. It allowed him to anonymously offer work to vetted private contractors. Now he not only had the analytical tools he needed, he also had the means of executing missions and collecting additional intelligence. He cracked his knuckles; it was time to go to work.

Chapter Thirty-Four

BEACH HUTS, LASCAR ISLAND

BISHOP SAT on a towel watching the sun set over the Pacific Ocean. He was drenched in sweat from another of Saneh's yoga sessions. She had surprised him with what she was calling her healing retreat. It was day one of three days down at the beach huts eating green things and contorting his body into painful poses. She hadn't even allowed him to make an alcoholic drink from the bar.

It was hard to admit but even at the end of the first day he felt rejuvenated. The dull weight of fatigue had lifted and his energy levels were renewed. Peeling off his T-shirt, he got to his feet and was about to walk down to the ocean when Saneh's sensual voice stopped him in his tracks.

"Hey, where are you going?"

He turned and let his eyes linger on her curves. The sports bra she wore did little to hide the fullness of her breasts. A smile crept onto his face as he spotted the slight protrusions from her nipples. "You cold?"

She rolled her eyes at him. "Are you ever going to grow up?"

He stepped forward and wrapped his arm around her waist. "Nope," he said as he leaned in and their lips touched.

She kissed him passionately and he slipped a hand down onto her buttocks. She reached around, grabbed his hand, and applied a gentle wristlock as she pulled away. "You smell terrible."

"How about a shower then?" He pushed against her so she could feel the bulge in his gym shorts.

She bit her lip. "OK."

He broke the wrist hold, grabbed her around the waist, and hefted her over his shoulder. She laughed as he slapped her bottom and carried her to the beach huts the team used for recreation. They had them all to themselves.

The shower was located outside the hut. A giant rose head hung over a slatted wooden floor surrounded by a bamboo screen. He placed her down under the shower and turned on the tap. She gasped as the water streamed onto her body. In a matter of seconds her long dark hair was slick against her back. Tilting her head up she let the cool water rinse the sand and sweat from her skin.

Bishop traced his fingers around her rib cage and hooked them under the sports bra. She lifted her hands over her head and he slipped the garment off tossing it on the floor. She kissed him again as he cupped her full breasts in each hand. Slipping his arms around her, he pulled her tight against him.

"Your turn," she said.

He peeled his T-shirt off and she traced her finger over the scars on his body as the cool water coursed over them. "You're a battered and broken man, Aden Bishop."

"Are you going to take care of me?"

"Do you want me to?" Her dark brown eyes locked on to his.

"More than anything." He kissed her again. For a moment he managed to block out everything but her. His world of loss and pain was replaced with the presence of this amazing woman. I'm not going to lose her again, he thought. Not now, not ever.

VANCE SAT with Chua in his office to talk through a post-mission debriefing. It was something they did after every operation. It helped identify strengths, weaknesses, and lessons to be learned.

Vance poured three scotch whiskeys. He and Chua raised one each. The third was a tribute for their fallen comrade. "For Aleks," he said as they downed their drinks. "OK, Chua, what's the go with MVI and GES? Did we shut those fuckers down for good?"

Chua coughed as he placed the tumbler on the table. "Man, that's strong. Yes. MVI's Venezuelan project is dead in the water and they're broke. I also just got word that Jordan Pollard was killed in prison last night. I'm trying to get more information but they're releasing nothing to the media and I don't have anyone with access."

"Assassinated?"

"It appears so, but I'm not sure by who. Bishop has a theory some guy called Larkin was out to get Pollard. He mentioned it in Caracas."

"Thomas Larkin," said Vance. "Sneaky self-righteous bastard when I knew him."

"We haven't been able to dig anything up on him, or confirm if that's the guy," said Chua.

"If he's still in the CIA he's going to be involved in something dark and deniable. That's the sort of guy he is."

Chua typed a note on his tablet. "Good to know, we'll keep working it."

"So MVI is done, right?"

"Yes, MVI was all Pollard. With him dead, it's over. No one is going to be suing the people of Mexico anytime soon."

"So that leaves Charles King and GES."

"Correct, and we don't know what happened to King. He's dropped completely off the radar. Flash is going back over everything we have but there's not a lot of depth to it. He's still running the numbers from the phone Bishop took off Pershing."

"We gutted them of operators and we've torn out their funding. What more could be left?" growled Vance.

"They had a number of CIA contracts. We're not sure if they're still running or if the FBI investigation shut them down."

"You'd fucking hope so. But, then again, I wouldn't put it past the CIA to ignore previous transgressions in the name of progress. OK, so we've dealt GES a serious blow. Let's monitor them and we can decide to take action when and if it is required."

"I concur," said Chua. "We add them to the watch list and go from there."

Vance poured another finger of scotch into his glass. He held the bottle over the other tumbler and raised an eyebrow questioningly.

Chua nodded.

Vance spoke as he poured, "I've got a bad feeling we've exposed ourselves."

"What do you mean?"

"The takedown at the CIA safe house was too close for my liking."

"We had to. We had to get Kurtz back."

"I know but there's no way the Company won't follow this up now."

"We can mitigate that. I'll get my team to do a counter-intelligence review. Search for any security weaknesses."

"I think we may need to do more than that."

Chua placed his drink down. "You want to initiate the dispersal plan and shut down the island?"

"No, but we need to be ready."

Next in The PRIMAL Series

vinci-books.com/primal-redemption

Secrets exposed. Loyalties tested. PRIMAL faces their darkest hour.

Turn the page for a free preview…

PRIMAL Redemption: Prologue

KUNAR PROVINCE, AFGHANISTAN, 2012

The four Blackhawk helicopters thundered through the night sky. Skilled pilots held the aircraft in formation as they weaved through the valley, beating their way toward an unsuspecting target. The birds had launched from Jalalabad forty minutes earlier as part of a larger force. The other aircraft, having already peeled off, headed to their separate landing zones or circled above waiting to dive down and provide close air support.

In the cabin of the lead airframe Staff Sergeant Shaun Clem glanced at the Suunto watch strapped to his heavily tattooed forearm. He whispered a prayer and looked up at the loadmaster in anticipation. The helmeted aviator manning the side machine gun turned inward and raised two gloved fingers.

"Two minutes!" Clem bellowed grasping the shoulder of the man next to him.

The call rippled through the helicopter and the soldiers conducted final checks on their equipment.

Clem increased the illumination on the red-dot sight mounted to his M4 carbine. He was feeling confident; his squad of nine men had performed similar missions countless times. They were Rangers and they were ready to lead the way.

"Thirty seconds!" yelled the loadmaster.

The squad leader felt the nose of the helicopter lift as the pilot flared to slow their descent. He adjusted one of the night vision tubes that hung from his helmet and gripped his carbine. Glancing around the cabin, he gave the boys a broad grin and unclipped his retention lanyard from the floor. "Here we go, Ranger buddies."

They touched down with a thud. Clem leaped through the open door into the maelstrom of dust thrown up by the rotor wash. They were now in the badlands. Jogging toward their RV he glanced over his shoulder to check that the two fire teams were following. He scanned the terrain to his front as the birds roared into the sky. The thud of rotors faded into the distance.

"Alpha Two-Zero, this is Alpha Two-One, we are in position," he reported as they approached the shallow wadi to the south of their objective. His squad fanned out providing all round security while he checked his map. The choppers had put them down only a few hundred yards from their target compound. He scanned the terrain around them. Through his night vision he could see the steep valley walls glowing green. They were the reason the helicopters had been forced to land so close to the objective. He was surprised that shots still hadn't been fired. Surely Terry Taliban hadn't slept through the racket of a helo assault.

PRIMAL Redemption: Prologue

He eyeballed the cluster of mud-brick walled buildings to their front. The intel guys had identified it as a key Taliban facilitation node. They had reports that weapons and IED components were being brought in from Pakistan for distribution. That's if the intel was correct. So often it wasn't. This could well be another dry hole.

"Alpha Two-One, this is Two-Zero, support by fire is in position. Commence infil," transmitted the platoon sergeant.

Clem acknowledged the call and shook the squad out into an assault line. With a wave of his hand they surged forward. His pulse quickened and he flicked his M4's safety off. Senses heightened, his finger was poised on the trigger. They were halfway to the high mud-brick wall when an AK barked, its muzzle flash bright through his goggles. The squad returned fire as they hit the deck. A gunner blasted the compound with a burst from his SAW machine gun.

"Bound forward!" bellowed Clem over the noise.

One team kept firing as the other four Rangers scrambled to a closer position. Like a well-oiled machine they leap-frogged until both teams reached the compound wall.

"Everyone good?" he asked when they were behind cover.

They checked in. No one had been hit.

Around them the valley echoed with gunfire as the other elements of the assault force made contact with the enemy. The radio was alive with call signs coordinating fire support. Clem glanced up as an Apache gunship sent its rockets streaking into the darkness. A moment later an explosion flashed on a hillside.

"OK, let's do this."

Clem's men stacked, one behind the other, on the

doorway into the walled compound. It was open and most likely covered by an AK-wielding Talib. He waited as one of his Rangers lobbed a 9-bang through the entrance. It detonated with a chain of sharp blasts and he charged inside.

He spotted a silhouette on the roof of the building to the rear and engaged, his finger pumping the trigger. The target fell. Behind him the rest of the squad swarmed inside the compound.

More gunfire broke out from the building and he felt the sting of rounds hitting the wall behind him. His machine gunner replied with a long burst. An AK barked again before the thump of a 40mm grenade silenced it. Clem rushed across the dust and smoke-filled courtyard weaving between piles of firewood, bundles of straw, and a tethered goat. The rest of the team followed.

He aimed his weapon through one of the windows and activated the IR flashlight. Invisible to the naked eye, the room was illuminated through his goggles. There were sleeping mats and blankets strewn on the dirt floor. He spotted an AK leaning against the wall. As he turned back toward the entrance he saw Rangers making entry. Gunshots rang out as he followed them in.

There were three bodies in the first room. One had taken the full force of the 40mm grenade. He was literally blown in half, his entrails smeared across the floor. The other two were bloodied corpses riddled with bullets.

"Good job," he grunted as he scanned the living area. The building was single-story with one adjoining room; the bedroom he had already cleared through the window.

"Holy shit," said his Alpha team leader, inspecting a stack of crates on the back wall. "We're fucking lucky, man.

If that guy hadn't taken the forty mike-mike to the chest it might have set this shit off. This right here is a crap load of one-twenty-two mill rockets."

Clem flipped his night vision goggles up and inspected the boxes using a light attached to his body armor. They were marked with Chinese characters. The team leader helped him lift one of them down and he prised off the lid with his multi-tool. Inside were two pristine olive-green rockets.

"Two-Zero this is Two-One, Objective Batman secure," Clem transmitted. "We've uncovered a major cache of rockets."

"Two-Zero, copy. Two-Two is taking fire from Objective Robin. Get a SAW gunner up on the roof, ASAP."

"Copy." He turned to his second-in-command. "Rig this to blow." Then he led the gunner out to the courtyard and up mud-brick stairs to the rooftop. His other fire team was already hunkered down pulling security. He glanced at the Taliban fighter he had shot, before positioning the gunner at the edge of the roof.

"Hey Clem, you might want to get back down here," transmitted his second-in-command over the radio.

He trotted down the steps and back inside.

The Ranger was standing over a hole in the floor. A heavy rug and a wooden cover had been hauled aside. "Chops found it."

Clem frowned. "Where's he at?"

"Down there."

He knelt by the hole and peered in. The beam from his flashlight revealed steps carved into the rock. They led down into a basement no bigger than a broom cupboard. He could see Chops standing looking at something.

"What have you got, Ranger buddy?"
"There's a guy down here."
"Taliban?"
"Nah bro, he's whiter than a bleached asshole and he's pretty fucked up."

PRIMAL Redemption: Chapter One

LANDSTUHL REGIONAL MEDICAL CENTRE, GERMANY

Landstuhl Regional Medical Centre was the largest US military hospital outside the United States. The three hundred and ten bed facility was constructed in 1953 and had been providing surgical treatment to American servicemen ever since. In the 1990s it had been expanded and with the commencement of operations in Afghanistan and Iraq it became the closest advanced surgical facility for critically wounded personnel.

Colonel Kevin Baker had been posted to the hospital for over a year. In that time the doctor had seen hundreds of mangled bodies come through the facility's operating theaters. Most were the victims of IEDs; home-made explosives that tore limbs from bodies, incinerated flesh, and caused horrific damage that he and his team would try, often in vain, to repair.

He yawned as he did his rounds. The previous night had

been exhausting with four new patients. He'd performed emergency surgery on three Marines who'd been blown up in Helmand province. Their Humvee had hit a stack of anti-tank mines. One of them had succumbed during surgery. The other two were clinging to life. If they made it through the next twenty-four hours he gave them a fifty-fifty chance of survival.

The fourth patient, a solidly built blonde-haired Caucasian, was an anomaly. Baker stopped at his bed and picked up the chart. Discovered in a Taliban stronghold during a raid, he had been imprisoned underground. His wounds were horrendous; he'd lost a leg below the knee. His right arm was mangled almost beyond repair and was infected with gangrene. Thick scar tissue covered his torso and one side of his square jaw was badly burned.

Baker shook his head. He had seen worse wounds but never this old. In his opinion the injuries had been inflicted well over a month ago and it was a miracle he'd survived with only the barest of field medicine provided by the Taliban. He was a hard man; the damage to his body was evidence of that.

Footsteps rang on the polished floor and Baker turned to greet one of the nurses. She flashed him a bright smile as she checked the IV bag hanging above the wounded man's bed.

"God knows how he survived," she said checking his dressings.

"Big guy's got the constitution of an ox."

She studied the patient's face. "He's handsome too, such a waste."

Baker turned his attention back to the chart he was holding. "His vitals are good. If we can get him out of the coma he should be OK. Have we had any luck identifying him?"

She shook her head. "No sir, we sent back a full set of prints. Heard nothing yet."

"Might take them a while. Did he come in with any personal effects?"

"No, nothing."

"It's strange. No one's mentioned any missing coalition soldiers."

"He might be a contractor or a journalist."

"True. So we've also sent photos through to ISAF headquarters?"

"Yes sir, they haven't got back to us either."

"Our first John Doe?"

"Looks that way." The nurse gave the unconscious man's mouth a dab with a cold compress then moved on to the next patient.

Baker spent a few more seconds checking the chart before hanging it on the end of the bed. He sighed. "Hang in there, buddy. You'll be alright."

Baker was sitting at his desk staring at the charts for John Blonde, as the nurses now called the mysterious casualty. In the seven days he had been at Landstuhl his vitals had improved dramatically. They now had the infection under control and his wounds had started to close over. However, he still hadn't come out of the coma.

He picked up the MRI report and read it again. The brain surgeon had identified significant bruising but that had begun to subside. He was baffled as to why the hulk of a man hadn't regained consciousness. He dropped the report and leaned back in his chair. What's more they still had no idea who he was. Everyone they had sent his fingerprints and photos to had come back with zero hits. It was as if the guy never existed.

"Dr. Baker."

The urgency of the nurse's tone told him something was wrong. She stuck her head into his office. "Sir, there's a bunch of men here and they're trying to take John Blonde."

He frowned, left his chair, and strode out of his office. He stormed past the duty desk and into the recovery ward.

There were four men in civilian clothing standing around the patient. His head nurse was glaring at them with hands on her hips. "What's going on here?" he asked as he arrived.

The men all turned toward him revealing their scruffy beards. He noticed that one of them was wearing a pistol on his hip.

"You do realize this is a hospital and weapons are not allowed."

"Hey bro, we're just here to collect the stiff," said one of the men as he chewed gum.

Baker clenched his jaw. "I'm not your, 'bro'. I'm a Colonel. Show me your identification." He thrust out his hand.

The man shrugged as he displayed his ID.

Baker checked it. It was as he suspected, they were CIA. "So, Mr. Weddell, do you have paperwork for the transfer?"

"Course I do." He reached into the pocket of his cargo pants, pulled out a piece of paper, and handed it over as he chewed.

Baker inspected the transfer document. It was correctly signed. There was nothing he could do.

"Are any of you by chance a doctor? I can only release this patient into the custody of a qualified medical professional."

The guy chewing dipped his head in the direction of one of his team. "Miller here is a medtech, that should cover it. OK boys, let's get the retard loaded up and get on the road."

Baker held up his hand. "I don't think you heard me. The receiving officer needs to be a doctor. It's standard operating procedure."

The team leader stared at him for a few seconds. "Look pal, I don't think you get what's happening here. The CIA is taking custody of a goddamn terrorist. You can bitch and moan about needing a doctor as much as you want but it ain't gonna change a thing. This asshole is coming with us."

Baker made eye contact with the head nurse. She shrugged. "Fine. But I want you to know that I will be lodging a formal complaint regarding this."

Weddell gestured for his men to grab the patient. "No problem. If I was you I wouldn't waste the time but if that's what you want to do, knock your socks off."

Baker watched as the men moved the unconscious patient onto the steel gurney.

The medic transferred the IV bags to the gurney. He took the paperwork from the end of the bed, folded it half, and stuffed it in his pocket. "We're ready."

The leader flashed Baker a broad smile. "Thanks, doc, been good doing business with you."

They wheeled the casualty into the corridor. Baker followed at a distance wracking his brain for a way to stop the transfer. Something told him if the patient left the hospital he was going into a far worse situation.

PRIMAL Redemption: Chapter One

Grab your copy...
vinci-books.com/primal-redemption

About the Author

Jack Silkstone grew up on a steady diet of Tom Clancy, James Bond, Jason Bourne, Commando comics, and the original first-person shooters, Wolfenstein and Doom. His background includes a career in military intelligence and special operations, working alongside some of the world's most elite units. His love of action-adventure stories, his military background, and his real-world experiences combined to inspire the no-holds-barred PRIMAL series.